B.J. BASSETT

the
GREATEST
SACRIFICE

AMBASSADOR INTERNATIONAL
GREENVILLE, SOUTH CAROLINA & BELFAST, NORTHERN IRELAND

www.ambassador-international.com

The Greatest Sacrifice: An Adoption Novel

ISBN: 978-1-64960-376-0
eISBN: 978-1-64960-373-9
Library of Congress Control Number: 2023939106

Cover design by Hannah Linder Designs
Interior typesetting by Dentelle Design
Edited by Katie Cruice Smith and Julia Anhalt

This is a work of fiction. Names, characters, and incidents are all products of the author's imagination or are used for fictional purposes. Any resemblance to actual events or persons, living or dead, is entirely coincidental. Any mentioned brand names, places, and trademarks remain the property of their respective owners, bear no association with the author or the publisher, and are used for fictional purposes only.

Scripture taken from the Revised Standard Version of the Bible, copyright © 1946, 1952, and 1971 the Division of Christian Education of the National Council of the Churches of Christ in the United States of America. Used by permission. All rights reserved.

AMBASSADOR INTERNATIONAL
Emerald House Group, Inc.
411 University Ridge, Suite B14
Greenville, SC 29601
United States
www.ambassador-international.com

AMBASSADOR BOOKS
The Mount
2 Woodstock Link
Belfast, BT6 8DD
Northern Ireland, United Kingdom
www.ambassadormedia.co.uk

The colophon is a trademark of Ambassador, a Christian publishing company.

the
GREATEST
SACRIFICE

To my daughter Dawn, who has a heart of gold

AUTHOR'S NOTE

The story began when my daughter Dawn discovered her birth family through an internet search. Her new family (as she refers to them) welcomed her with open arms.

Later, during a conversation, Dawn said, "Mom, you know that if my birth mother ever became homeless, I'd take her in." Yes, I knew she would because she is the most generous person I know.

When I told my daughter Kathy what her sister said, Kathy responded, "Dawn has a heart of gold." Thus, the working title and seed of an idea for the book you hold in your hands. (The title was later changed to *The Greatest Sacrifice*.)

This story addresses several very sensitive topics, including underage drinking, rape, abuse, unwed pregnancy, adoption, and immorality. For many readers, these are difficult issues to face, but I wrote *The Greatest Sacrifice* to share the Gospel. And what is the Gospel for if not to heal people from their sin? In fact, the Bible addresses these difficult topics as well. From King David, who murdered his best friend and forced himself on his friend's wife, to the woman at the well, who had five husbands and was living with a man who was not her husband, we see over and over in Scripture how the Gospel redeems what humanity destroys.

I chose to focus on the points of view of the birth mother, adoptive mother, and adoptee because I have walked the road of adoption in my own life and wanted to show each member of the adoption triad. Although adoption laws and policies were far different than they are today and adoption itself is more open today than it was back when I adopted my daughter in the '60s, there are still many false assumptions about each person in the triad.

In *The Greatest Sacrifice*, the characters experience horrendous trials and find God's love, forgiveness, and grace—the same love, forgiveness, and grace that is available to all of us who will accept God's free gift of salvation. My hope is that you will read this story and come away with not only a better understanding of the adoption journey but also a better understanding of Who God is and what He can—and will—do for those who seek Him.

Acknowledgments

To my daughter Melanie, my encourager and first editor, thank you.

To my critique group, Scribes 202—Julie Arduini, Marie Bast, Kathleen Friesen, Laura Hilton, Linda Hoover, Heidi Kortman, Linda Maran, and Christy Miller—thank you not only for your expertise but also for being my prayer warriors.

To Katie Smith and the Ambassador International staff—thank you for your belief in *The Greatest Sacrifice* and for seeing it to fruition. Bless you.

Last but not least, to my tribe—you know who you are—my family, friends, and readers who have read my books and blessed me with your kind, encouraging words—thank you all from the bottom of my heart.

With appreciation,

B.J. BASSETT

CHAPTER 1

Annie

1967
ORANGE COUNTY, CALIFORNIA

Annie Costa sobbed into her pillow. Her monthly curse, accompanied by cramps, was uninvited and not welcomed. How much more could she take? Month after month, year after year, the reminder of Annie's infertility crushed her hopes. And Joe's refusal to consider adoption was yet another crushing disappointment for her.

Nothing ruffled Joe, the golden boy of Orange County, California—the real estate mogul with ten offices to oversee. He was like the guy spinning all the plates and doing a great job. Not one plate fell.

Annie heard the shower turn off. She sat up, wiped her tears, and pushed her feet into her slippers, heading toward the bathroom as he entered the bedroom.

"Good morning, sleepyhead." He leaned in to kiss her, but she pulled away.

"Morning," she mumbled with her head down. *Don't look at him. Avoid his dreamy blue eyes.*

Lines appeared across his forehead, his tone low. "What's wrong?"

"The same old thing." Her words sounded accusatory, and she recoiled from his touch.

"Oh, hun, I'm so sorry." He dropped the towel onto the floor and began to dress. He grabbed a freshly ironed shirt from the closet. "I'm running late. We'll talk tonight."

Left alone with her emotions, Annie let the water heat up as she began to undress. She stepped into the shower and let the hot water pulsate against her back. What was there to talk about? He wouldn't change his mind about adopting a baby, even after six years of marriage and not conceiving. She had to give him credit, though. He did what he was supposed to do. At least, he considered he'd done his part. He'd been tested, and there was no reason he couldn't father a child. The test verified he had a high sperm count. *So, I'm the problem. Not him.*

Turning off the shower, she quickly toweled off and began to get dressed in her tennis whites. She was meeting her best friend, Jenn, at the country club for their Wednesday tennis game.

As Annie ran a comb through her wet hair, she allowed her thoughts to wander.

All I've ever wanted is to be a mother. What have I done wrong? If there is a God, why is He punishing me?

From the time she was little, Annie had always looked forward to being a mother. Even long after her friends had discarded their dolls, Annie had clung tightly to hers, still rocking them to sleep, "feeding" them, and changing their clothes. She even mothered every animal she met, from the homeless kitten she had found shivering in the rain to the squirrel she had later rescued from that same cat's claws.

"Maybe it's just not meant to be," Annie told her reflection in the mirror. But saying the words out loud only made the pang in her heart more intense.

Looking at the clock, she shook herself out of her melancholy and hurried to finish getting dressed. She didn't want to keep Jenn waiting.

After the game, she and Jenn showered and dressed in the locker room, then headed to their favorite outdoor café on the beach. They sat across from each other and ordered Shrimp Louis for lunch. While waiting for their food to arrive, Annie sipped her iced tea, plucked a roll from the breadbasket, and buttered it.

"You weren't on top of your game today. Something wrong?" Jenn asked. They had been best friends since seventh grade, and Jenn knew her better than anyone.

Annie lowered her head. "Another month without getting pregnant."

Jenn reached over and placed her hand over Annie's. "I'm so sorry."

"Me, too." Annie struggled to keep the tears from flowing. "You know how much I've always loved children. I can't imagine my life without them." She lifted her head to find Jenn's comforting smile.

"I wish you'd make an appointment with Dr. Anderson. He's the one I told you about who does private adoptions."

"Isn't a private adoption illegal?"

"No, I know that many couples have adopted through Dr. Anderson."

"Besides, why would I make an appointment? You know Joe isn't interested in adopting." Annie didn't like the sound of her bitter voice. Did it sound as awful to Jenn as it did to her?

"Maybe there is something new you could try. I don't see why you wouldn't try every option available. My friend Kathy is Dr. Anderson's office manager, and I've heard he's the best," Jenn persisted.

"We have tried everything, even the temperature thing. And Joe was so good about it. He'd run home from the office every time my temperature spiked. I'd like to call it making love, but it was more like performing on demand." Annie smiled. "He was a trooper."

"I remember."

"Are you sick of hearing about my baby drama? Or, should I say, lack of baby drama?" Annie searched Jenn's face for a reaction. She'd know if Jenn was telling the truth or not.

"Are you kidding? I've loved you since the day we met in Mrs. Evans' homeroom, silly."

"It isn't Joe. He's been tested. It's me. I must be infertile. And I don't know who I'm angrier at—myself for being unable to get pregnant or Joe for not considering adoption. Every time I mention adoption, he changes the subject."

"Don't be so hard on him or yourself. I know Joe. Talk to him. Joe loves you. When you tell him how much you want a baby, I'm sure he'll eventually change his mind. Besides, how do you know you're infertile unless you see a doctor?"

Annie avoided Jenn's eyes. "Maybe I'll look into it. Now, enough about me. How did your date go last night?"

"I won't be seeing that one again!" Jenn began rattling off the details of her evening, and Annie did her best to listen to her best friend. She loved her friend and hoped that someday, Jenn would meet Mr. Right.

The conversation turned to lighter topics, and soon, they asked for their checks.

"Fashion Island has a new shop that just opened," said Jenn as they walked out of the restaurant together. "Why don't we check it out? A new outfit will cheer you up."

Later, Jenn rummaged through the beach bags as Annie sorted through the clothes rack. Annie selected a few outfits, slung them over her arm, and passed Jenn as she headed toward the dressing room. "I'm going to try these on."

"Let me see how they look."

"Will do. I never do anything without your approval," Annie teased. "Even marrying Joe."

It was Jenn who'd dated Joe first, but she was getting over a bad breakup at the time. So, she decided to work for him instead. She had introduced Joe to Annie, and the rest was history. Annie stepped out of the dressing room wearing eggshell-colored, linen pants that flared at the bottom and a matching tunic top over her tall, slender frame. "What do you think?"

Sitting on a red velvet Victorian settee, Jenn flipped through a magazine. She looked up and grinned. "It's perfect. Get it."

Annie returned to the dressing room to change. *Jenn is always able to get me out of a bad mood.* When Annie emerged, she marched to the sales counter and purchased her new outfit.

Jenn linked her arm through Annie's as they exited the shop together. "Don't you feel better now?"

"I must admit that you're always good at pulling me out of a bad mood." Annie laughed at her friend, who was more like a sister. "Thanks for putting up with me."

"We've been through too much together for me to ever let you go," said Jenn. "Besides, who else can I complain about my bad dates to?"

With bolstered spirits, the two friends said their goodbyes and went their separate ways—Jenn back to work and Annie to the grocery store to purchase ingredients for supper.

After picking up Joe's favorite meal—steaks, russet potatoes, and items for a green salad—Annie headed home. She drove up the steep driveway to her estate in Laguna Hills, overlooking the Pacific.

She smiled, remembering Jenn's words. *Joe loves me. I should be the happiest woman in the world—a successful husband and a beautiful home in paradise. I have everything. Everything except a baby. Will this ache I feel ever end?*

She parked her Mercedes, hurried into the house, and set the food on the kitchen counter.

After putting the groceries away, she looked at the clock. It was only three o'clock. She still had plenty of time before Joe would arrive home from work. She decided she would clean up around the house a little bit before starting supper.

It didn't take her long to spruce up the house, so she went into her bedroom and snipped the tags off her new outfit. She put it on, added gold hoop earrings, and dabbed her favorite delicate fragrance on her neck and wrists.

She headed into the kitchen to prepare dinner, hoping to have everything ready before Joe arrived home.

She turned from the kitchen sink when Joe entered. "You're early," she said.

He held a bouquet of red roses with baby's breath and ferns interspersed in the arrangement. "I am, but for a good reason." He set the flowers on the kitchen counter. "The idea of adopting a baby made me feel like a failure, but after doing some soul-searching, I realize why it's so important to you."

Her heart pounded inside her chest. Was it possible he'd changed his mind about adoption? She teetered on her tiptoes to reach a vase from the cabinet above the refrigerator. He stepped behind her, grasped the vase, pulled it off the shelf, and handed it to her.

"I'm sorry it took me so long to figure it out. If you still want to adopt, I'm willing to look into it with you."

She turned and grabbed him into an embrace and held on for dear life like he was a lifeline. "Thank you." The tears choked any other words from being uttered.

The following day, Annie picked up the telephone book from the drawer, flipped through it, and then ran her finger down the page until she reached Dr. Edward Anderson. She dialed the number, and when the receptionist answered, she scheduled an appointment. Maybe a baby was in her future after all.

CHAPTER 2

Stevie

Stevie Shaw stood on the damp lawn at the Santa Ana Cemetery. She looked at the ground to avoid seeing her daddy's cheap casket.

"Stephen Michael Shaw . . ." the priest droned on.

We're Catholic in name only. We never attend Mass.

She stood beside her mother, dressed in a new black dress. Aunt Betty had bought both Stevie and her mother the proper attire for the ceremony. The new black patent leather pumps pinched Stevie's feet as the narrow heels sank into the ground.

Why would Aunt Betty buy her high heels? Stevie couldn't even walk in them. Was she trying to turn Stevie into a girly girl when all Stevie wanted was a pair of cleats and a baseball mitt—and to go back in time before cancer took her daddy away?

The ceremony was over quickly. Stevie's mother came up beside her as they looked at the place where the men had lowered the casket.

"It'll be okay," her mother tried to reassure her. "We'll be okay."

Stevie sat in the living room corner—as far away from everyone as possible. "It's hard to lose a father," someone said. "I'll keep you in my thoughts and prayers, dear."

If I hear that one more time, I'm going to scream.

When Aunt Betty opened the front door and accepted the casserole Mrs. Graham offered, Stevie jumped up and rushed toward the front door. "Come in," Aunt Betty greeted Mrs. Graham and Stevie's best friend, Rachael.

"Come with me." Stevie grabbed Rachael's hand and led her to her bedroom, shutting the door behind them. "I'm not sure why Aunt Betty even came here." Stevie plunked down on her bed, pulling Rachael down beside her. "Why would she come all the way from Ohio? Aunt Betty and my mom have never gotten along. She flew in and took over. Mom's always called her sister Bossy Betty."

After an awkward silence, Rachael wrapped an arm around Stevie. "A bunch of us are going to the beach tonight. Can you come? My cousin Nick is visiting, and he'll be there."

There was a tap on Stevie's bedroom door. "May I come in?" Aunt Betty whispered as she stuck her head in the room.

Stevie shrugged her shoulders. "Yeah."

Aunt Betty walked over to the bed and patted the top of Stevie's head. "I wanted to make sure you're okay."

"Fine. I'm fine," Stevie stated.

Aunt Betty squeezed her large body next to her on the bed. "I'm aware of how you took care of your father. No sixteen-year-old girl should have the responsibility of taking care of her dying—" Aunt Betty changed the subject fast. "Friends are important during times like this. I'm glad you have Rachael to talk to."

What a perfect opportunity. "Aunt Betty, if it's okay with Rachael's mother, can I sleep over at their house tonight?" Stevie put on her most innocent, pleading face.

"I'm sure it'll be okay with my mom," Rachael interjected.

"Go. Have fun. Summer's almost over. I'll tell your mother," Aunt Betty said and left the room.

Seriously? Did she really say have fun*? Give me a break.*

The sunset dipped into the horizon. Rachael's cousin, Nick, swaggered over and eased down beside Stevie at the beach party. At nineteen, he'd matured since his last visit to California two years ago. He was different than the boys at school. He was a man, not a kid. Blond chest hair peeked out from his opened shirt. "Hi, Stevie, remember me?"

"Rachael mentioned you'd be here tonight." Stevie brushed the sand off her feet.

"I heard about your dad. I'm sorry."

"Thanks. He was very sick," Stevie said. "People say it was for the best." *Don't cry in front of Nick.*

"This will help you feel better." He handed her a bottle.

She took a sip, then swallowed. It burned going down. She grimaced and handed it back to him.

"It numbs the pain," Nick said, putting the bottle to his mouth. Then he passed it around the circle of party-going teens. When it was empty, other containers appeared. Stevie joined in, taking her turn each time the numbing drink came around. After that, everything and everyone became a blur.

Stevie turned to the girl next to her and held out her hand. "Hi. I'm Stevie. What's your name?"

"I'm Cindy. We're in Mrs. Hill's English class together."

"Nice to meet ya." Stevie shook her hand.

A blurry figure approached. "Rach? Is that you? Daddy died. Did you know my daddy died?" Stevie began to cry.

"Yeah. I do. I think you've had too much to drink. Let's go home." Stevie felt Rachael's arms around her, trying to get her to her feet, but Stevie's legs wouldn't hold her up. Rachael gave up and sat down in the sand next to her friend.

"Nicky is helping me numb the pain," Stevie slurred.

"I can see that. Where is he?" Rachael looked at the crowd as the party began to break up.

"He went to get a blanket out of his truck. Isn't he the sweetest?" Stevie cooed.

"How thoughtful of him," Rachael said wryly.

"Are you mad? Don't be mad." Stevie closed her eyes and lay back on the sand. Their voices sounded far away, and she was unable to contribute to the conversation.

"Cindy, will you stay with Stevie until I get back?" Rachael pleaded.

"Sure. But everyone's leaving. I don't want to miss my ride."

"Do you know where there's a payphone? Unfortunately, all the concession stands seem to be closed."

"There's probably one on the pier," Cindy suggested.

"Thanks. I promise I'll hurry."

As Rachael left in search of a payphone, Cindy sat down next to Stevie. "I'm sorry about your dad," she said.

"Thanks," Stevie mumbled. Her head was spinning, and she didn't want to talk about her dad with someone she barely knew.

Thankfully, just then, Nick appeared.

"Nick, I thought you went to get a blanket," Cindy questioned.

"I did. I left it over by the lifeguard station. I thought we could move over there. It's more sheltered. But it looks like the party's over."

"Yeah. I told Rachael I'd stay with Stevie until she gets back, but I gotta go. My ride's leaving," Cindy said.

"It's okay. I'll wait with her."

Cindy looked uncertain. "I don't know . . . Stevie doesn't look so good."

"I'll be fine," Stevie slurred, rocking back and forth in the sand.

Cindy stood up and waved when the driver of the car honked at her.

"I promise I'll watch out for her," said Nick.

With the sound of another honk from her ride, Cindy hurried off, glancing back at Stevie one more time before getting in the car.

Stevie and Nick were alone.

Stevie stirred. "You came back." She felt Nick's arms around her as he carried her, then placed her on a blanket. *Are his lips on mine? What's happening?* Then blackness overcame her again.

The morning sun woke Stevie. She turned to see Rachael lying beside her. Stevie's head pounded, and her body ached. She turned away from Rachael in time to puke in the sand. "Yuck," she moaned and lay back down.

Rachael got up and stood in front of Stevie, blocking the sun. "You were so bombed last night. I guess it'd be stupid to ask how you're feeling."

"Where is everyone?" Stevie gazed at the empty beach.

"They all left. It's just us."

"Nick, too?" Stevie asked.

"Yeah, the jerk. He left us here. He didn't even try to help me get you home."

"Will your mom be mad that we stayed out all night?"

"I found a payphone and called her last night. I said I was staying at your house."

"Good idea. But if our mothers ever find out, they'll probably agree that one of us is a bad influence on the other and insist we never see each other again. I don't know what I'd do without you," Stevie said.

"I tried to get you home; but your legs wouldn't hold you up, so I decided to stay here with you."

"Rach, I gotta . . ."

"Come on." Rachael leaned down, grabbed Stevie's hand, and gently pulled her to her feet. Then, putting her arm around Stevie's waist, Rachael guided her toward the public restroom. "Come on. I got you."

After trudging through the sand, Stevie entered a stall.

"Rach," she said, panic rising in her throat. "Something's wrong. There's blood in my panties, and it's too soon for that time of month."

"What? Should I call someone?"

Stevie flushed the toilet and stepped out of the stall, hurrying to the sink to wash her hands and face. "No! I'm . . . maybe . . . I don't know . . . I can't let my mom know I was out partying. Who knows what she'll do?"

"But, Stevie, we need to get you checked out! What if something happened to you? Do you remember anything at all?"

"The last thing I remember is Nick carrying me over to the blanket, and I thought I felt his lips on mine. But, I mean, I didn't hate it. I *wanted* him to kiss me." Stevie shook her head. "No, Rach. Promise me. You can't tell anyone about this!"

Rachael sighed. "I think this is a bad idea, but I promise." She brushed her hair out of her eyes and gave herself a last look in the mirror. "Let's go before our moms start wondering about us."

Chapter 3

Annie

Wearing an oversized paper gown, Annie sat on the edge of the exam table. Her gaze kept focusing on the clock as she waited for the doctor to enter. She breathed deeply to slow her pounding heart. Eventually, the door opened, and an average-sized man with a fringe of gray hair around his ears and none on top entered. He held out his hand.

"Hello, Annie, I'm Dr. Anderson."

Annie accepted his handshake. "Hello." His hand was soft. *Of course, his hand would be smooth. He's a doctor, not a carpenter.*

A nurse with a pleasant smile followed him into the room and closed the door behind them.

"So, you want to have a baby." He set her patient chart on the counter.

"Yes," Annie confirmed. "My husband and I've been trying for six years without success."

"Well, that's plenty of time to try. Let's see what's going on." He positioned the pillow for her to lie down. "Scoot down to the end of the table for me." He sat on the rolling stool.

Sure. Easy enough for you to say. You're not the one in the stirrups! At least, I shaved my legs.

"I like the name Annie. My mother's name was Ann. Did you know that Annie means gracious and merciful?"

"I think I've heard that before."

"I'm going to use the speculum now. Try to relax. It'll be over soon."

So that's what that invasive metal instrument is. A speculum. Whoever invented it must have hated women. His name was probably Mr. Speculum.

He stood. "Almost done." He continued the uncomfortable examination. "You have a tipped uterus, but that shouldn't prevent you from becoming pregnant."

He pulled off his rubber gloves and pitched them into the trash can with the pop-up lid. Then, moving back to Annie, he helped her sit up. "You can get dressed and meet me in my office." He smiled. "Gracious and merciful Annie."

Annie clutched the paper gown at her neck and exhaled. *I like him. He has a good bedside manner, even during the worst experience.*

With a compassionate smile, the nurse handed Annie a packaged towelette. "Dr. Anderson's office is at the end of the hall. Have a nice day, Annie."

In his office, Annie glanced around the room at all the diplomas and certificates as she waited. Finally, he entered, went around, and sat behind his rich mahogany desk. Leaning back in his chair, he said, "It says on your information form that you want to adopt. Does your husband feel the same way?"

"He didn't at first. But Joe knows how much I want a baby."

"Well, that's the funny thing about men. We want our kids to look like us." He sat up and folded his hands on his desk. "I'll tell you what

I think will be agreeable with both of you. I'd like to do a procedure first. If you don't get pregnant in three months, we'll move forward with an adoption. How does that sound?"

Annie nodded.

"During the procedure, we'll inject a dye into your fallopian tubes—to make sure there's no blockage. You'll be sedated. So, you'll feel like you've had too many martinis."

"I have no idea how that feels. I don't drink."

Not sure why I told him that.

"Be sure to have your husband or someone else with you. You won't be able to drive afterward." He searched Annie's eyes. "I think it would mean a lot to your husband to realize we tried this before moving forward with an adoption. Are you up for it?"

"Yes. Thank you, Doctor."

"You're welcome. Kathy, my office manager, will schedule the hospital, and I'll see you there." He stood, came around his desk, and held her hand between his. "Annie, I assure you, I'll do everything I can."

Annie had to tell Joe her news. So instead of going home, she'd decided to surprise him at his office.

She entered the double doors of Joe Costa Real Estate and was greeted by Mallory, the receptionist. A large bouquet of red roses sat on the edge of her desk, not unlike the arrangement Joe had given Annie only weeks before.

"Hello, Mrs. Costa. Joe isn't here. He's at a Rotary meeting." Mallory looked annoyed to have Annie there. *What is it about her that rubs me the wrong way?*

"When do you expect him to return?"

Appearing flustered, Mallory straightened the items on her already neat desk. "He didn't say. May I leave him a message?"

"No. No message. I'll see him later." Annie began to leave, then asked, "What about Jenn? Is she in?"

"I'm afraid she's out, too. She's showing a house to a prospective buyer."

The phone rang, and Mallory answered, "Joe Costa Real Estate, how may I help you?" She paused. "I'll connect you." Mallory pushed a button on the phone and excused Annie with a look. "Have a nice day, Mrs. Costa."

"You, too." Annie slumped as she turned to leave.

Just then, Jenn came through the door. "Annie! How did your doctor's appointment go?"

Very aware that Mallory was listening to their conversation, Annie whispered, "Not here. Can we go somewhere?"

Slipping her arm through the crook of Annie's, Jenn directed her, "Let's go to the courtyard." In the middle of the office building with floor-to-ceiling windows was a piece of heaven. Annie had chosen the flourishing plants and statues herself. She was sure Joe had given her the project only to keep her mind off what he considered her "obsession" with having a baby.

They sat on one of the benches along the path that ran through the courtyard. "So, tell me," Jenn pleaded.

Annie straightened. "Dr. Anderson is wonderful. He's so kind and gentle.

"I've heard nothing but good things about him. Everybody loves him."

"Since Joe wasn't all that keen on adopting at first, Dr. Anderson is going to blow my tubes open."

Jenn cocked her head.

Annie went on. "He said if I don't get pregnant in three months, he'll find a baby for us to adopt."

"No wonder you're so excited." Jenn hugged Annie. "I couldn't be happier for you."

"Dr. Anderson even knew the meaning of my name. Can you believe it?"

"What does it mean?"

"Gracious and merciful." Annie looked at her hands, folded in her lap. "I came to tell Joe about my appointment. I'm disappointed he isn't here."

"Who isn't here?" Joe walked up behind the women. "What a nice surprise. Mallory told me you were here." He sat next to Annie and put his arm around her shoulders. Then, leaning around her, he asked, "Did you make that sale today, Jenn?"

"Not yet. They're picky. I'll find them something, Boss. You know me. I don't give up."

"That's for sure." He smiled, then looked at Annie. "What have you been up to today?"

Annie stiffened. "Don't you remember? I told you I had an appointment with Dr. Anderson." *How could he forget something so important to me?*

"That's right," Joe said. "What did he say?"

"Well, he wants to do a procedure to blow open my tubes. But if that doesn't work, then he can help us start the adoption process." Annie shifted nervously, waiting for Joe to shut down that idea.

"Whatever makes you happy makes me happy. You know that." Joe wrapped his arm around her, giving her a reassuring squeeze.

"Hey, Boss, there's an important call for you," Mallory interrupted, calling out the office window into the courtyard.

"Sorry, ladies. That's my cue to get back to work." Bending over to kiss Annie goodbye, Joe whispered, "It will all be all right, darling."

I sure hope so, she thought to herself.

CHAPTER 4

Stevie

Stevie tried to button her flared jeans without success. Finally, with a huff, she pulled on a long, button-down shirt over top her jeans to hide the buttons. Rummaging through her discarded clothes on the floor, she un-earthed her science textbook. Stevie discovered her history tome wrapped in her bedspread on top of her bed. Where was her English book? She had to find it. There was an open book test today in English.

"Mama," Stevie yelled.

She rushed to the kitchen, but Mama had already left for work.

On the table, she spied her English book and a note in her mother's scrawled handwriting.

Stevie,

I'm sorry I was so angry with you last night about the detention notice. It's just that you're smart, and I don't want you to end up like me.

I love you, and I'm proud of you.

Love, Mom

Next to the note was the detention notice for ditching physical education. Her mother had signed it per the school's instructions. Stevie hated P.E.—mostly because of undressing in front of nosy, giggling girls with prying eyes. She knew they would notice the extra weight she had been adding to her once-small frame.

It had been four months since that intoxicated night on the beach. She couldn't remember any of the details of what had happened, but she was certain to always remember the consequences. She knew she was used goods now and doubted that any man would ever want her if he knew the kind of girl she was.

Stevie tromped to the school bus stop just before it was due to arrive. Before, she liked going early and talking to the other kids while waiting for the bus, but not anymore. Was it because she was grieving the loss of her dad? She only knew she didn't want to be with anyone except Rachael. And Rachael lived on the other side of town, so she didn't ride the bus to school.

She hadn't heard from Nick since he had left her on the beach. Did he know anything about how she had ended up this way? Should she ask him? Oh, why couldn't she remember?

Sitting on the bus, Stevie thought over how much her life had changed in just the last few months. Her mother had become more difficult as she took on the burden of being a single parent. They had already had a difficult relationship before her dad had died; he had always been their buffer, able to soothe both of them and bring laughter into their home. There was no laughter anymore.

She sighed. What would her father think of her if he knew she might be a pregnant teenager? Would he have been as disappointed in her as she was in herself? Closing her eyes to stop the flood of doubts assailing her, Stevie slept the rest of the way to school.

At lunch, Stevie was munching on an apple when Rachael sat down across from her. She took her lunch items out of the paper bag and spread them before her. "Sorry I'm late. You going to the game tonight?"

"Nah."

"Come on, Stevie. A bunch of us are decorating the gym for the winter formal after the game. It'll be fun."

"I'm not interested in any of that stuff anymore." Stevie sighed.

"You've dropped out of everything." Rachael cocked her head to one side. "You stopped going to Future Teachers of America, drama club, drill team—"

"I'm not sure I want to be a teacher anymore. And I don't need drama club. My life is enough drama. Drill team isn't for me right now." Stevie looked down. "I still belong to the Honor Society. That is—if I keep my grades up."

"Didn't Brad ask you to the dance?"

"I told him no," Stevie said.

"Why? He's a nice guy."

"Maybe I don't deserve a nice guy." Stevie squashed her paper bag and dumped it into the trash can. "He doesn't know who I really am."

"Stevie, you didn't do anything wrong. It was my loser cousin, Nick, who took advantage of you. He raped you."

"But—"

"But what?" Rachael's perfectly shaped eyebrows arched.

"It's my fault. I was the one who drank myself into unconsciousness." Stevie looked down at her hands in her lap. "I don't remember anything about being raped. I guess I'm lucky that I don't remember. And besides, maybe I wasn't raped. Maybe I asked for it . . . " Stevie's voice trailed off as the panic began to rise up in her throat again. Shaking herself back to the present, Stevie turned her attention back to Rachael. "Besides, my mother can't afford to buy me a dress for the dance."

"We're the same size. You can borrow one of mine."

All of Rachael's formals were expensive and gorgeous. "Thanks, Rach, but I'm not going. Can we talk about something else? Please."

"Okay."

"My mother signed my detention slip. She was so mad at me last night. I've never seen her like that before." Stevie rubbed her tummy; the queasiness had returned. "She's changed. It seems like she's angry a lot since Daddy died."

"Anger is part of the grieving process."

Rachael probably read that in a book.

"I'm angry, too." Stevie stopped rubbing her stomach. "Mostly at God."

Rachael didn't say anything.

"Mama left me a note this morning. She said she was proud of me. I wonder if she'd still be proud of me if I told her . . . " Stevie changed the subject. "Have you heard from Nick?"

"No, but my aunt and uncle called my parents. I guess my dear cousin Nick got himself into trouble with the law in New

York before he came to visit us. My aunt and uncle thought being with my parents would be a positive influence on him, but he's disappeared." Rachael leaned closer. "No one knows where he is, not even his parents."

"I'm not sure how I feel about him. I probably should be irate. Instead, I'm mad at myself. Do you think I'm bad?" Burning tears threatened to spill over. Rachael came around to Stevie's side of the table. She scooted close and put her arm around Stevie.

At first, Stevie laid her head on Rachel's shoulder. Soon, she straightened and wiped her tears. "Sorry. My emotions seem to be all over the place." She changed the subject. "So, why were you late for lunch today?"

"I had to turn in my article for the newspaper."

"You are always doing something, Rach. We used to spend every day together during lunch, and now I'm lucky if I see you once a week. What's up with that? Do you really like being so involved in everything?"

"Yeah, I do. We're going to be juniors only once. And I want to be a part of it all." Rachael took a bite of her tuna sandwich. "I'm sorry you don't feel the same way."

"Well, my situation is a little different. In reality, it's a lot different." Stevie pitched her apple core into a nearby trash can.

"I get it." Rachael stopped eating and gazed at Stevie. "You still haven't told your mother, have you?"

"No."

"Stevie, you've got to tell someone. And you've got to go to a doctor. You haven't been yourself since that night. You've been gaining weight, but you're always sick. And you're always falling asleep. Do you think you could be pregnant?"

"I'm no longer nauseated in the mornings. I can't be pregnant. It was just that one time, and I don't even remember if anything happened. But what could it be?"

"I don't know." Rachael sat silently for a moment. "My mother said when a woman is pregnant, she needs to take special vitamins."

"And of course, she would know because she works for a doctor."

"If you're not going to tell your mom, then tell mine. She'll help you."

"Help me? How?"

"Doctor's appointments are confidential. And if you aren't pregnant, your mother will never find out. And it's possible you could miscarry. I guess it happens a lot in the beginning."

"Your mom wouldn't tell mine?" Stevie tilted her head, frowning.

"I don't think she would. She keeps all her work stuff to herself. She feels that her patients deserve privacy." Rachael unwrapped a snack cake and bit into the gooey treat. "Plus, Dr. Anderson is highly respected, and he does a lot of adoptions, too."

"Adoption? I'm not giving away my baby. I can't. I won't. And no one can make me." Although she believed every word she uttered, did she have the strength to stand firm and keep her baby? She mentally shook herself. *I am* not *pregnant!*

"But, Stevie, you're just a kid. How are you going to take care of a baby?"

"Rach, this is a silly conversation because I'm *not* pregnant!"

The bell rang signaling that lunch was over.

Rachael jumped up. "We'll talk about this later. Can't be late to class. See ya."

"After school?"

"Not today. I've got a lot to do before the game."

Stevie plodded to P.E. *I can't get another detention. It would break Mama's heart. It will break her heart even more if I am pregnant!* Worry clouding her mind, Stevie followed the other girls into the locker room.

CHAPTER 5

Stevie sat at the Grahams' large oak dining room table, more nervous than she'd ever been while taking a geometry test. Tonight, she and Rachael planned to talk to Mrs. Graham privately after dinner when the dishes were washed, dried, and put away.

What will Mrs. Graham think of me?

"Rachael, will you please pass the potatoes?" Mr. Graham reached his hand out to accept them. "So, Stevie, I haven't seen you at the basketball games. How come?"

"Ah . . . too much homework."

"Even on Friday nights?" Mr. Graham eyed Stevie as he scooped a second helping of potatoes onto his plate.

"Dad, you're not in court. Please don't treat Stevie like she's on the witness stand," Rachael pleaded.

Whether she knew it or not, Mrs. Graham came to Stevie's rescue, too. "Phillip, speaking of court, how's your case coming along? Any new developments?"

"I'm sure you'll read about it in tomorrow's *Register.* I got her off. The spoiled, little starlet is guilty. I'm not sure why I agreed to represent her. Sometimes, I hate what I do." He wiped his hands on his napkin.

"It's our legal system. Everyone deserves a fair trial." Mrs. Graham smiled sweetly across the table at her husband. "And it's the jury's decision, not yours."

Phillip Junior, Rachael's little brother, whom they affectionately called Buddy, interrupted. "May I be excused, please?"

"Yes, Buddy," Mr. Graham said. "You want to shoot some hoops later, after our dinner digests?"

Buddy grinned. "Is the Pope Catholic?"

Mr. Graham scooted his chair away from the table. "Thanks for dinner, Kathy. I don't know how you work all day and come home and provide us with a gourmet meal every night." He walked to the other end of the table, bent down, and kissed his wife on the cheek. "Well, I'll leave you ladies to your girl talk now."

Girl talk. Had Rachael told her dad? Stevie glared at her, but Rachael didn't seem to notice as she stood and began to clear the table. Mrs. Graham went to the living room while the girls did the dinner dishes.

"Did you tell your dad I'm pregnant?" Stevie whispered angrily.

"Of course not." Rachael gave her a disappointed look. "I'd never do that. Plus, you don't even know for sure you're pregnant."

"Then why did he say *girl talk*?"

"Duh. Because we're girls. And we talk. Stevie, get a grip."

Stevie placed a plate on the counter and began to cry. "I'm sorry, Rach. It's just . . . "

Rachael wiped her hands on a tea towel. Then she hugged Stevie. "I'm sorry."

With the kitchen duties finally completed and hearing the basketball bouncing outside, Rachael and Stevie walked into the living room, where Mrs. Graham sat reading. "Mom, we need to talk to you. Privately."

Mrs. Graham placed a bookmark in the book she was reading and put it on the coffee table.

"Can we talk in my room? We don't want to be interrupted by Dad or Buddy when they come in."

"Sure." Mrs. Graham followed the girls to Rachael's bedroom.

I feel like I'm going to my execution.

Rachel held Stevie's hand as they lowered themselves onto Rachael's bed, while Mrs. Graham took the pink, velvet bedroom chair across the room. She leaned back against the chair.

"Mom, Stevie was raped."

"Raped?" Mrs. Graham sprang from the chair and joined them on Rachael's bed. Putting her arm around Stevie, she asked, "Can you talk about it?"

Stevie hiccuped a sob. "It's my fault. If only I hadn't—"

Mrs. Graham rubbed Stevie's back.

"He said the alcohol would make my pain go away," Stevie said, looking at her hands folded in her lap.

"So, you know who did this to you?" Mrs. Graham pulled back to look at Stevie.

Rachel moved to the chair Mrs. Graham had vacated. "It was Nick, Mom."

"*Our* Nick?" Mrs. Graham gasped. "I think one of you better start at the beginning and tell me everything."

After a long silence, Rachael said, "The night of Mr. Shaw's funeral, a bunch of us kids went to the beach." She avoided her mother's eyes. "Some of them got drunk. Stevie passed out, so we slept on the beach all night."

"We'll talk about your part and the drinking later, young lady." Mrs. Graham glared at Rachael. "Did you report the rape?"

She turned to Mrs. Graham. "Please don't blame Rachael. It's my fault. I passed out, and I don't remember anything."

The words tumbled out of Rachael's mouth. "Stevie thinks she might be pregnant."

Stevie took the pillow from Rachael's bed and held it protectively in front of her.

Mrs. Graham rocked Stevie for a long time as she sobbed out all the feelings that had been welling up inside of her for so long. Mrs. Graham was like a second mother to her. Stevie spent more time at their house than she did her own.

"Have you told your mother?" Mrs. Graham asked in a low voice.

"No," Stevie choked out.

Rachael interjected, "We thought if she isn't pregnant, her mother wouldn't have to know."

"Your mother needs to know you were raped," Mrs. Graham said in her professional voice. "You don't want to carry this secret. It could have consequences later." Mrs. Graham pulled back and looked at her. "When was your last period?"

"The first week of August." Stevie wiped at her tears.

"There are all sorts of reasons your cycle could change. You may not be pregnant." Mrs. Graham rubbed Stevie's back.

"What sort of reasons?" Stevie asked.

"It could be from stress after your father's passing. You're as thin as a rod. It could be from an eating disorder. How have you been eating?"

"M-my appetite's not been great, but I'm not starving myself, if that's what you mean. But I must be putting on weight because my clothes have been tighter." Gripping Mrs. Graham's arm, Stevie begged, "Mama is so sad right now, and I don't want her to find out. Please, Mrs. Graham."

"I'll make an appointment for you with the doctor I work for—Dr. Anderson. I'll get you in right away. Then we'll go from there." Mrs. Graham hugged Stevie again. "Don't worry. It could be as simple as not having a regular menstrual cycle. And you aren't alone. Rachael and I are here for you. But you do need to be honest with your mother. Maybe after your doctor's appointment, we can talk to her together."

"Thank you." Stevie wiped the rest of her tears and continued to hug the pillow.

"And, Stevie, I'm furious with my nephew. What he did is a crime. You're only fifteen, and he's an adult. That's statutory rape. If he ever shows his face here, he'll pay for what he did to you. And I plan to tell his parents what he did." Mrs. Graham stood and returned to her chair by the bed. "Now, I believe we need to have a long talk about lying and drinking."

"Please. Please don't report it. It's my fault." Stevie rocked back and forth.

"Let's deal with one thing at a time, okay?" said Mrs. Graham. "But one thing I want you to know for sure is that this is not your fault. You made some bad choices that night—that's true—but that does not mean that it was okay for Nick to force himself on you. He took advantage of you in a weak moment. And we are not going to let him get away with it."

Stevie sighed. *Would Mama be as understanding as Mrs. Graham?*

Mrs. Graham continued to rub her back. "You said you didn't remember the rape."

"Uh-huh."

"Although you don't remember it, you may have trauma from it."

"Really? Like what?" Stevie searched Mrs. Graham's eyes.

"You may experience flashbacks, mood swings, depression. There are all sorts of symptoms rape victims go through." Mrs. Graham continued to soothe Stevie's anxiousness with her gentle stroking.

Mrs. Graham's knowledge about rape victims answered a lot of questions about how Stevie had been feeling lately—mood swings and depression. Knowing she wasn't crazy helped a little. Yet she still had to face the possibility of being pregnant. She exhaled a deep sigh, trying to release the tension in every muscle in her body.

They talked for a while, and then Stevie excused herself. It was getting late, and she needed to get home. She felt so much lighter knowing Mrs. Graham was in her corner.

Seated in a chair across from Dr. Anderson's desk, Mrs. Graham held Stevie's hand, waiting for Dr. Anderson to speak.

"It's nice to see you, Stevie." He looked over the top of his glasses. "The results of the test are back, and you *are* pregnant."

Stevie gulped as Mrs. Graham squeezed her hand.

Dr. Anderson's voice was calming. "You are young, and you have choices. You can keep your baby, or you can place your baby for adoption."

Stevie stiffened. *How can he even suggest that I give my baby away? This man doesn't know me at all!* She sat up straight. "I want to keep my baby."

"You may feel that way now. But you may change your mind later. It'll be very hard to care for a baby and go to school. You'll need lots of support from others." The doctor glanced over at Mrs. Graham and then back at Stevie. "I understand the baby's father is not available."

Stevie nodded.

"If you want to press charges, then we can do a rape kit on you to provide you with evidence against him."

The idea of going to court and having people judge her for what she had done made her sick at heart. "No. I-I just want to move on and forget about him. I just want my baby."

"I understand your feelings. You also have options. There are couples who, for one reason or another, cannot have children. However, they can love and care for your baby. I can help you make all the arrangements. But you don't need to decide today."

He stood. "I'd like to see you once a month. Kathy can schedule your appointments." He handed Stevie a bottle of pink and blue pills. "Please take these vitamins daily, so you'll have a healthy baby. Now, if you ladies will excuse me, I'm due at the hospital. One of my patients is in labor." He smiled and patted Stevie's shoulder before he left his office. "Everything is going to be okay."

Is it?

CHAPTER 6

"I'm pregnant." Sitting on Rachael's bed, Stevie plucked at the pink gingham bedspread.

"So, was the exam horrible?" Rachael held up her hands and shook her head. "No. Don't tell me. I don't want to know."

"Dr. Anderson was nice enough. Although, I didn't like him suggesting that I place my baby for adoption. No one seems to understand how I feel. I don't want to give away my baby. I want to keep it." Stevie fell back onto Rachael's bed and gazed at the ceiling. "Mama is off tonight, so after dinner, your mother is going to come to my house when I tell Mama I'm pregnant. Telling Mama is going to be even worse than the doctor's exam. I know it will."

"Don't worry. Your mother loves you. Look how my mother reacted when we told her that Nick raped you."

"Your mother and my mother are different. Plus, it isn't your mother who has a pregnant teenage daughter." Stevie inhaled as if it would ease her fear of telling Mama she was pregnant.

"Do you think your mother will make you have an abortion?" Rachael's forehead wrinkled.

Stevie hesitated. *Would she? Surely not! No matter how angry she got, Mama would never go that far.*

"She'll probably ground me for the rest of my life, but I don't think even Mama would stoop to that." Stevie rubbed her belly over the baby that was growing inside her.

Seeing Stevie's worried face, Rachael changed the subject. "I wish you'd come to the dance! It'll be so much fun. Wanna see my dress?"

Pushing thoughts of her mother to the side, Stevie oohed and aahed over her friend's beautiful gown. But try as she might, worry gnawed at her. *Will Mama make me give up my baby? Will she kick me out of the house? Is it going to hurt to give birth? Oh, what am I going to do?*

Stevie left Rachael's house an hour later, promising to call her friend after the conversation with her mother. She didn't know what to expect, but she couldn't shake the feeling that things would not end well.

"Dinner's ready," Mama called.

Stevie trudged to the kitchen, pulled one of the chairs out, and sat on it.

"I thought I'd make fried chicken for a change instead of wolfing down a TV dinner between jobs." Mama smiled.

"Maybe I could help make dinner more often," Stevie offered.

"That would be nice; but you have homework, and you already keep the house picked up, plus do the laundry." Mama brushed her graying brown hair away from her face.

"You work so hard. I want to help." Stevie pushed the mashed potatoes with the country gravy around her plate.

"You're not eating. Is something wrong?"

"No. Dinner's nice, Mama. I'm just not hungry."

"Are you sick? It's cold and flu season."

Before Stevie could answer, the doorbell chimed, and her stomach knotted even more.

"I'll get it." Mama rushed to the door and opened it. "Hi, Kathy. We're finishing dinner. Come in and join us." Mama closed the door behind Mrs. Graham.

"I brought an applesauce cake. I know Stevie likes it."

Mama accepted the cake. "Thank you. It looks delicious. Will you have a piece with us and some coffee?"

"Sure." Mrs. Graham pulled out a chair and sat between Stevie and Mama. She patted Stevie's leg under the table as Mama busied herself brewing coffee and slicing the cake. The two adults talked about all the non-essential things people talk about—the weather, gossip, work.

"Stevie, do you have homework?" Mama asked.

"I did it earlier." Stevie twisted her hands in her lap.

The coffee had turned cold, and the cake plates sat empty, except for a few crumbs.

"Margaret, Stevie has something she needs to tell you."

"What is it?" Mama, suddenly nervous, turned and peered at Stevie.

Stevie began to sob. In between gasps, the words erupted. "I'm pregnant."

Mama's face went ashen, and she was silent for several minutes before speaking. "Have you seen a doctor?"

Stevie's cries increased to hiccuping. Unable to go on, Mrs. Graham took over. "I took her to the doctor I work for—Dr. Anderson. He examined her."

"I see. And why did you take her to the doctor and not me?" Mama glared at her.

"Stevie was hoping she wasn't pregnant . . . And she didn't want to hurt you." Mrs. Graham tried to put her arm around Mama, but Mama shrugged her off.

"And I feel somewhat responsible." Mrs. Graham placed her hands in her lap. Mama cocked her head, glaring at Mrs. Graham. "The kids were at a beach party. It was my nephew who raped Stevie." Mrs. Graham looked at her hands.

Expressionless, Mama stood and began to clear the table. No doubt, she was probably mulling things over in her mind. She didn't even offer Mrs. Graham more coffee. Stevie wiped her tears, and the room was quiet.

"I'm so sorry that my nephew did this—"

"You should be!" Mama turned around angrily. "What were you thinking, letting the girls go to a party alone on the beach? Why weren't you taking better care of them?" The angry words cut through the room like a knife, and Mrs. Graham winced at the onslaught.

"If you want to press charges—"

"Of course, we do! We're going to get that boy for what he did!" Mama was shouting now, tears rolling down her cheeks.

"Mama, stop!" Stevie stood, her legs shaky underneath her. "I don't want to press charges. I just want to move on—and keep my baby."

At this, Mama sat down, exhausted by her tirade. She put her head in her hands.

"The doctor gave Stevie some options I can go over with you if you like," Mrs. Graham tried again.

"Just go," Mama said wearily. "This is a family matter."

Mrs. Graham rose. "Stevie has some prenatal vitamins and doctor appointments scheduled. If I can be of any help, don't hesitate to call me." She leaned down and hugged Stevie. Then she grabbed her purse, slipped it over her shoulder, and reached for the door handle.

Mama mumbled under her breath, "I think you've done enough." She grabbed her cigarettes with shaky hands. Plucking one from the pack, she lit it. "I feel humiliated." She inhaled and blew out smoke. "How could you have gone to a doctor with her instead of me? How does that look? Did Kathy Graham pay for your doctor appointment as well?"

Stevie avoided her eyes. "No. I did."

"And how did you do that?" Mama flicked ashes into the ashtray.

"My babysitting money." Stevie stood, grabbed the tissue box from the counter, and returned to the table. "I was trying to protect you—in case I wasn't pregnant."

Mama began to pace. "Was there drinking at the beach party?"

"Yes."

Mama stopped pacing and glared at Stevie. "Didn't I warn you about the consequences of drinking? Did you initiate sex? How were you dressed? Tell me everything, and don't leave anything out. Do you understand me? Because I'll be able to tell if you're lying." Mama stopped pacing and got in Stevie's face, her nicotine breath overpowering her.

"It was the night of Daddy's funeral. Nick said the alcohol would ease my pain. I believed him, and I drank too much. I don't remember anything else." Stevie stood and turned to leave the room.

"You sit yourself down, young lady. I'm not through with you."

Stevie eased back down onto the chair.

"How could you not remember something that traumatic?"

"I don't know. I just don't."

"It doesn't make sense."

"I blacked out." Stevie searched her memory. "Maybe that's the reason I don't remember it."

"And do you like this boy?"

"I thought I did." Stevie blew her nose.

"Have you told him that you're pregnant?"

"No. He left town." Stevie wadded the tissue in her hand.

"Well. Isn't that just great?" Mama stood behind her chair, stubbed out her cigarette in the ashtray, and lit another one.

Stevie mentally focused as she tried to gain courage. "I want to keep my baby."

"Over my dead body."

Stevie rushed on before she lost her nerve. "I'll go to school and find a job. I know I can do it."

"You have no idea how to take care of a baby. And who is going to take care of it when you're at school? Or at work? Not me. I won't help you. You will not bring a baby into this house. Do you hear me? Adoption is your only option. Haven't I suffered enough with your father's death? You had a future. Now, look what you've done. Your father would be so disappointed in you."

Mama left the kitchen, went to her bedroom, and slammed the door behind her.

Stevie's shoulders slumped. *What am I going to do?*

CHAPTER 7

That night, Stevie crept down the hall to Mama's bedroom. Putting her ear to the door, she heard her mother's even breathing of sleep. Stevie tiptoed back to her bedroom and packed a tote with a few items. After stuffing her babysitting money deeply into her coat pocket, she grabbed a blanket and her pillow. Stevie needed to clear her head, think, and devise a plan to keep her baby, no matter what. And it was impossible to do it in the house polluted with cigarette smoke.

The Grahams would take her in, but that would be the first place Mama would look for her. Stevie quietly pulled the front door shut until she heard it click. She left the little house in Santa Ana, not sure where she'd go.

She boarded the bus and tried to avoid the driver's curious stare as she dropped money in the coin slot. A few passengers got on and off the bus as Stevie tried to think. She would have stayed on it all night, except the driver called, "Tustin. End of the line."

After Stevie disembarked, she wrapped her blanket around her shoulders to ward off the cold night. She wasn't sure if she shivered from cold or fear. Leaving the sidewalk, she tramped through the orange grove, grateful for the moonlight and lack of eerie animal noises.

Across from the orange grove, a new development was being built. The homes were in different stages of completion. She tried the doorknobs of the ones that looked ready for occupancy. After a few tries, she found one of the doors unlocked. Was it fate? She pushed inside and moseyed through the new home with wall-to-wall carpet and finished bathrooms. She had to use the bathroom so badly. She plopped down her things and used the facility. Moonlight filtered through the freshly painted, newly built home. She was so tired, she wandered into the bedroom and spread her blanket and pillow on the floor. She'd leave in the morning before the workers arrived.

In the morning, sunlight streamed through the window. After using the bathroom, she gathered her things and left the house, hoping it would still be unlocked when night fell.

Stevie stashed her things behind a shrub in the park, then strolled along the paths around the development. At midmorning, she sat on a bench at the playground and watched children playing. Their mothers pushed them on swings or visited with other mothers. Stevie daydreamed about what it would be like to live here with her baby. Someday, she'd have a beautiful house. And she'd bring her baby to the park to play.

Mama's wrong. I have a future.

A young mother scooted close to her on the bench. "I just moved here. Which street do you live on?"

Stevie shook her head. "I'm only visiting."

"Be careful, Todd," the stranger called to her preschooler playing on the slide as she moved the stroller back and forth with her foot. "I'm Deana." She smiled. "And you are?"

"Stevie."

The baby in the stroller stirred. Deana picked her up and placed her on her lap. "Libby, meet Stevie."

"She's adorable."

"Thanks. But our little Libby wasn't so adorable last night. I couldn't get her to go to sleep for the life of me. No matter what I did." Deana did look tired. "You're so young. You probably don't have kids yet."

"Not yet, but I'm due in May," Stevie rubbed her tummy.

"Really? Who is your doctor?"

"Anderson."

"You're lucky. I heard he's the best. I wanted him, but he wasn't accepting new patients." Deana cocked her head as she bounced Libby on her lap. "How'd you get so lucky?"

"My friend's mother manages his office."

Deana perused Stevie. "You look so young. How old are you, anyway?"

"Sixteen."

"I don't want to discourage you, but I hope you realize what you're getting yourself into. Being a mother is constant. My husband is a big help, so I'm more fortunate than some. And my mother takes the kids one night a week, so I can get a good night's sleep."

Stevie chewed her bottom lip. Why was everyone so negative? Dr. Anderson wanted her to place her baby for adoption; Mama refused to help her; and now, Deana made motherhood sound like a nightmare.

When a screech came from the play area, Deana handed Libby over to Stevie and rushed to her screaming son. With his head lodged between the bars, it took a while. Eventually, she was able to turn his head at an angle and free him. Todd's screaming subsided to crying.

"It's time to go," Deana said.

Since Todd refused to be put down, Stevie placed a fussy Libby in the stroller, and Deana left with both bawling children. "Good luck. I hope I see you again," she called over her shoulder as she pushed Libby in the stroller while Todd wrapped his legs and arms around his mother like a monkey.

How long could Stevie stay in the empty house? It was Christmas break, so she didn't have to worry about missing school, but her money and food would eventually run out if she didn't find a job. On the third day, it rained, so she decided to stay inside the house and hoped she wouldn't be discovered.

It was still raining the next day. She was cold, hungry, and lonesome. Stevie knew she couldn't do this anymore and needed help. She walked to the corner convenience store to use the payphone. When Rachael answered, Stevie whispered, "Rach, it's me."

"Stevie! Where are you? Your mother is worried sick. She's been calling every day and asking if we've heard from you."

"I had to get away. I needed time to think." Stevie began to cry. "Rach, my mother said she wouldn't let me keep my baby."

"Oh, Stevie. Let us come and get you. My mom and dad will let you stay with us. They love you, Stevie. You're like one of theirs," Rachael said.

Stevie gave Rachael the address of the convenience store. She hung up the phone and slid down to the floor of the booth. Under her damp blanket, pillow, and tote, Stevie was a wet heap. Sheltered from the downpour, she waited to be rescued.

Stevie's eyelids fluttered open. Her mouth felt like cotton as she tried to swallow. "Where am I?"

A gentle hand touched hers. "You're in a hospital, and we're going to take good care of you."

Tired, dizzy, and thirsty, she asked for water. As she sipped the cool water, Stevie spotted a needle in her arm. Her eyes followed the tube up to a bag of liquid high above her. She gasped. "Is my baby okay?"

"Your baby is fine."

Stevie closed her eyes but could hear the conversation around her hospital bed.

"We're hydrating her, but I want to keep her overnight for observation. I'll release her in the morning."

Mama's guarded voice said, "Thank you."

Soon, there were only two voices in the room—Mama's and Mrs. Graham's.

"I can't afford to take time off from work," Mama said.

"I understand." Mrs. Graham's soothing voice was a balm to Stevie. "Tomorrow is my day off. I'll pick her up and bring her home with us. Is that okay with you?"

"It's too much to ask."

"You didn't ask. I offered. You're grieving, and so is Stevie. You both need to give yourselves time. And I'd like to do this for you."

Before Stevie fell asleep, she heard Mrs. Graham. "Stevie is not only grieving the loss of her father but also the possible loss of her unborn baby to adoption. We need to give her as much love as we possibly can."

Physically, Stevie started feeling better under the care of the Grahams. Mrs. Graham fussed over her, making sure she rested well and ate healthy meals. She even reminded her to take her prenatal vitamins every day. But emotionally, Stevie was a wreck. She was frantic to find ways to keep her baby.

One night, Mrs. Graham found Stevie studying in the living room. "Stevie, I think we need to talk about your baby. I know you're going back home with your mom tomorrow, and I wanted to have a chance to talk with you before you leave."

Stevie put her books aside, knots forming in her stomach from what she dreaded to hear.

"I know you love your baby and want to do what's best for him or her," began Mrs. Graham. "But keeping your baby when you're still a kid yourself is no way to show that love. God made this baby for a good purpose, even if the circumstances leading to this precious life were evil. He tells us that when man does evil against us, He can turn it around and make it for our good."

Stevie looked down at her hands, tears welling up in her eyes. "But how can I let someone else raise my baby?"

"Stevie, Dr. Anderson is a good, kind man. He will find just the right couple to parent your baby. Adoption is really the best choice, sweetheart." Mrs. Graham patted Stevie's hands as she rose to leave the room. "And give your mom a break, too, okay? She loves you, but she's still grieving and trying to handle all of these things on her own. She may not always give you the answer you want to hear, but she does want what's best for you. I'm praying for you, Stevie. I hope you'll consider what I've said."

Stevie could barely nod, then ran to Rachael's room to cry on her best friend's shoulder.

A couple of months later, Stevie noticed classmates diverting their eyes when they passed her in the hall. After a few instances, she called Rachael one night after school. When she answered, Stevie said, "I know it's late, but I need to talk to you."

"Shoot," Rachael said while yawning.

"Do you think everyone at school knows I'm pregnant? They won't look me in the eye."

"I don't know. Maybe some do. Barbara Baker asked me if you were pregnant. I told her it was none of her business. No one likes 'Big Mouth Babs,' anyway."

"That's what worries me. Everyone will know if she finds out, which she probably will."

"Well, don't you think you're starting to show a little? Even in the baggy clothes, you can't hide that you've put on a little, um . . . weight. People are going to notice." She paused before adding, "Look, Stevie, your true friends will still be your friends no matter what, so don't worry about it."

Stevie could tell Rachael was tired by the sound of her voice. "Did you finish your English essay?"

"Just now. You?"

"It'll be late. I can't concentrate."

"It'll affect your grade."

"I know."

There was silence on Rachael's end of the phone.

"Thanks, Rach, for being my best friend."

"Of course."

"Good night."

"See you tomorrow." Rachael hung up, leaving Stevie to ponder who her true friends were.

CHAPTER 8

Annie

Annie removed her coat and wrapped it over her arm. "Dr. Anderson, I'd like you to meet my husband, Joe."

Joe reached out his hand. "Good to meet you, Dr. Anderson."

Dr. Anderson gripped Joe's hand. "You, too, Joe. Please have a seat." He cleared his throat. "I've asked you both to come in today, so I can get to know you better. Medically, there is no reason Annie isn't able to become pregnant. Yet, for one reason or another, it hasn't happened."

Annie squeezed Joe's hand. "Why? We've tried everything."

"Joe, I understand from Annie that you were originally apprehensive about adopting. How do you feel about it now?" Dr. Anderson took off his glasses and laid them on his desk.

"It's true. In the beginning, I wasn't keen on adopting, but I'm fine with it now." Joe met her gaze. "I know how much it means to Annie."

Dr. Anderson asked questions about their backgrounds, finances, and faith. Finally, he leaned back in his chair. "I may have some good news. Three of my patients are due to deliver in May. Barring any complications, one of those babies will be yours. One of my patients is an unwed teen without support from her family and no way to provide for a child. She's healthy and has a good medical history."

He hesitated. "With private adoptions like this, the birth mother has six months to change her mind after she signs the relinquishment form. For some adoptive parents, it can be heartbreaking to have a baby in their home only to have it taken away before their case goes to court for the final adoption." Dr. Anderson looked at them and waited.

Joe responded, "We've researched and discussed the pros and cons concerning adoption, including the possibility of the birth mother changing her mind." He cleared his throat. "Annie's familiar with heartbreak. Being unable to get pregnant has broken her heart every month for several years. There are no guarantees in life. And we're ready to take the risk as adoptive parents."

My hero. The man I love and the father of our future children. Taking a tissue from her purse, Annie dabbed at her tears of joy.

"My dear, you already have a mother's glow." Dr. Anderson rose. "I understand. While it's true birth mothers sometimes do change their minds, I'm optimistic for you. I'll keep in touch."

"Thank you, Doctor," said Joe, sticking out his hand. He then offered his hand to Annie, pulling her to her feet and escorting her out of the office.

Holding hands as they exited the medical building, they headed for their car. Joe said, "I think we need to celebrate. How about an early dinner at PJ's?"

"I'm so excited. I'm not sure if I can eat."

"Then we'll drink to the good news. You've wanted this for a long time." Joe opened the passenger door for Annie and waited for her to get in, then walked to the driver's side, slid behind the wheel, and drove away.

Later, with their plates in front of them, Annie ate more than she could have imagined—onion rings and a cheeseburger. She even stole a french fry from Joe's plate and dipped it in ketchup before dangling it in front of her mouth.

Joe leaned back in his chair and smiled.

The faster she ate, the quicker she talked. "We need to shop for baby things—diapers, clothes, a crib, a stroller . . . " She gulped. "Joe, we need to make one of the spare rooms a nursery."

He grinned. "Slow down. You're going to give yourself indigestion or worse. We have four months to prepare."

"But what if the baby comes early?" She wrinkled her nose. "Do babies come early?"

"You're asking the wrong guy. Maybe you should make a list of questions to ask Dr. Anderson the next time you talk to him."

"Okay." Annie sipped her Coke through a straw until she made a slurping sound.

"You've got me all excited, too. The stores stay open until nine o'clock tonight. Would you like to go to the hardware store and buy paint for the nursery?" Joe asked.

"Could we?" Clasping her folded hands to her breast, she remembered the same feeling on Christmas morning when she was a little girl.

Fifteen minutes later, they stood in the paint aisle, and they scanned the swatches. "Since we don't know if we're having a boy or a girl, pink and blue are not an option."

Joe held up a green sample. "What about this?"

"It reminds me of mint chocolate chip ice cream."

"So, that's good? Right?"

"It's a possibility."

She showed him a light yellow. "What do you think of this one? It looks like lemon meringue pie."

He stepped closer and whispered in her ear, "Does this mean I'm going to have to get up at all hours of the night to run out and get lemon meringue pie and mint chocolate chip ice cream for your cravings?" He grinned.

She playfully punched his arm.

"Ouch." He grabbed his bicep.

Annie held the color samples in her hand and wandered to the wallpaper book. Joe followed close behind. After spotting the children's section, she flipped through the pages—sports themes for little boys and cherubs for either. There were pages and pages of baby animals of all shapes and sizes—the bunnies and the lambs were Annie's favorites. There were rainbows and hot air balloons. "What do you think? Do you like any of these?" She looked up at her handsome husband.

"I think you'll know it when you see it."

She turned a few more pages. "Joe, look." She pointed to the sample of teddy bears. "It'll coordinate perfectly with the mint green paint."

"If that's what you want, let's order it."

They purchased the paint and walked out of the store with a synchronized spring to their steps.

"I think the nursery should be closest to the master bedroom."

"Okay by me." He stored the paint cans in the trunk.

"Do we need to hire someone to paint the room?" Annie searched his eyes.

"I think we should paint it together. Are you up for it?"

"Really?"

"Sure. It'll be fun. I'll take tomorrow off."

"Oh, Joe, I've never been so happy."

The following morning, Annie made them a hearty breakfast of scrambled eggs, ham, and wheat toast—two slices for Joe and one for her. Excited to get to their project, they didn't linger over a second cup of coffee.

Joe prepped the empty room, taping around the windows and doors. Using a roller, he painted three walls, leaving one wall for the wallpaper when it arrived. Annie followed behind him. She dipped a paintbrush into the paint and began to work around the molding of the windows, closet door, and bedroom door.

"We need to shop for a crib, changing table, dresser . . . and I'd like to get a rocker." Annie turned to see if Joe was listening.

He playfully dabbed a spot of paint on her nose.

"Oh, no. You didn't just do that." She chased him around the nursery with her paintbrush poised to retaliate. Joe dodged her again and again. Then he changed strategies and took the offense. Joe grabbed her around the waist from behind with one arm and wrestled the paintbrush away from her. After setting it on top of the paint can, he carried her to their bedroom.

CHAPTER 9

Stevie

Although it was a warm, spring day, Stevie wore a bulky sweater to conceal her baby bump.

At their lockers between classes, Stevie met Rachael and latched onto her arm like a vise. "Rach, I've got to talk to you."

"Ouch!" Rachael rubbed her arm before she pulled out her math book from her locker. "What's wrong?"

"There isn't any time to talk between classes—and you're always so busy. I don't work tonight. Can I come over to your house after school?" Stevie pleaded. "Please, Rach. My mother said it was okay with her."

"I've got a junior prom committee meeting after school. Wait for me in the quad, and my mom will pick us up after the meeting. Can you stay for dinner? My mom's been asking about you. She'd love to see you. Tonight is taco night. And you love my mom's tacos."

The bell rang for the next class to start.

"I'll be in the quad," Stevie yelled as classmates rushed through the hall to their next class.

Stevie did her homework in the quad while she waited for Rachael and her mother. At five o'clock, Mrs. Graham pulled up in her blue station wagon. Rachael ran up just then, and she and Stevie piled in the backseat with upholstery that still smelled new.

"How was school?" Mrs. Graham glanced at them from the rearview mirror.

"I told the committee that you agreed to be a chaperone at the prom," Rachael said.

Stevie listened as Rachael sat on the edge of the seat and leaned toward her mother, her arms resting on the back of the front seat. She gushed about the decorations of colorful streamers, balloons, and the cardboard cutout of a record at the entrance. "We'll pass through it. And all the lights will be off, except for a strobe light."

Soon, they were pulling into the driveway. Stevie was relieved to end the string of conversation about the prom. She was exhausted and starving.

After entering the house, Stevie followed Rachael into her bedroom. Rachael set her books on her desk and plopped on her bed. Stevie edged toward the bed, but she no longer felt comfortable lying on her stomach. So she lay on her side, facing her best friend. "I'm bummed," she said.

"Why?"

"Coach Ross cut me from the softball team." Stevie searched Rachael's expression. "I don't mean to brag, but I'm the best second baseman on the team."

"Everyone knows you are." Rachael reached over and rubbed Stevie's arm. "I'm sorry."

"You know how much I love to play the game."

Rachael listened.

"I think Coach Ross suspects that I'm pregnant. And that's why she cut me from the team." Stevie's hands balled into fists. "I'm not sure how much longer I can hide this baby."

When the baby kicked, causing Steven's belly to visibly ripple, Stevie unclenched her fists.

Rachael sprang to a sitting position and stared. "What was that?"

"The baby's kicking." Stevie smiled. Taking Rachael's hand, Stevie placed it on her belly.

"Amazing." Rachael stared in wonder.

"I know." Stevie smiled.

After moments elapsed, Stevie said, "Rach, my plan has to work. I can't give my baby away to strangers. I'm the baby's mother. You understand, don't you?"

Rachael eased her hand away from Stevie's belly. "I realize it's selfish of me, but I want us to spend our senior year having fun together. I don't want you to have to take care of a baby." She lay back down and looked toward the ceiling. "Speaking of, how is your plan coming along?"

"Okay, except my grades are dropping. I'm just so tired all the time with going to school and working with my mother at night. If I don't get my homework done before the night shift starts, I try to do it when I get home from work. But some nights, I skip it and fall asleep because I'm exhausted." Stevie didn't tell Rachael that she had stolen a bottle of vodka hidden in her closet and sometimes drank from it—trying to dull her pain of feeling lost, lonely, and unloved. The pain never went away for very long.

"You won't like what I'm about to say, but I'm going to say it, anyway. Maybe you should quit the job and concentrate on school."

Stevie glared. "Never. I need to work to show my mother that I can do both, so she'll change her mind and let me keep my baby." Stevie rubbed her belly, making cooing sounds. She walked over to the full-length mirror attached to the bedroom door and gazed at her profile.

"After the baby is born, who will take care of it while you're at school?" Rachael arched her eyebrows and pursed her lips, reminding Stevie of a fish.

"Mrs. Godsey, our neighbor, takes care of kids. She's a sweet, old lady; and she likes me. I plan to ask her. I'll offer to clean her house in exchange for babysitting."

Rachael sat on the edge of her bed, looking at Stevie's reflection in the mirror. "Don't you ever think about adoption and having fun during our senior year?"

"Girls," Mrs. Graham's voice rang out from the kitchen, "it's time to set the table."

"Sure, I think about it," said Stevie. "But then I feel the baby kick, and I think how much worse my life will be if I give this baby away." She walked out the bedroom door with Rachael close behind her.

Everyone helped get dinner ready. Mr. Graham finished chopping lettuce and tomatoes and grating cheddar cheese. He brought the serving bowls to the table. As Stevie set the plates at each setting, Rachael grabbed the taco sauce from the refrigerator. Stevie realized she felt more at home here than at her house. The Grahams were like the family she dreamed of having someday. She smiled, remembering seeing Mr. Graham kiss and hug Mrs. Graham in the kitchen as they worked side by side.

Mrs. Graham placed the serving dish filled to the brim with tacos in the middle of the table, and they all sat down. While everyone was busy loading their plates with food, Stevie felt uncomfortable, as though someone was staring. She glanced around to see Buddy scrutinizing her.

Scooting his chair close to the table, Buddy cocked his head toward his mother. "Mom, does Stevie look like she's going to have a baby?"

Mrs. Graham reached her hand over and held Stevie's hand under the table. "Yes, Buddy, Stevie is going to have a baby."

"That's impossible." His brown eyes grew as big as basketballs. "She doesn't have a husband."

CHAPTER 10

Annie

Annie leaned against the doorframe of the completed nursery, daydreaming. Everything was ready. Days before, she'd watched Joe assemble the cherrywood crib. The rich wood of the crib, dresser, changing table, and rocker all matched.

Joe sidled up next to her and slipped his arm around her waist. "Happy?"

"Very." She laid her head on his shoulder. "I'd like to buy large letters to spell out the baby's name and put them on the wall above the crib, but since we still don't know if it will be a boy or a girl, I have to wait. Patience is not one of my strong points."

He winked. "I know."

"We still need to decide on a name." She looked into his blue eyes. What color eyes would their baby have? Blue? Brown like hers? Or hazel?

Joe intertwined his fingers with hers and led her to the family room. "It's time to get back to business."

"What business?"

"This." He pointed to the books on the coffee table. Then he pulled her down next to him onto the cushy sofa.

Strewn across the coffee table was every book Annie could find on childcare and one on baby names. There was even the fourteenth volume of *Childcraft,* titled *You and Your Child.* The rest of the set was shelved in the bookcase. Joe had bought the entire set from a door-to-door salesman. Joe always thought bigger was better. One day, he'd even come home with a giant teddy bear. It was too big to sit in the rocker, so it sat in a corner in the nursery.

Annie picked up the dog-eared baby name book. "I've enjoyed taking up Dr. Anderson's hobby of finding the description of names. I want our baby to have a meaningful name. I still like Zoey. I'm just not sure about the middle name."

"And you still agree with Joseph Michael Costa the Third for a boy?"

"Maybe. I wouldn't want your family to disown us." She grinned.

"You? Maybe. Me? Never." He leaned in close to her. She could feel his breath on her cheek. "I'm their pride and joy."

"Don't I know it." She flipped through the book. "I think I'd like the middle name for a girl to be Elizabeth. It was my mother's name."

"Zoey Elizabeth Costa. That sounds nice." He laid his head on the back of the sofa and looked upward. "Remind me—what does Zoey mean?"

"Life."

"Yes, I think that's it. This baby is bringing new life to our home," agreed Joe. "I'm getting more excited the closer we get."

Annie sighed contentedly. This was what she had hoped would happen. She was so relieved that Joe had come around to the idea of adoption. But the waiting was excruciating. She tried to distract herself but often found herself standing in the nursery, dreaming of the day they would finally bring their baby home.

She set down the name book and picked up one of the childcare books from the coffee table and began reading.

"I'm hungry for popcorn. Are you interested?" Joe asked.

She set the book aside. "I'll make us some."

"You're engrossed in what you're doing. I'll pop it."

After he returned, he pushed the books to the side and placed the large bowl in the middle of the coffee table. The doorbell chimed. "Who could that be at this hour?"

She shrugged her shoulders. "Got me. We're not expecting anyone, are we?"

He answered the door, and Jenn followed him into the living room.

"I thought you had a date tonight." Annie wrinkled her brow.

"I did. And it couldn't have ended soon enough for me." She plunked down next to Annie on the sofa. "The guy was so boring, I thought I'd fall asleep with my head on my plate."

"That bad?" Joe offered her some popcorn.

"No, thanks. I'm full. At least I got a meal out of the guy."

"So you'd rather be with a couple of old, married people than checking out the dating scene?" Annie asked.

"I would. You two are comfortable. And I like comfortable." She leaned back onto the sofa and propped her feet on the coffee table.

Joe tossed a popcorn piece and caught it in his open mouth. "So, what was so bad about your date? Bad breath? B.O.? Horns?"

"He talked only about his job. It wasn't a conversation. He just droned on and on about how to package meat of all things." Jenn sighed. "You cut the fat off the meat, but not all of it. You leave some fat. You place the meat in the little Styrofoam tray with a blotter under it to soak up any blood. You wrap the film over it. You—"

"Okay. We get it. He isn't Mr. Right." Joe laughed and scooped up a handful of popcorn.

"So, what are you two doing besides munching on popcorn?" Jenn grabbed one of the books on the table.

"We're discussing baby names," Annie said.

"Oh, yeah." Jenn thought for a moment. "Jennifer is a nice name. Don't you think so?"

"I do. I've always loved your name." Annie smiled.

Jenn put down the book she was holding and picked up the book of baby names. She found the girls' names inside the book, beginning with "J." "It says Jennifer means 'fair one,' 'blessed spirit,' and 'white enchantress.' And the characteristics include giving, sharing, loving, caring, and loyal."

Joe added, "Just like a puppy dog." He grinned and threw a popcorn kernel at her.

"I like to be with people I care about."

"And we like being with you, too. I'm just sorry your date turned out to be awful." Annie reached over and squeezed Jenn's shoulder.

"Oh, well. It's not the end of the world. What's that cliché? There are more fish in the sea."

"But is it a fish you want?"

"No, Joe. For sure, not a big mouth bass like you," Jenn bantered with him.

"Don't forget that I'm your boss." He smiled.

"Yeah, you, too. You two act like brother and sister." Annie shook her head.

Joe yawned. "I'm done in. I think I'll excuse myself and let you ladies continue without me. See you tomorrow, Jenn."

"Good night." Jenn turned back to face Annie and Joe walked out of the room. "It *is* late. I should probably go."

Annie walked her to the door, and they hugged while saying good night. Annie watched until Jenn drove away, feeling lucky to have such a loyal friend.

Chapter 11

Stevie

Stevie felt fat and ugly as she slumped in a chair, watching Rachael and the committee put the finishing touches on the decorations for the prom.

"There." Turning toward Stevie, Rachael asked, "What do you think?"

"It's nice." Stevie placed her hand on her aching lower back and tried to rub the pain away without success.

Rachael checked her watch. "We'd better scoot. Mom will be here to take me to my hair appointment. You're still going with me, aren't you?"

"Sure." She was grateful for any time she could spend with her best friend between school, work, and Rachael's busy schedule. She wouldn't miss it.

At the salon, Stevie listened as her friends tittered about their dates and plans for the evening, starting with a steak dinner at Megan's house. Three couples planned to arrive at the prom in a limo. She sighed, knowing she could have been a part of the memorable evening.

Giggles filled the beauty salon. How long had it been since she'd laughed? Since the night she'd gotten so drunk and lost her virginity? Or was it even before that? Did she ever even chuckle after Daddy was diagnosed with inoperable cancer? A stream of water slid down her legs and puddled on the salon floor. Stevie looked down. "Mrs. Graham!"

Sitting in the waiting area, Rachael's mother looked up from one of the outdated magazines she was perusing.

"I think my water broke! And I've made a mess."

The laughter stopped, and the teens gawked at Stevie.

Mrs. Graham and a beautician, who carried towels, rushed to Stevie's side. "Don't you worry about a thing, honey," the stylist said as she handed a towel to Stevie and wiped the floor with the other one.

Helping Stevie to her feet, Mrs. Graham said, "Rachael, can you get a ride home from one of the other girls?"

Megan gaped. "My mother will take her home, Mrs. Graham."

"Thank you, Megan."

Rachael's mother smiled and put her arm around Stevie's waist. "I think we'd better get you to the hospital."

By the time Mama arrived at the hospital, Stevie's labor pains were five minutes apart. How much longer would it be?

"I'll be leaving now," Mrs. Graham said. She released Stevie's hand, her face full of compassion. Stevie needed to let her go, yet Mrs. Graham was like her lifeline. Their hands slipped apart.

Mama took the chair vacated by Rachael's mother and grasped Stevie's hand between her rough ones. "I'd do this for you if I could," Mama said.

For hours, between the painful contractions, Stevie imagined what was happening at the prom. Who would be the prom king and queen? If not the queen, she would have been one of the royal court. She'd been popular before that ill-fated night. Stevie winced from another labor pain.

Mama rubbed Stevie's hand. "You're a brave girl. Soon, it'll be all over. And you can get on with your life."

Stevie turned her face away from Mama. Rage boiled inside her like a witch's brew, feeling like she was losing the battle to keep her baby and hating Mama's words—"get on with your life." If she could, she would grab her baby and run away. But where would she go? Mama wasn't going to help her keep her baby. During Stevie's pregnancy, Mama hadn't budged in her firm conviction of not letting Stevie bring her baby home. Like Daddy once said, *Your mother is as stubborn as a mule. But deep inside her, she has a soft heart.*

Stevie winced from another contraction. They were stronger and closer together now. No contraction was as painful as the ache in her heart of having to give up her baby. She knew even if Mama saw the baby after it was born, she wouldn't change her mind. She was as determined as Mama, but Mama had won.

After the nurse arrived and checked Stevie's progress, she said, "It's time. Mrs. Shaw, you may have a seat in the waiting room."

"Dr. Anderson is on his way, dear. It won't be long now," said one of the nurses in green scrubs as she wheeled Stevie into the delivery room.

Stevie knew May 11, 1968, would forever be etched in her mind and heart. The following day, depression engulfed her like the black mourning veil Jackie Kennedy wore when President Kennedy died. Stevie had been glued to the TV during the funeral coverage, and she'd never forgotten the image of Mrs. Kennedy standing between Caroline and John John nor the picture of John John saluting his father's casket—the father who would never see John John grow up.

Stevie stared at the relinquishment paper lying on the hospital rolling table in front of her. Once she signed it, she could "get on with her life." Isn't that what Mama and everyone said? Nauseated, she pushed the papers away.

Later, when the nurse entered her room, Stevie asked, "Is my baby a boy or a girl?"

The nurse avoided Stevie's question and checked her vitals.

"Please," Stevie begged.

The nurse hesitated. "A girl."

"I want to hold her."

"For your sake, it's better you don't." The nurse straightened Stevie's bedding while Stevie sat in a chair, watching.

"Did you ever place a baby for adoption?"

"Well . . . no."

"Then how do you know?"

With her head down, the nurse quickly left the room.

Later, after visiting hours were over, Stevie left her hospital bed and looked both ways down the hall. When the corridor was clear, she shuffled to the nursery and scanned the plastic bassinets. She spotted the only one that didn't have a name written in large block letters. The baby bed held a little bundle, wrapped tightly in a blanket, like a papoose. All she could see was a perfectly shaped head with tiny ears, nose, and a sweet mouth. A wisp of blonde hair covered her head like a cap. Stevie stared for a long time until she felt weak.

"I love you, sweet girl. No matter what happens, I always will," she whispered, then she wandered back to her room. She would remember the features of her perfect daughter forever because they were etched in her heart.

With trembling fingers, she dialed Rachael's number from the room phone and waited for her to answer.

"Rach, Mama hasn't changed her mind. She's forcing me to give up my baby. I'd rather die. What am I going to do?"

"Stevie, I'm sorry. Really, I am. But maybe it's for the best."

Stevie slammed down the phone and began to weep uncontrollably. Her body shook with each sob.

The following morning, Mama arrived to take her home. Mama eyed the unsigned document.

"Mama, did you see her?"

"No."

"Won't you please change your mind? I'll be a good mother. I can do it. I know I can."

"Stevie, I haven't changed my mind. What kind of life do you want for her? Do you want her to be with babysitters all the time while you go to school and to work? Or do you want her to have a mother and a father to love and care for her? You, of all people, are aware of what it's like to have a loving father. Don't you want that for your baby?" She sat next to Stevie on the bed and put her arm around her. "You'll have other children someday. And you'll be a great mother." *Is that a tear in Mama's eye?* "Do the right thing."

Stevie's trembling hands covered her ears, yet Mama's words echoed in her head. *Get on with your life. Do the right thing.* She mulled over Mama's words.

Was she selfish, wanting to keep her baby all to herself, not giving her every opportunity? How could she be so selfish?

Stevie had tried so hard to keep her baby, doing everything in her power for her plan to work, yet she'd failed. She picked up the pen and signed the official document, waiving her parental rights.

Although the nurse had given her a pill to dry up her milk, it hadn't worked. Her breasts swelled with life-giving nourishment, yet her arms were empty.

CHAPTER 12

Annie

Her hand shaking from excitement, Annie dialed Joe's office number. She stood on one foot and then the other.

When Joey answered, Annie exclaimed, "Daddy, you'd better get home. We have a baby girl."

"When?"

"She was born yesterday, and the birth mother signed the waiver of her parental rights." Her heart pounded inside her chest. *Breathe, just breathe.* "Dr. Anderson said we could go to the hospital and see her."

"I'm leaving now. Meet me in front of the house."

Annie hung up the phone and jogged to the master bedroom, squealing. She changed her clothes, looked in the mirror, and combed a strand of her ebony hair into place. Then she grabbed her purse and waited in the front of the house for Joe to arrive.

Shortly, Joe's red Corvette came to a complete stop at the curb, and Annie jumped into the passenger seat.

"We should probably take your car. More room to bring her home."

"We can't bring her home until tomorrow. The pediatrician needs to examine her."

"What's wrong with her?" His brow was furrowed.

"Nothing." She patted his leg. "All babies are examined before they leave the hospital. Now go."

Per Dr. Anderson's instructions, when they arrived at the hospital nursery, they knocked on the door.

A nurse in a white uniform opened the door. "May I help you?"

Joe said, "We're the Costas. Dr. Anderson said we were to ask for Mrs. Pearson."

She smiled. "I'm Laurie Pearson. I've been expecting you. Stand at the window, and I'll bring your baby." She closed the door, went to one of the cribs, and lifted a little bundle wrapped in a pink blanket. Bringing her to her side of the glass, she held up the baby for them to see.

Not taking her eyes off Zoey, Annie leaned into Joe's side as he placed his arm around her.

The nurse lifted the blanket away, showing them Zoey's full length—her arms and legs, hands and feet. Zoey stretched, yet her eyes remained closed. Although Mrs. Pearson didn't rush their staring at her in wonder, it didn't seem long enough. She returned the baby to her bed, and then she rolled the crib close to the glass. Mrs. Pearson gathered some papers from her desk, then came out of the nursery to speak to them.

"Dr. Mills will examine your baby tonight or first thing in the morning. Plan to pick her up around noon. Bring a diaper bag with diapers, something for her to wear home, and a receiving blanket. If you decide to use Dr. Mills as your pediatrician, I've enclosed his phone number. There is an infant care booklet, diaper service brochure, and other information inside." She held up a large envelope. "Tomorrow, we'll send home a couple of cans of formula with your baby, but you'll need to buy more." She handed the envelope to Annie.

"Thank you so much," Annie said.

"You're very welcome." Mrs. Pearson shook their hands and returned to her post.

Clutching the envelope to her breast, Annie and Joe couldn't take their eyes away from their sweet daughter.

Eventually, one of the nurses in the nursery stepped to the window, smiled, and pulled the curtain closed.

Joe looked down at Annie. With a raised eyebrow, he said, "I guess visiting hours are over."

"For us, they are. Dr. Anderson provided us with private time to see our baby. It isn't regular visiting hours."

"Well, let's go, Mommy. Before we head home, we have formula to pick up." He placed his hand on the middle of her lower back and guided her to the parking lot.

At home, she took inventory of the packed diaper bag for all the necessary items. She mentally checked off each item—diapers, receiving blanket, pacifier, and the outfit she'd chosen to bring Zoey home in—a yellow terrycloth sleeper with a bunny embroidered in white.

Satisfied, she padded to the master bedroom, slipped into a nighty, and slid next to Joe's warm, sleeping body. Annie snuggled close to him. His even breathing should have lulled her to sleep, but it didn't. She was too excited to sleep.

The following morning, Annie and Joe watched one of the nurses dress Zoey in her going-home outfit Annie had carefully chosen and brought to the hospital. Soon, they slid into the front seat of Annie's Mercedes parked in the hospital parking lot.

Annie turned her gaze from Zoey, who was asleep in her arms, to Joe. "Drive carefully, Daddy. We have precious cargo with us."

Like her, he couldn't take his eyes off their daughter wrapped in a pink baby blanket, one tiny hand gripping Annie's finger.

With his hand on the key in the ignition, Joe pensively looked at Annie and asked, "Happy?"

"Happier than I could have ever imagined." She wiped a tear off her cheek.

"So, those are happy tears then?"

"The happiest."

While Joe drove, slower than usual, Annie cradled Zoey's head covered in soft blonde fluff. Then she ran her hand over Zoey's skin. "Her skin is so silky." She buried her nose in Zoey's neck. "And she smells delicious."

After arriving home, Annie placed Zoey in her crib, and together, standing side by side with their arms around each other's waist, they stared at their daughter.

A few weeks later, the doorbell chimed, waking Annie from slumber. She checked to see if Zoey was still asleep in her bassinet next to the sofa where Annie had fallen asleep. She staggered to the door and looked through the peephole. Seeing it was Jenn, she opened the massive door. "Good morning."

"I woke you. I'm so sorry."

"Don't think anything of it. Zoey has her days and nights mixed up, so I sleep when she sleeps. At least, I try." Annie tucked her hair behind her ear.

"How is Angel Baby today?" It was the nickname that only Jenn called her.

"Wonderful. Come see for yourself." Annie led Jenn into the family room and stood beside the bassinet. "Want some coffee?"

"No. If I have any more, I'll float away." Jenn stared at Zoey as she slept. "Can I hold her?"

"Sure." Annie poured herself a cup of coffee. "It's okay if you wake her. She needs to eventually switch to being awake during the day and sleeping at night."

Jenn cradled Zoey in her arms and watched her sleep. "Joe was telling me that you're up all night."

"I don't mind it." Annie watched Jenn holding Zoey. "She's my world now. I'm the luckiest woman alive."

"What about your charity work?"

"What about it?"

"Don't they need you?" Jenn's eyebrow lifted.

"Someone else needs to step forward. I paid my dues volunteering for several years."

"I won't argue with you about that," Jenn said.

"Zoey is my life."

Jenn caressed Zoey's soft head of blonde fluff. The baby's hair was as light as Annie's was dark. "I miss playing tennis with you. Sharon is okay, but she isn't any competition like you are. Are you sure you won't consider a babysitter?"

Taking a sip of her coffee, Annie made a face and shook her head.

"What about Joe's mother?"

Annie shook her head more vigorously this time.

Changing the subject, she asked Jenn if she had been on any interesting dates recently.

Jenn sighed. "There's not a lot to choose from these days," she complained. "We can't all find our Joe out there."

An hour later, Jenn checked her watch. "Gotta run. I have an appointment to show a house." She placed sleeping Zoey in her bassinet and hugged Annie goodbye.

Annie fell onto the sofa, exhausted. In a few minutes, she was sound asleep as well.

When Zoey was six weeks old, Annie felt guilty for neglecting Joe, so she planned a candlelight meal in the dining room. She'd cooked the spaghetti sauce all day just like his mother had taught her. A fresh green salad and garlic bread completed the meal. Zoey was asleep in the nursery when Joe arrived home. Annie wore a black dress that clung to her curves. It was Joe's favorite.

"What's this?" Joe smiled.

"Dinner." She placed her arms around his neck. "You like?"

"Yes, I like." He ran his hands down her sides until cries from the nursery stopped him.

Annie had learned the cries—wet, hungry, and bored. This one sounded different—like she was in pain. Annie rushed to the nursery and picked her up, holding Zoey on her shoulder, patting her back.

"You go ahead and eat," Annie said to her dejected-looking husband. "Dinner will get cold."

"What about you?"

"I'll warm up mine later." She paced, unable to soothe her precious baby.

At midnight, she was finally able to get Zoey to sleep. Exhausted and feeling inadequate, Annie stepped into the shower and let the warm water massage her back while Joe slept.

In the morning, while Zoey slept, Annie researched *Baby Care* for colic symptoms. She left a message for the pediatrician, asking if Zoey's formula needed to be changed.

Later, when the phone rang, she clutched the receiver with both hands like a lifeline.

"Annie, this is Dr. Mills."

"Doctor, thank you so much for returning my call. I appreciate it."

"You're welcome. Since it's probably colic, like you say, you can change the formula if you'd like. Try not to worry. Colic is common in infants, and she'll outgrow it. But if you'd feel more comfortable bringing her into the office, you can make an appointment."

After saying goodbye and feeling somewhat reassured, Annie hung up the phone.

The following week, Joe brought home take-out from Chin's. He set the boxes on the table, unknotted his tie, and took a crying Zoey from Annie's arms. "You eat." He began to pace. "You're okay. We love you, baby girl. Shh." When that didn't work, he laid her across his muscular arm on her tummy and rubbed her back.

As the weeks turned into months, Joe started to come home later and later. When Zoey was three months old, he walked through the door to her crying. He reached for Zoey. "I'll take her for a drive. Maybe the motion of the car will soothe her. Besides, you need a break. Why don't you go out somewhere? Maybe call Jenn."

Annie knew she was giving him a blank stare as Joe closed the door. She shuffled to the bathroom and undressed. Letting the hot water pour over her, she began to sob.

On Saturday afternoon, Annie turned to Joe and suggested, "Why don't we have an early dinner tonight?"

"Great idea. I'd like a pleasant, quiet dinner with my wife." He kissed her.

After firing up the grill on the patio to put the steaks on, they heard Zoey begin the nightly ritual. Joe ran his hand through his curly, dark hair, looked at Annie, and said, "My mother said to let her cry. It won't hurt her."

Annie turned and met his pleading eyes. She screamed, "I don't care what your mother said. Zoey is in pain. You've seen how she arches her little back, and her bloated tummy fills with gas. I'm not about to let her suffer in pain alone." Then she rushed to the nursery.

CHAPTER 13

Stevie

Stevie dozed, lying on the beach blanket while Rachael swam in the surf.

After Rachael plodded through the sand toward the blanket, she sprinkled water on Stevie's belly.

Stevie sprang to a sitting position. "What in the—"

"It's just water. It won't hurt you." Rachael plopped down beside her.

"I was asleep. Thank you very much." Stevie lay back on the blanket.

"You've been depressed all summer. Since . . . "

"Since I gave my baby away?" Stevie shot back.

"Yeah. Stevie, you're my best friend, but . . . "

"It isn't fun to be with me anymore. Right?"

"We're young. It's supposed to be the best time of our lives."

"So, I suppose you agree with everyone else that I need to get on with my life."

"I understand how much you hate those words, but yes." Rachael turned toward Stevie. "I miss how you used to be. There's nothing you can do to change what happened—or, should I say, the decision other people forced on you?"

"You mean, my mother." Did Stevie's words sound as angry as she felt?

"Well, yeah."

Stevie flopped over onto her stomach. "I can't pretend to be happy when I'm not."

Rachael turned over, too, and let a handful of sand run through her fingers.

"I've got to get out of my mother's house. I hate living there. My clothes and hair always smell like cigarette smoke."

Rachael continued to play with the sand as she listened.

"Originally, I saved my money so Mama would let me keep my baby and take care of her. But since that didn't happen, I have another plan. I'm going to get an apartment as soon as I have enough money saved."

"Is that why you're still working nights?"

"Exactly, Einstein." Stevie chuckled and punched Rachael on the arm.

"Now, that's the Stevie I remember." Rachael bumped her back. "Don't look now, but Jerry Osborn and Mike Mulligan are coming toward us."

Both girls sat up as the boys approached. Jerry, a stocky football player, and Mike, a lanky basketball star, stood beside the girls' blanket. After an attempt at awkward conversation, they eventually sat on the edge of the blanket. Jerry sat next to Rachael, and Mike sat at Stevie's feet, buried in the sand. Mike had teased Stevie in middle school, but he'd been nicer to her in high school.

"So, do you know which classes you have yet?" Mike asked.

"Not yet. Our schedules will probably be posted next week," Stevie said.

"I've been at football practice every day for the last month." Jerry played in the sand.

"He can't even go swimming. It might sap his strength," Mike teased.

"Bummer," Rachael interjected.

"At least I made the team." Jerry looked at Mike with his perfect white teeth, evidence of years of wearing braces.

"What about you?" Mike looked at Stevie. "Want to go for a swim?"

"Me?" Stevie pointed to her chest. "Uh, I can't get my hair wet. I have to go to work tonight." *Dumb, Stevie. Really dumb.*

"Really? Where do you work?" Mike asked.

Stevie looked down at her lap. "I clean office buildings."

"Oh, yeah? Good for you. My parents wanted me to get a job for the summer, but I couldn't find one. To be honest, I didn't try very hard. I just wanted to have fun this summer—before our senior year," Mike said.

"Has it been fun?" Rachael asked.

"Sort of. Except for Jerry's schedule." Mike nodded toward Jerry. "We got to get home by two o'clock for him to get ready for football practice." He looked at Stevie. "Are you sure you don't want to go swimming? I'll make sure you won't get your hair wet."

"And how do you propose to do that? Waves are unpredictable." Stevie couldn't see his eyes behind the sunglasses, but she knew they were blue—a beautiful shade of blue.

"If one came toward you, I'd pick you up and hold you above them." He stood. "Plus, I'm tall. Very tall."

Stevie giggled. "I can see that."

The four teens walked to the edge of the surf and stood in the water, talking, the water lapping at their legs. Eventually, Jerry said, "We gotta go. Practice."

Mike turned to the girls. "There's a party at Clark's house tonight. Want to go with us?"

Rachael thought for a minute. "Sure. But I have to ask my mom."

Mike looked at Stevie.

"I'm working," Stevie said.

"That's right. You can't get your hair wet." He grinned. "Maybe another time. I can only hope, can't I?"

"Come on, man, we gotta go." Jerry turned to Rachael. "I'll come by your house at seven. I hope your mom says yes."

The girls walked with them as far as their blanket, then watched them trudge through the sand toward the parking lot.

"Do you think your mom will let you go to Clark's party?" Stevie asked as she lowered herself to the warm blanket.

"Probably. Clark's parents are always home, so there isn't any drinking. And my mom likes Jerry. She's been friends with his mother since high school."

"Rach, do you think Jerry and Mike know?"

"About what?" Rachael searched her beach bag and pulled out the suntan lotion.

"That I had a baby?"

"I don't know. No one talks to me about it. Probably because we're best friends." Rachael reapplied the lotion to her arms and legs. "Do you hate Nick?"

Stevie swallowed hard. "Not really. I probably should, but I don't. Instead, I hate myself."

"I wish you didn't. All of us were drinking that night—some more than others. You made a mistake. Everyone makes mistakes." Rachael handed the tube to Stevie. "Will you do my back?"

Stevie smoothed lotion over Rachael's tan shoulders. *But my mistake left me with a hole in my heart. Rachael doesn't understand. No one does.*

Stevie usually did the vacuuming and mopping at work, yet tonight, she'd switched duties with Mama. The vacuum droned in the background of the empty office building as Stevie moved from work area to work area, emptying wastepaper baskets into the large trash can she pushed around. Taking a dust rag from the cleaning cart, Stevie dusted one of the desks, picking up Joe Costa's nameplate. She'd learned to be thorough, wiping away every dust particle. She moved around to the other side of the desk and gasped when she spotted a double picture frame. On one side of the silver frame was a birth announcement, and on the other, a picture of her baby. With her hand covering her heart, she read the words.

Announcing the birth of our baby

Zoey Elizabeth Costa

Born May 11, 1968

Seven pounds, four ounces

Nineteen inches long

It took her breath away as Stevie stared at the picture for a long time. She'd recognize her baby anywhere. After a while, her eyes focused on another portrait on the desk. It was of an elegant-looking woman, probably in her late twenties, wearing opera-length pearls. Her hair was parted in the middle and pulled away from her face. Stevie's eyes darted back to her baby's sweet face. Her heart ached. Mechanically, Stevie finished dusting the rest of the office. She didn't plan to tell Mama. It was her secret.

On the ride home from work, Stevie cracked the passenger window to try and relieve the acidic smoke in Mama's old Chevy. Tears blurred her vision as she stared out the window at the closed strip malls and sleepy neighborhoods.

Entering the house, Mama lit a cigarette.

"Night," Stevie mumbled as she went down the hall to her bedroom. "Goodnight."

Stevie closed her bedroom door and went to her closet. She grabbed the vodka bottle from under her dirty clothes. She unscrewed the cap and gulped the pain-killing liquid. The words echoed in her head—*get on with your life.*

How?

CHAPTER 14

The following morning, Stevie dragged herself out of bed at eleven o'clock, her head pounding like a jackhammer on concrete. She staggered to the fridge and poured herself a glass of orange juice. After unscrewing the cap on the aspirin bottle, Stevie popped down a couple of them with juice. She was glad Mama wasn't at home.

She opened the drawer, grabbed the telephone book, and flipped through the pages. Finding the alphabetical names listed beginning with "C," she ran her finger down the columns—Costa, Joseph and Annie, 1010 Ocean Vista, Laguna Beach. She'd found her baby.

With her head still pounding, she dialed Rachael. "Rach, can you borrow your mom's car today?"

"We're going shopping for school clothes. We're leaving in a few minutes. Do you want to go with us?"

Not really, but if it's the only way . . . "Okay."

"We'll swing by and pick you up in a few," Rachael said.

Stevie hung up the phone and wrote Mama a note saying she went shopping with Rachael, then went to her room. She pulled on jeans and a V-neck t-shirt, easy to pull over her head to try on garments. Stevie didn't plan to buy many school clothes because she was saving her money to rent an apartment.

She grabbed her purse and pulled out the bank savings book. It was silly for her to look because she was aware of the exact amount written in it—$327.19. It might be enough to rent a small apartment if she had someone to share the expense with her. But what about money for food? And she needed a car, unless she found a place near the bus line. Who would share the rent with her? Everyone else seemed happy living with their parents—everyone except her.

A car horn beeped, and Stevie locked the front door and climbed into the backseat of Rachael's mother's station wagon. Stevie was dying to tell Rachael about what she'd discovered about her baby. After arriving at Fashion Island, they couldn't ditch Rachael's mother. Mrs. Graham shopped with them, making comments about every item they saw or seemed interested in trying on.

In the dressing room, Stevie whispered, "I've got to talk to you."

"So, talk," Rachael whispered back.

"Not here. I don't want anyone to overhear us." Stevie pointed to the occupied dressing rooms on either side of them.

"It must be important."

"It is."

Later, after what seemed to Stevie to be a grueling amount of time, Rachael's mother said, "I need to do an errand in town. I'll be back at five o'clock to pick you up. I'll meet you at the entrance."

"Thanks, Mom."

"Yeah, thanks, Mrs. Graham." Stevie blew out the breath she'd been holding all day.

As they watched Mrs. Graham walk away, Stevie turned to Rachael. "Do you have more shopping to do?"

"Nah, this was last-minute stuff." Rachael held up several bags. "The other things are at home. What about you? Only one new top?"

"Yeah. Saving my money." Stevie grabbed onto Rachael's arm. "Let's get a Coke."

They sat outdoors at a round table with their drinks. "So, what's so important that you've got to tell me?" Rachael asked as she put her shopping bags in a wrought iron chair next to her.

"I know where my baby is."

"No way."

"One of the office buildings I clean is Joe Costa Real Estate. He has a picture of my baby on his desk."

"How can you be sure it's your baby?"

"I told you about sneaking to the nursery after she was born. I know it's her and where they live."

Rachael's mouth gaped.

"I looked up their address in the phonebook—Joe and Annie—and they live in Laguna Beach. That's why I want you to borrow your mother's car—so we can see where my baby lives."

"Stevie, that's creepy."

"No, it's not!" Stevie balled her hands into fists. "You don't understand how I feel. No one does."

"No, I probably don't. I don't think anything good will come from seeing where the adoptive parents live. It'll only bring you more heartache than you already have."

"I've got to. If you don't want to help me, I'll find someone else." Stevie wiped her tears with her finger and searched in her purse for a tissue.

"Okay, I'll ask, but I don't think you should do it."

They stood at the entrance to Fashion Island and waited for Mrs. Graham to pick them up. After sliding into the car and settling the shopping bags on their laps, Rachael stuttered, "Mom, can I borrow the car tomorrow?"

"Rachael, do I need to remind you that Sunday is family day and how much your grandmother looks forward to our visit?" Mrs. Graham glared at Rachael. "I can't believe you'd even ask me to borrow the car on Sunday."

"I'm sorry," Rachael responded.

"It's my fault, Mrs. Graham. I asked her if she could drive me somewhere."

"Where do you need to go?" Rachael's mother looked in her rearview mirror at Stevie in the backseat. "Maybe I could take you there now."

"No, thank you." Stevie wiped her sweaty hands on her jeans. *Please, Mrs. Graham, please drop it,* she thought.

"Stevie, I'm here for you—whatever you need." Mrs. Graham signaled and turned into the next lane.

"I appreciate it." Stevie's words came automatically. It was Mrs. Graham who had introduced her to Dr. Anderson, and he'd encouraged her to place her baby for adoption. She'd always liked Rachael's mother, but she didn't trust her with what she planned to do.

And Mama was no different—not supporting Stevie by helping her to keep her baby. Stevie couldn't ask to borrow Mama's car either. No doubt, she'd grill Stevie about where she planned to go, too. The only person Stevie trusted with her secret was Rachael.

The following week, school started; and after getting off the bus in the afternoon, Stevie went to work with her mother. Rachael had something to do every day after school. It didn't matter because Mrs. Graham had the station wagon at work, anyway. So, Stevie was left with no wheels and no way to get to Laguna Beach. Stevie took Friday night off from work so she could go to Rachael's sleepover and celebrate her birthday. After the party quieted down, the girls slipped into their sleeping bags in the living room. Stevie kept her eyes closed for what seemed like hours, but she couldn't sleep because of the whispering. She overheard Megan tell Kerry, "I heard that Mike Mulligan likes Stevie and wants to take her out."

"Nice guys don't take out girls like Stevie." Kerry's whisper came even softer.

"It wasn't her fault. I heard she was raped," Megan said.

"Well, my mother said no decent boy would ever marry her because she's spoiled goods," Kerry said.

"Shh."

"She can't hear us. She's asleep."

Tears crept out of Stevie's closed eyes. She no longer belonged in the group. Stevie wished she had her bottle of painkiller with her, but she only drank alone. She'd wait until she got home. Morning couldn't come soon enough.

Saturday morning, Mr. Graham and Buddy came into the living room where the teens were in different stages of wakefulness, some whispering, others with their eyes still closed. Mr. Graham roared, "Everyone outside." He led Rachael out the front door. Outside, Mrs. Graham operated the movie camera. In the driveway was a yellow VW Beetle with a huge bow on top.

"Happy birthday, darling," Mrs. Graham said from behind the camera.

Stevie joined the others with their verbal awes over Rachael's birthday gift. But inside, her happiness for Rachael was shadowed by Kerry's words echoing in her head: *nice guys don't take out girls like Stevie.*

The following Saturday, Rachael picked up Stevie at her house. They stopped at a gas station in Laguna Beach and asked for directions to Ocean Vista. Rachael drove the winding tree-shaded street and stopped at the mansion perched on top of the hill. Rachael turned around at the dead end, pointing her new bug down the hill, and parked across from the house.

"I don't like this." Rachael turned off the ignition and set the brake. "What if someone sees us? Or asks us what we're doing here?"

"We'll say we're lost." Stevie stared at the house, surrounded by a wrought-iron fence.

"Stevie, this is crazy. What do you plan to do?"

"I'm not sure. I need to see where my baby lives."

"You've seen it. Can we go now, please?"

The wrought-iron gate began to slide open.

Rachael gasped, started the ignition, and put the bug in gear.

They passed a Corvette coming up the hill as they were going down.

"Are you satisfied now? You're stalking them." Rachael smacked the palm of her hand on the steering wheel.

"No, I'm not. I'm watching over my daughter."

They were silent as they drove along the coast.

Stevie asked, "Who lives on a street overlooking the ocean?"

"Rich people."

"I plan to write a letter," Stevie said.

"To the adoptive mother?"

"No, to Zoey."

"She can't read."

"I've never known you to be snippy." Stevie looked out the window as they turned inland toward Santa Ana. "She'll be able to read them someday. If you were adopted, wouldn't you want a letter from the person who gave life to you? I would."

"If you want to write a letter, fine. But you should stay away. You're obsessed. And I don't think it's good for you."

That night, Stevie took a new spiral notebook and wrote "Letters to My Daughter."

September 21, 1968

My darling daughter,

Today I saw where you live. I'm watching over you, my precious baby. I've loved you since before you were born. I hope someday you will be able to forgive me for giving you away.

Love,

Your First Mother

She closed the notebook and hid it at the bottom of her top dresser drawer. She grabbed the vodka bottle from her hiding place and took a sip. Rachael knew all her secrets—except this one. She cradled the bottle to her chest.

Chapter 15

With the windows rolled down in the yellow bug, Stevie rode around town with Rachael. When Rachael pulled into the neighborhood gas station, a young man came from the garage wiping his hands on an oil-stained rag.

Standing beside the driver's door, he said, "Howdy."

"Two dollars' worth," Rachael responded.

After inserting the nozzle into the gas tank, he washed the windshield, smiling through it at Stevie. "Hey, Beautiful. Can I take you out sometime?"

Caught off guard, Stevie smiled and giggled. The name embroidered on his shirt read "Gary."

After he finished pumping the gas, he went to the driver's door, leaned down, and looked over at Stevie. "How about—"

Rachael shoved two dollars into his hand.

He pushed out his lower lip as Rachael sped away.

"That was rude." Stevie turned to look out the back window.

He shrugged his shoulders, watching them drive off.

"You don't plan to go out with him, do you?"

"Maybe."

"He's, like, in his twenties. Maybe even thirty."

"So?" Stevie pulled down the visor and looked into the mirror. "He thinks I'm beautiful."

"You *are* beautiful. It seems you're the only one who doesn't believe it."

The following Saturday, Rachael was busy doing a fundraiser with the basketball cheerleaders. Stevie borrowed Mama's car, offering to put some gas in it. In Mama's old Chevy, she pulled up to the pump Gary was servicing. She rolled down the window when he approached the driver's side. "Fill it up, please," she said with a smile.

"You're back."

Stevie rushed on while she still had the nerve. "I wanted to apologize for my friend. She left before I could accept—"

He grinned. "A date?"

She looked down at her lap. "Yes."

His grin broadened before he turned toward the gas tank. When he returned, he said, "*Finian's Rainbow* is still playing. Have you seen it?"

"No."

"It's a musical. Do you like musicals?"

"Yes. I loved *The Sound of Music*." Her heartbeat sped up.

"Would you like to go next Friday night?"

"I work Friday nights . . . And there's a problem."

"What's that?" He cocked his head to the side.

"My mother insists on meeting you before she'll allow me to go on a date with you."

He leaned into the car. "Not a problem. I'm great with mothers."

"Can you come for dinner next Sunday?"

"I work until five. Will six o'clock be okay?"

When another customer pulled up behind her, Stevie handed him the money for the gas and pulled over to the side of the station. She wrote her address on a piece of paper, walked over to the pump, and handed it to him.

He stuffed the scrap of paper in his pocket. "See you Sunday, Beautiful."

Beautiful. He thinks I'm beautiful.

That night, Stevie joined Mama in the living room, her feet up on the hassock, watching *The Lawrence Welk Show.* Gone were the days when Daddy and Mama danced. Daddy would whirl Stevie around the room, too, until she collapsed on the sofa.

The perfect time came when a commercial interrupted the show. "Mama, I met a boy who wants to take me to a movie—*Finian's Rainbow.*"

"Do I know him?" Mama blew smoke into the hazy room.

"No. I just met him."

"Where?"

"He's a mechanic at a gas station Rachael goes to." For some reason, mechanic sounded better than a gas station attendant.

"I'll have to meet him before I allow you to go out with him. Invite him over for dinner some Sunday. I'll make fried chicken." Mama ground out her cigarette butt into the overflowing glass ashtray.

The conversation ended when Bobby Burgess danced into their living room.

Stevie helped Mama the Sunday Gary was due to come for supper. She cleaned the house and set the table. The doorbell rang as she finished spraying a flowery scent around the house. *As though that would help.*

After looking in the mirror near the entry for any last-minute touch-ups, she opened the door. He was wearing what looked like a new pair of jeans and a blue button-down oxford shirt. His dark hair was slicked down, and he smelled like soap. Although his fingernails were stained with grease, it was obvious to her that he'd cleaned up for the occasion. He held a bouquet of white daisies. "These are for your mother," he said.

"Stevie, let the young man in." Mama was at her side.

"Mrs. Shaw, these are for you." Gary handed the flowers to Mama. *Good move, Gary.*

Mama was as giddy as a schoolgirl. He sure knew how to win her over. "Dinner is ready. Please sit there across from Stevie." She pointed to one of the chairs.

"Here. Allow me." He pulled out the chair at the head of the table for Mama.

Mama blushed. "Thank you." After picking up her napkin, she spread it over her lap, then passed the platter of chicken to him. "Stevie tells me you're a mechanic."

"Yes, ma'am. I'm saving to buy my own gas station someday," he said.

"So, you have a goal. I like that."

"My cousin, Ted, will be my partner in the business. Ted's going through a rough time now, so he lives with me."

"That's kind of you." Mama patted her lips with her napkin.

Gary smiled at Stevie, sitting across the table from him.

"Did you know that after Stevie graduates, she plans to go to college?"

"To be honest, I didn't. We haven't had an opportunity to get to know each other. That's why I'd like to take her on a date."

Mama passed the platter. "Have another piece of chicken."

"Thank you. It's delicious. Colonel Sanders better watch out. Your fried chicken is the best I've ever had."

Mama blushed again.

Later, they adjourned to the living room, where Mama took out a cigarette. But before she could light it, Gary pulled a lighter out of his pocket and lit Mama's cigarette for her.

Stevie felt like she was watching a tennis match as the two conversed.

After he left, Stevie helped clean up the kitchen.

"Gary is a nice young man," Mama said as she stored the leftovers in the refrigerator.

"So, can I go on a date with him?"

"Well, I don't know. He seems too old for you . . . I'd feel better about it if it was a group date . . . or if I chaperoned. I'll have to think about it." Mama walked away.

What? Stevie dialed Rachael's number, and after she answered, Stevie ranted, "You're not going to believe this. My mother wants to chaperone my date with Gary. Rach, I'll die. I'll just die. What am I going to do?"

"Doesn't she know no one does that anymore?"

"She's living in the dark ages." Stevie twisted the dishtowel in her hand. "She also mentioned a group date. Could you and your date go with us Saturday night?"

"Sorry, I have to babysit."

"I know what I'm going to do. I'll tell her I'm staying overnight with you, but instead, I'll go out with Gary."

"I don't want to be any part of it. After the last time we lied to our mothers, it took a long time for my mother to trust me again."

Mama entered the kitchen.

"Bye, Rach." Stevie ended the call by hanging up the phone on the wall.

"Gary does appear to be a nice young man—polite, kind, and a gentleman. Plus, he came to dinner for me to check him out. I've changed my mind. You can go on a date with him."

Stevie hugged her close. "Thank you, Mama."

"I'm not an ogre. I was young once, too."

When the doorbell rang on Saturday night, Stevie tingled from head to toe. She wore her favorite outfit—a red plaid skirt, white blouse, and a black vest with black flats. Stevie decided not to wear her coat because the elbows were worn thin. She opened the door.

"Wow!" Gary's eyes were huge as his gaze scanned her up and down.

Stevie smiled. "Mama, I'm leaving now."

"Have a good time. Remember, be home by eleven o'clock," Mama shouted from the hall.

"Nice car," Stevie said as he opened the passenger door for her. "What is it?"

"A '64 Mustang," he responded.

"I don't know much about cars."

"Most girls don't." He drove down the boulevard toward the theater. "Your stuck-up friend has a nice ride."

"You mean Rachael? She's not stuck-up; she's my best friend."

"Well, I hope I'll be able to change that." He looked over at her and winked. "I plan to be your best friend."

They made it to their seats in the darkened theater as the overture played. "Would you like some popcorn?" Gary asked.

"Sure."

"I'll be right back."

When Gary returned, he sunk into his seat, handed Stevie a couple of napkins, and held the buttery popcorn between them. She was already engrossed in the Irish fable, always putting herself in the place of the heroine. She'd been Maria in *The Sound of Music*, and now she was Sharon in *Finian's Rainbow*.

She was thinking of Daddy during the singing of "How Are Things In Glocca Morra?" A tear slipped onto her cheek. With her left hand, she wiped it away. Embarrassed, she hoped that Gary wouldn't notice. He interlaced his fingers with her right hand.

Later, with Gary's jacket draped over her shoulders, he walked her to the front door. Standing under the porchlight, he said, "I had a nice time tonight."

"Me, too."

"Will you go out with me again?"

"Okay." *Of course, I will.*

"With you going to school and both of us working, Saturday night might be the only time I can take you out."

They lingered on the porch talking for a while. Then he kissed her on the cheek. "It's cold out here. You'd better go inside." She handed him his jacket before he walked toward his car, turned, and said, "I'll call you."

She went inside the house and dreamily leaned against the door. Mama was asleep on the couch, a burned-out cigarette in her nicotine-stained fingers. Stevie walked down the hall softly singing the words from *Finian's Rainbow*.

CHAPTER 16

Annie

Annie spied Jenn's car pulling up the driveway through her kitchen window. She put the finishing touches on lunch with a sprig of parsley on the crab salad plate with the gold edging and was about to put the rolls in the oven to warm.

Jenn rapped on the massive front door, then entered. "Yoo-hoo," she called.

"I'm in the dining room," Annie responded.

Jenn spied the salad. "Yum. Looks great."

"Have a seat and pour yourself some iced tea while I get the rolls," Annie called over her shoulder as she went toward the kitchen. "Unless you'd like something warm to drink, since it's cold outside."

"Iced tea is good."

Annie returned, placed the rolls on the table, and took her seat. "Now, do you only have an hour, or did the boss give you an extra-long lunch today?"

"Well, you know him better than anyone. What do you think?" Jenn took a roll from the basket and buttered it.

"Well, since it's you and you're having lunch with me, I'll say Joe said to take as long as you'd like."

"Pretty much." Jenn pierced a cherry tomato with her fork and popped it into her mouth. "How is Angel Baby?"

"Napping. Ever since Zoey got over colic, she's a different baby. It's like going from nights of agony to bliss." Annie sighed. "She's a perfect baby now. I can't believe the difference." Annie sipped her iced tea.

"It's obvious. You look more rested now than you did during Zoey's first five months."

"No doubt because Zoey is sleeping through the night. I'm even sleeping late now." Annie leaned back in her chair and smiled. "I put toys in her crib after she falls asleep at night. In the morning, when she wakes up, she plays with them and then falls back to sleep until about ten o'clock."

"That is a change." Jenn arched a brow. "I wonder how many mothers can say they have it that easy."

Annie scooted her chair back and got up from the table. She grabbed some photos and returned, handing them to Jenn. "These were taken the day Zoey's adoption was official." Annie replaced her napkin on her lap and took a bite of salad.

Jenn went through the color photos one by one.

"She wore the blue dress you gave her—with the smocking."

"I thought I recognized it." Jenn looked up from the pictures. "So, are you less worried about Zoey being taken away from you since it's official now?"

"Do you remember how I tried not to get attached when we first brought her home? How I tried to think of it as babysitting her?"

"I do."

"Well, that only lasted for a second. She's been ours since the moment we brought her home. But to answer your question, I no longer worry that she'll be taken away. And that's a very peaceful feeling."

Jenn set the pictures aside. "You must have two sets of these. Joe showed them to me as well as everyone else in the office and every client, too."

Annie smiled. "How about dessert? I made a banana cream pie."

"I can't."

"Sure, you can." Annie went to the kitchen. When she returned, she carried two dessert plates. Just then, cooing noises came from the nursery. "You finish your dessert while I change Zoey, and you can see her before you have to go back to work."

Jenn nodded with her mouth full of pie.

When Annie came back out to the dining room carrying a smiling Zoey, Jenn wiped her mouth with her napkin and reached out her arms. "Angel Baby."

Zoey eagerly went into Auntie Jenn's embrace.

CHAPTER 17

Stevie

The week after Christmas, while cleaning the office building of Joe Costa Real Estate, Stevie pushed the vacuum around each desk, chair, and file cabinet. At Joe's desk, she looked up and froze. Instead of the double frame birth announcement and Zoey's photo, now there was a color picture of Zoey sitting on Annie's lap under a Christmas tree. Joe sat next to them, holding Zoey's tiny, chubby hand. She wore a red dress, and her blonde hair had a curl on the top of her head. She ran the machine back and forth as she stared.

Mama startled her when she approached and yelled over the noisy vacuum, "What's the matter with you? You're going to wear out the carpet."

The following day, while Mama worked at her day job, Stevie grabbed her spiral notebook. She lay on her pink bedspread and began to write.

January 7, 1969

My Darling Daughter,

December was very hard for me, thinking about my first Christmas without you. If anyone knew how I felt, I'm sure they'd say I was selfish, thinking only of myself. I'm sure your parents love you very much, and they can give you whatever you'll ever want or need. So, your first Christmas was no doubt captured in pictures and maybe home movies, too.

I want you to know about me and what happened. My daddy, your grandfather, had just died, and I was very sad. So I went to a beach party and drank too much. I drank so much that I don't remember what happened that night. Please, never drink too much. I was sixteen.

Your biological father, Nick, is Rachael's cousin. Rachael is my best friend. Nick was visiting. He left the day after the beach party, and no one knows where he is. He is handsome with light blond hair. Rachael says he was a towhead as a boy. You have his hair. I know because I saw you when you were in the hospital nursery. In my hospital room, I begged the nurse to let me hold you, but she wouldn't let me. So when no one was looking, I crept down to the nursery. You were beautiful with perfect features—ears, nose, and a tiny rosebud mouth. Your light blonde hair covered your little head like a cap.

I wanted to keep you, but no one would support my decision. I even worked nights to earn money to prove I could raise you. Your grandmother was firm in her decision not to let me keep you. After you were born, she wouldn't even look at you. If she had, she would have changed her mind. Your grandmother isn't a bad person. She's just overwhelmed with life. Daddy was sick for a long time. With the medical bills, it was too much for her. She'd put all her dreams in me, and now I'm a disappointment to her.

People, even Rachael, tell me to get on with my life. I'm trying, but it's hard.

Well, my darling daughter, that's a little of your history. I hope you'll be able to receive my letters someday and realize that I loved you from the beginning.

Love,

Your First Mother

CHAPTER 18

In school, everyone was talking about the winter formal. She'd invited Gary to the dance, and he'd agreed, even though he was twenty-three. She knew he'd do anything to make her happy. Between school and work, they managed to squeeze in more dates to movies and nice restaurants and talk on the phone daily, sharing their dreams. There were no secrets between them. At least, she didn't think there were any. She'd told him everything.

Stevie and Rachael had already decided to shop at Fashion Island. Stevie was in her bedroom that evening, writing an essay for her English class.

"Stevie, phone," Mama yelled.

Stevie plodded to the kitchen and answered, "Hello?"

"This is Mike—Mike Mulligan."

"Hi, Mike."

"Would you like to go to the Winter Formal with me?"

"Thanks for inviting me, but I'm going with someone else."

"Oh." There was silence on his end of the phone, then he said, "Maybe some other time."

"Sure." *Why did I say that? I should have told him I have a boyfriend. At least, I hope he is my boyfriend.*

"Well, I'll see you at school."

"Bye." She hung up the phone feeling somewhat regretful. She liked Mike. She would have said yes if he had asked her before she had met Gary. Gary was different than any of the boys at school—maybe because he was older. He knew how to treat a girl. And he was kind to Mama.

But Nick had been older, too. She'd trusted him when he said alcohol would numb her pain. He was right, but it was only temporary. After the alcohol wore off, the pain of grieving the loss of Daddy returned. Could she trust Gary?

After stowing their formals in the backseat of Rachael's VW, they slid into the front seat. "Rach, can I leave my formal at your house? I don't want it to smell like smoke."

"Of course. Why don't you plan to get ready for the dance at my house?"

"Mama will want to take pictures of Gary and me."

"Don't worry. I'll have my mom invite her over to our house. She can take all the pictures she wants."

"You're the best. How did I get such a good friend?"

"Lucky, I guess." Rachael accelerated, and the little yellow bug zipped down the street toward Santa Ana.

After Mama and Mrs. Graham took their fill of pictures, Stevie and Gary sat in the front of Gary's Mustang, while Rachael and Jerry piled in the backseat.

"Hey, man," said Jerry, greeting Gary. "Nice ride."

"Yeah, I know, right?" Gary ignored Jerry's outstretched hand and revved the engine. "Just don't get any dirt in my car, okay?"

Stevie saw Jerry glance over at Rachael, but she shrugged off the worry that crept into her heart. She was sure Gary didn't mean to be so rude. He was just excited about the dance. He had confided in her that he didn't get to go to his high school dance because he had dropped out before he graduated.

Soon, they entered the high school gym under hanging snowflakes and everything covered in white.

Dancing with Gary was much different than dancing with Daddy. Daddy could do all the dances—swing, polka, tango, Charleston, fox trot, and the waltz. She loved it when Daddy jitterbugged with her. Gary only stood in one place and swayed to the music. Stevie put her arms around his neck, and she loved the warmth and feel of his arms around her waist.

With their heads touching each other, he whispered, "I love you."

She felt something for him, too. She wanted to spend all her time with him when she wasn't at school, working, or studying. His deep voice over the phone filled her with a sensation she couldn't describe in words. Sometimes she couldn't even eat. She'd never felt this way before. Could it be love?

Later, Stevie and Rachael excused themselves and went to the restroom. Standing in front of the mirror, Stevie took her lipstick out of her evening bag. "Jerry sure is quiet tonight. It isn't like him."

"He doesn't have anything in common with Gary. Besides, he doesn't like him."

Stevie looked at Rachael in the mirror. "Why?"

"Just a vibe he has."

"What vibe?"

Rachael ran her hands down her powder blue formal with the high empire waist, smoothing the satin fabric. "He can't pinpoint any one thing. He doesn't trust him."

"He doesn't even know him." Stevie dropped the lipstick into her purse and snapped it shut. "Do you feel the same way Jerry does about Gary?"

Rachael avoided Stevie's eyes. "I think he's too old for you, but you already know that. Why didn't you let Mike bring you tonight? I know he asked you."

"Because I'd already asked Gary. You know he's my boyfriend."

"Well, your boyfriend is a grease monkey."

"And you're a snob."

Rachael looked as though she'd been slapped. Pivoting on her satin pumps, she exited the girls' restroom.

"Rach, I'm sorry." But it was too late. Rachael was gone, and the music had drowned out Stevie's apology.

The next day, Stevie dug out her notebook and snuggled under the covers with it. She began to write.

February 16, 1969

My Darling Daughter,

I've met someone. His name is Gary Gilbert. He works at the gas station where Rachael gets gas. He doesn't only pump gas; he's a mechanic, too. And he wants to buy his own gas station someday. I asked him to go to the Winter Formal with me, and he said yes.

When I was pregnant with you, I saved my money, hoping I'd be able to keep you and take care of you. I used some of that money to buy a dress. It is white with a red satin sash. It's the first high school dance I've gone to since my sophomore year. I'm a senior now. After graduation, I plan to go to college, but I haven't decided on a major yet.

I told Gary about you, and he said it didn't make any difference to him. He still likes me. What he really said was, "I love you."

I made a terrible mistake at the dance last night. I said something unkind to Rachael, and I'm so ashamed of myself. I don't know if she'll ever forgive me. I hope you will never make the same mistakes I've made, but you will always be kind and think before you say something to your best friend that you'll regret.

Love,

Your First Mother

CHAPTER 19

Stevie gathered her dirty laundry from her closet floor and spied the bottle of vodka underneath. "I don't need you anymore," she mumbled as she kicked the closet door shut on her way to load the washer. She stuffed her clothes into the machine, set it to wash, then headed back to her room. Stevie picked up the bottle of clear liquid. "Bye-bye," she said and dropped it into the wastebasket. "Gary loves me. And I'm doing fine without you."

Stevie had continued to work nights, cleaning alongside her mother, so she could watch over Zoey—or at least, so she could see photos of her on Mr. Costa's desk. Every minute she wasn't at school or working, she was either with Gary or on the phone with him.

She ran to answer the ringing phone in the kitchen. "Hello."

Gary's intoxicating voice responded, "Hi, babe."

"Hi." She was glad Mama was doing errands so she could talk to him privately.

"How are you, beautiful?"

She slid down and sat on the floor, absentmindedly wrapping the yellow, coiled phone cord around her finger. "Missing you."

He groaned. "I miss you, too—more than you'll ever know. I'm dying when I'm not with you. We have to be together."

"It isn't realistic. I've got school, and we both have work."

"There is a way. I have a surprise for you. I'll be there to pick you up in ten minutes. Wear that cute number you wore on our first date." He hung up.

She jumped up, hung up the phone, and raced to her bedroom to change her clothes. *A surprise?* She shook with excitement.

After getting dressed, she scribbled a note to Mama. When she heard Gary's car arrive, she rushed outside and jumped into the passenger seat.

"So what's the surprise?" She tickled his side.

"Cut it out." He grinned. "You'll just have to wait and see."

She playfully pushed out her lower lip.

"Pouting will get you nowhere." He pulled down the visor against the afternoon sun.

Soon, he parked at their favorite spot, on a cliff in Little Corona overlooking the Pacific, with the sun sparkling off the surf. He pulled out a box from his pocket and opened the lid. A tiny diamond ring was inside. "Babe, will you marry me?"

She threw her arms around his neck. In her enthusiasm, she almost pitched the ring box into the backseat. She kissed him all over his face—his cheeks, forehead, and chin. "Yes! Yes! A thousand times, yes!"

Gary placed the ring on her finger as he gazed into her eyes. "Happy?"

"The happiest." She held out her hand and scrutinized her engagement ring.

"I want to get married right away."

"But I'm still in high school."

He turned away from her.

"What's wrong?"

"I told you I had a way for us to be together. I have an apartment. We both have jobs. We can make it work, and now you're trying to sabotage it."

She wrapped her arms around his dejected shoulders. "No, I'm not. Just until after I graduate. It won't be long. I promise. Then we'll be together forever."

They held each other and kissed hungrily until the sun dropped further into the ocean.

Later, they shared one more kiss before he dropped her off in front of the house. Stevie strolled up the walkway. She stopped before opening the door and taking off the ring; she tucked it into her pocket. She'd wait until Mama was in a good mood before she'd tell her she was engaged. For now, it was her secret—hers and Gary's.

At the end of the week, when she heard Mama open the front door, she closed her science textbook, leaving it on top of her bed. She went down the hall toward the kitchen and met Mama carrying a pizza box. "I couldn't think of what to make for dinner, so I decided to pick up a pizza before we head to work."

After eating, they stored the leftover pizza in the refrigerator. Mama grabbed her purse, and Stevie followed her to the car and slid in the passenger side. A few blocks from work, Stevie cleared her throat. "Mama, you like Gary, don't you?"

"I do." Mama looked over at Stevie, her forehead wrinkled.

"He's asked me . . . to marry him."

"After college, you mean," Mama stopped at the red light and glanced at her again with piercing eyes.

"No. We want to get married after I graduate from high school in June," Stevie said, crossing her fingers and tucking them under her thighs as if that would help Mama agree. Maybe even give them her blessing. "I know it's sudden, but we love each other."

"What about my dream of you going to college?" Mama glared at Stevie. "It's still your dream, too, isn't it?"

"I still plan to go to college. I've applied to Cal State." Stevie touched Mama's arm, "I can do both—be married and go to college. It'll be hard, but I can do it."

Mama frowned against the glare of the setting sun through the windshield. She was quiet—probably thinking.

Stevie kept silent, too. *Don't make waves. Just let Mama think about it.*

Mama exited the freeway. Without looking at Stevie, she said, "I want more for you than I had." She sighed. "My dream was for you to experience dorm life and college friends, but of course, I can't afford that. I need to face facts. I like Gary well enough. I just wanted more for you."

"Gary makes me happy. He's good to me." Stevie uncrossed her fingers. "I was hoping you'd be happy for us."

Mama parked the Chevy and dropped the ignition key into her purse. "It's too sudden. You need more time to get to know each other."

Stevie sat up straighter. "I know all I need to know about him. Mama, I love him, and he loves me. We're asking for your blessings."

"You're so young."

"You married Daddy when you were eighteen."

"That was different. We grew up together." Mama opened the door and climbed out of the car.

Stevie squared her shoulders and trudged behind her. *Gary and I will be married with or without your blessing.*

Parked under a tree at the park, Stevie pulled away from Gary and leaned back against the passenger door. The back of her head rested on the steamed-up windows of his Mustang. Stevie buttoned her blouse.

Gary laid his head on the back of the seat, staring at the roof of the car. "Come on, babe. Don't stop now. You know I love you."

"I love you, too. It's just—"

"You're afraid of getting pregnant again." He faced her. "I told you, I've got protection."

Stevie was silent.

"Why are you such a prude?" He hit his fist on the steering wheel.

Stevie shuddered.

"Are you going to be like ice after we're married?"

"No, of course not."

"I hope not because a guy has needs."

"Please, Gary, it'll be different after we're married. I promise."

He flipped on the defrost lever and drove her to her house.

"I'm sorry."

"Yeah. Me, too. But remember, when we're married, if I don't get it from my wife, I'll get it someplace else."

Stevie sat up taller. "Are you threatening me?"

"No. I'm just telling you how it'll be if you act like this after we're married."

"It won't be a problem." She wouldn't turn her husband away. She loved Gary.

He stopped the car in front of her house and waited for her to get out.

"Will I see you tomorrow?" Holding the car door open, Stevie leaned into the car to see him behind the wheel.

Gary stared out the windshield. "I guess," he mumbled.

She closed the door and watched him as he sped down the street. *He's moody. Things will be better after we're married. He just loves me so much, he can't wait to be with me. Everything's fine.*

During lunch period at school, Stevie sat across from Rachael. Although they'd made up after their argument during the Winter Formal, Stevie knew Rachael still didn't like Gary, and that put a strain on their friendship.

"Are you still mad at me?" Stevie asked.

"For what?"

"For what I said at the dance."

Rachael grabbed Stevie's hand across the table. "We both said things we can't take back, but we've always gotten over our differences in the past."

"Except this time." Stevie looked down. "You still don't like Gary, do you?"

"I'm trying to like him for your sake. It's just that you seem depressed. You've been moping around for a couple of weeks. What's wrong?" Rachael leaned toward Stevie.

Of course, I'm depressed. It's my baby's first birthday soon—the baby I gave away. "I've got a lot on my mind."

"Someone who's about to get married should be happy. What is it? Wedding jitters?" Rachael took a bite of her apple.

"Maybe." Stevie pushed her half-eaten tuna sandwich into her lunch sack. "Although it's going to be a small wedding with only a few guests and cake at the house afterward, Mama is overwhelmed."

"My mother can help. She'd love to do it."

"Your mother and dad have always been nice to me. But Mama would probably be overwhelmed no matter how much help she got. She's not like your mother. Everything makes her nervous." Stevie sipped her milk through the paper straw and then added the empty carton to the rest of her trash in her lunch bag.

"My parents miss seeing you. Why don't you come over tonight?" Rachael smiled.

"Can't tonight. I've got to go to work."

"Why are you still working? I thought you took that job when you were trying to save money to . . . "

"To take care of my baby?"

"Well, yeah."

"I like having my own money. It's security for my future," Stevie said.

Rachael cocked her head.

"You probably wouldn't understand because your parents always give you whatever you want. I don't mean to be unkind. It's just a fact. Besides, working at Joe Costa's Real Estate, I see pictures of Zoey." Stevie wadded up her lunch sack and pitched it into a nearby trash can. "I need to go to the restroom before class. See you tomorrow."

"Bye."

A couple of days later, Stevie sat on her bed. She ran her hand over the cover of the notebook. As she began to write, a lump formed in her throat.

May 11, 1969

My Darling Daughter,

Today is your birthday. It's a very hard day for me because I love you, and I want to celebrate your first birthday with you. Maybe someday, we will be together. I can only hope that you are happy.

Next month, after I graduate from high school, Gary and I will be married. Maybe then, I'll find happiness, too.

Love,

Your First Mother

A tear fell onto the page, blurring the words. Stevie wiped it away without success, causing her last words to be one long, inky smear. She closed the notebook, buried her head in her pillow, and let the tears flow.

Will my heart ever heal?

CHAPTER 20

Annie

Sitting at her dressing table, Annie applied black mascara to her long eyelashes while Zoey napped. Where was Joe? He promised he'd be home in time to help her with the party preparations for Zoey's first birthday. Annie stepped into her new dress and managed to zip up the back. She pushed her feet into turquoise flats. When she heard a car approaching that didn't sound like Joe's, she glanced out the window and saw Jenn.

Annie opened the front door to see Jenn's arms filled with wrapped gifts. She said, "Let me help you. Joe was supposed to be here."

"He's still at the office." Jenn stepped inside the entry. "He asked me to come instead—to give you a hand."

The hair on the back of Annie's neck rose. "He knows I haven't entertained since Zoey was born. And we're expecting fifty people."

Jenn followed Annie, her heels clicking on the marble entry floor. In the living room, they placed the presents on the table designated for the gifts. "You're a pro as a hostess. I don't understand why you're worried. It's probably like riding a bike. You never forget."

A sweet sound came from the nursery. "Mama. Mama."

"I'll get her changed and dressed." Annie headed down the hall toward the nursery.

"What can I do?"

"There are dishes of nuts and mints on the kitchen counter. Will you place them around the room?"

"Sure, I can do that."

Annie returned a few minutes later carrying Zoey. Zoey wore a turquoise dress, like her mother, with patent leather shoes and white, lace-trimmed socks. Lacy panties were pulled over her diaper. Annie set Zoey down on the floor, and Zoey toddled to Jenn, her arms out.

Jenn placed her hand over her heart. "Angel Baby! You're walking!"

Zoey giggled as she reached Jenn's open arms before she fell.

"Hurray!" Jenn clutched her in a hug and raised Zoey's arm into the air. "The winner."

Annie grabbed the orange sherbet out of the freezer and began scooping it into the punch bowl. "Has Joe been acting odd at the office lately?"

Jenn furrowed her brow. "No. Why?"

"Just a feeling."

"Is he acting odd at home?"

"Forget it. It's probably my over-active imagination." Annie put the empty sherbet carton in the trashcan under the sink. Taking the cake out of the box, she placed it on the bar, poking a single candle in it. After stowing the box in the laundry room, Annie brushed off her hands.

Jenn held up Zoey to see her cake. "Look, Angel Baby, it's your birthday cake. Isn't it pretty?" Zoey reached a chubby, dimpled hand toward the creamy icing, but Jenn was quick and backed away from the cake. "Not yet. Later. We have to get a picture of this for posterity. Isn't that right, Mommy?"

"Huh?"

The doorbell rang with the first of the guests arriving.

A few minutes later, Joe walked through the door. He greeted everyone with his charismatic personality, and soon, he was filming Zoey's first birthday with the state-of-the-art camera he'd bought when Zoey was born.

Later, with the party winding down, Annie looked out the kitchen window to see Joe in a tense conversation with his receptionist as they stood beside her car. Although she couldn't be sure, it looked like Mallory was crying.

She had a sinking feeling in the pit of her stomach that something wasn't right, but she pushed the thought away as she put on her best smile and said goodbye to her guests.

That evening, after cleaning up from the party and putting Zoey to bed, Annie slipped her silk nightie over her head while Joe lay in bed, watching Johnny Carson. "Is anything wrong?"

"Huh?"

"You're distant." Annie climbed into bed beside him. She had noticed a growing distance between them over the last few months. At first, she thought it was just the exhaustion from Zoey's colic, but now, she wasn't so sure. The sinking feeling was back.

"It's work." Joe didn't even look at her, so engrossed was he in watching his show.

"Talk to me." She leaned toward him.

"I talk to people all day long. I'm tired and just want to unwind, okay," he snapped. Joe had never been one to be harsh before.

Tears filled Annie's eyes, and she sniffed. "I'm sorry."

Joe hesitated, turned down the television, and finally looked at her. "No, I'm sorry. I didn't mean to snap at you. I'm fine. Really. It's just been a long day." He kissed her on the cheek and turned back to his show.

But Annie couldn't rid herself of the feeling that something was wrong. Joe had kissed her on the cheek like she was a child, not his wife. Sighing, Annie turned off her bedside lamp and closed her teary eyes against the drone of the TV.

The following day, Annie dialed a longtime family friend.

"Jim Thorp, private investigator."

Annie walked into the small, musty bungalow that had been converted into an office. Jim removed his feet from the desk. He stood, reaching out his hand to her. "Annie, it's been a long time."

She switched Zoey to her left hip and accepted Jim's handshake. "Since my wedding, I think. I thought you might have retired." She took the seat he showed her.

"Not me. I don't think I'll ever retire. I like catching the bad guys and seeing they get what they deserve."

Annie settled Zoey on her lap.

Jim Thorp had been a friend of her mother's since before Annie's parents were married. Although she hadn't seen him since her wedding day, she was confident in him professionally.

Still not trusting anyone to babysit Zoey, Annie brought her along to Jim's office for her appointment.

He leaned back in his big chair, steepling his fingers. "How are you?" he asked.

"Not so good." The nausea she'd felt since seeing Joe and Mallory together loomed.

"You said on the phone that you'd like to have your husband investigated. Is that right?" Jim leaned across his desk toward her.

"Yes. And I don't want Joe to find out. Ever. In case I'm paranoid. I wouldn't want him to think I didn't trust him. So please, send your bill to me."

"Of course. If you decide to move forward with this, I assure you it will be confidential."

His pen poised above a legal pad. "Now, tell me why you are suspicious of . . ."

"Joe."

"Sorry. Yes, Joe. I remember now. Forgive me. It's been a long time since your wedding."

Zoey played contentedly in Annie's lap with the colorful plastic keys on a ring. She put them in her mouth and drooled.

With her hand, Annie wiped the drool off Zoey's chin. "Joe's been distant for a while. I don't have any proof. That's why I contacted you. Because of my father, I've always had trouble trusting men. But I thought Joe was different."

"Besides him being distant, is there anything else?" Jim looked up from the legal pad.

"I did see him having a serious discussion with his receptionist. He was gripping her upper arms and talking real close to her face. He looked angry. And it looked like she was crying."

"What's her name?"

"Mallory Mitchell. I don't know where she lives."

"That's okay. It'll be easy enough to find out."

Zoey banged the toy keys against the desk. "I'm sorry," Annie said as she pushed the chair back.

"No problem. This old desk has seen worse than that." He smiled. "She's delightful and so pretty. Like her mother."

"Thank you." Annie hugged Zoey closer. Should she tell him that Zoey was adopted? No. What difference would it make?

"Is there anything else for me to go on?"

Annie searched her brain. "Not that I can think of."

"So, if I hear you right, you think Joe may be having an affair. Is that correct?"

"Yes. I think it's a possibility. But I need to know for sure. Whenever I try to talk to him, he just shuts me down. I'm not like my mother. I won't be a victim and bury my head in the sand. I believe she died of a broken heart because of all my father's affairs. I'll never understand why she didn't leave him," Annie said.

"I'd always hoped your mother was happy. I cared about her very much." Jim looked off into the distance. Then he folded his hands on top of his desk. "I'll get on this and contact you when I have something. I'll write a report on my findings and take photographs if necessary. Then, if it'd be more convenient for you with the baby, I can deliver the information to you at your home." He stood.

"Thank you, Jim." Annie rose and hefted Zoey onto her hip.

"I hope you're wrong—for you and your little girl." He smiled at Zoey and reached out his hand to her.

Zoey latched onto his finger. "Da-ddy."

CHAPTER 21

A couple of weeks later, Jim Thorp called and said he'd be stopping by. After putting Zoey down for a nap, Annie paced the floor, wringing her hands as she waited. The doorbell finally rang. Annie rushed toward the front door, and then she slowed her steps. Did she want to see the results of Jim's investigation?

She opened the door and showed him into the living room. "Would you like something to drink?"

"I could use a cup of coffee if you have some made." He sat on one of the white brocade sofas, holding a manila envelope in his hand.

Annie returned with a steaming mug of coffee, along with cream and sugar, and set them on the glass coffee table. She sat across from Jim on the matching sofa. "Is it bad?"

She tried to search Jim's eyes, but there was nothing there. He must have done this so many times before. His job seemed like a police officer's—telling a widow that her husband was dead. But Joe wasn't dead. Hadn't she sat across from Joe this morning at breakfast, with Zoey sitting in her highchair between them—like a happy family? Then why did she feel as though he was dead?

Jim continued to hold the manila envelope as he spoke. "I've interviewed employees at a hotel in San Clemente." He kept a careful eye on Annie as he spoke. "Your husband registered as Mr. and Mrs. Sal Santini." He let the information sink in for a minute. "A couple

134

of months ago was the last time they stayed there. The bellhop said there was an argument. He heard Mr. Santini say, 'It's over.'"

Annie, numb and drained, stared at him, unable to speak.

Jim continued, "The bellboy said that's when it got loud. The woman yelled, 'If you don't want your wife to find out about us, you'll pay big time.'" Jim handed Annie the envelope. "My report and photos are enclosed. I'm sorry, Annie." He waited. After taking a sip of the coffee, he frowned.

Annie stood, her hands trembling. "Let me warm that up for you."

Jim put a gentle hand on her shoulder. "There's no need."

They both sat back down.

Jim said, "Even though you had your suspicions, this is never easy to hear. I'm sure this comes as a shock. Is there someone you can call to be with you?"

"I have a friend, but she's Joe's friend, too. I would never put her in the middle." Had Jenn known about the affair and never told her? Thoughts swirled in her head like a kaleidoscope. "I have my daughter. She'll get me through this. Children always help in times of crisis, don't you think?"

"I've heard that to be true." *Were those tears in his eyes?*

Annie stood. "Thank you. I'll be fine."

He put his arm around her shoulder and gently squeezed her arm as she walked him to the door. "I know you will."

After he left, her hands shook as she read the report. She refused to look at the pictures, her stomach feeling full of bile. She vowed she never would.

As she shoved the envelope in a drawer, Annie formed a plan of the steps she'd take. She would not be a victim of an unfaithful husband as her mother had been. Instead, she would take charge of her life. Anger welled within her, but she pushed it down, determined to be strong for herself and for her daughter.

When Zoey woke from her nap, Annie played with her on the floor in the family room, even though she felt dead inside. Before Joe was due to arrive home, Annie went into the bedroom and freshened up. Then she made a dinner of her favorites, not Joe's. She baked chicken, sautéed fresh vegetables, and prepared a fruit compote.

Joe came through the door and entered the kitchen with his tie loosened. He sorted through the mail, while Zoey offered him a Cheerio. "Da-ddy."

He leaned down and kissed her. Then he went to the sink and kissed Annie on the cheek. "How was your day?"

"Oh, you're familiar with how my days are. They're all pretty much the same."

"Uh-huh." He sat at the table, continuing to look through the mail, oblivious to the storm brewing inside his wife.

After dinner, per their evening routine, Annie cleaned up the kitchen while Joe bathed Zoey. It gave Annie a break from Zoey and Joe an opportunity to bond with his daughter.

Annie waited until after playtime with Zoey and bedtime stories. Once Zoey was down for the night, Annie stepped to the end-table drawer, pulled out the envelope, and flipped off the TV. From across the room, she flung the envelope at Joe. It landed in his lap.

Dazed, Joe picked it up. "What's this?"

"You can read it for yourself." She remained standing, her fists on her hips.

Joe pulled out the enclosures and glanced at them. She wasn't sure if he saw the pictures or not. He looked up. The color drained from his face. He moved toward her. "I'm so sorry."

When he reached for her, she backed away and glared at him. "Don't you dare touch me."

He dropped his hands to his sides. "It's over with Mallory. It has been for a couple of months."

"I'm aware of everything." Her palms began to sweat. *Don't waver. Don't let him sweet-talk me with all his charm.*

He stammered, "I never wanted you to find out. That's why I've been paying her."

"If that's supposed to make me feel better, it doesn't. You're no better than my father. You're a cheater just like him." She raised her voice. "And cheaters never change."

"I'm not your father."

She turned away from him, and her chest tightened. *Don't cry. Please, don't cry.*

"I made a mistake." When she turned back toward him, he reached out to touch her but stopped. "Please, Annie, please forgive me. I love you."

"Forgive you?" She spit out the vile words that had been inside her. "I can't even stand to look at you." She swung her arm and pointed to the front door. "Get out."

He stood. With slumped shoulders, he slowly walked to the door, shutting it behind him.

Spent, Annie eased down into a chair. It had taken everything within her power to stand up for herself. *I will not be a victim.*

Much later, after a crying binge, she dialed Jenn. "I know it's late, but . . . can . . . you . . . come over?"

"What's wrong? Is it Angel Baby?"

"No."

"I'll be right there."

Fifteen minutes later, Jenn walked through the door. "What's wrong?" she asked.

Annie pulled Jenn down beside her on the couch. "Joe cheated on me." She searched Jenn's expression. "Did you know?"

Jenn gasped. "No, I didn't."

"How could you not have known? You see them every day."

"Who?"

"Joe and Mallory." Annie plucked a tissue out of the box beside her.

"You're kidding!"

"Does it sound like I'm kidding?" She stared at Jenn. "I wouldn't kid about something like this."

"No. Of course, you wouldn't." Jenn shook her head as if in disbelief. "Are you sure?"

"I hired a private investigator. I have his report. And pictures. Trust me. It's true."

Annie reminded Jenn of how her mother died young of a broken heart because of her father's infidelity.

"I remember. You even disowned your father." Jenn took a breath. "Zoey has a grandfather who doesn't even know about her?"

"Yes. And I plan to keep it that way." Annie wiped at her tears.

They talked late into the night. Finally, Jenn yawned and she said, "I'm staying with you tonight."

"You don't have to."

"Come on. Let's try to get some sleep if we can." Jenn pulled Annie to her feet and headed toward the bedrooms and sleep.

The last time Annie looked at the lit clock, it was three in the morning. She must have slept for a couple of hours because she awoke at five, quietly got up, trying not to disturb Jenn in the bed beside her. Annie showered, dressed, applied her make-up, and groomed her hair. She was ready to face the day when she heard Zoey.

Sitting with Zoey as she ate her breakfast, Annie heard Joe come through the front door as Jenn came down the hall from the bedroom.

"I'm leaving now. I'll call you later," Jenn said. Spotting Joe, she brushed past him and mumbled, "You blew it."

"Da-ddy." Zoey reached out her arms to him while Annie washed off Zoey's breakfast from her face and hands.

Joe took her out of the highchair and held her. He looked as if he'd been in a war—his wrinkled clothes, unshaven face, and bloodshot eyes were the opposite of Annie's polished look. She was thankful the application of eye drops had worked for her.

"We need to talk," he said.

She didn't offer him anything, not even coffee.

"I know we can get through this."

"Do you now?" She was determined not to let him penetrate her hard shell of anger.

"Annie, I love you and Zoey." He took a breath. "I promise I'll never cheat on you again." His bloodshot eyes watered. "Please give me another chance."

"I can't. I don't trust you."

He set Zoey on the floor, where she toddled to her toy basket, pulling out the ball with the different shapes to put into it.

"I was frustrated when you were obsessed with getting pregnant. I needed someone to talk to."

"You could have talked to me."

"Not really. We both needed someone with objectivity. Later, when Zoey had colic, Mallory listened to my frustration."

Annie sat taller. "You will not blame Zoey and me for your unfaithfulness. Ever. Do you understand me?"

"I realize there is no excuse for what I did. I'm trying to figure out why I did it. Annie, I had everything, and I blew it."

"Because you're selfish. Please get your things and leave."

Joe went to gather his belongings from their bedroom. Annie sat down and sipped on her coffee while she waited.

When Joe appeared with a suitcase in hand, Zoey toddled to him, "Bye-bye, Da-ddy."

He scooped her up in his arms and held her close.

Annie kept her tears at bay until he closed the door behind him. Then she rushed to the door and locked it. Turning to see Zoey playing with her toys, Annie darted into the kitchen for a drink of water to soothe her dry throat from all the crying she'd done the night before. Holding the glass, her hand shook. She felt numb. Would she ever feel again? She hated him for what he'd done to her. To their family.

Jenn popped in at dinnertime. "I brought Chinese."

"Thanks, but I'm not hungry. You want something to drink?"

"A cup of tea would be nice." Jenn set the little white boxes on the table. "Hi, Angel Baby." After kissing the top of Zoey's head, Jenn pulled out a kitchen chair. "How are you doing?"

"I'm . . . I don't know."

"Well, you sure look a lot better than he does. He's been sitting at his desk with his head in his hands all day." Annie didn't respond. Jenn poked the chopsticks into the sweet and sour pork and pulled out a chunk of meat. "Mallory's gone. He fired her." She chewed on some pork before continuing. "A temp took her place."

"It's too late. The damage has already been done. It's no use closing the barn door after the horse has already run away."

CHAPTER 22

Stevie

After withdrawing money from her savings account, Stevie left the bank with a spring to her step. She walked toward her favorite dress shop, where in the past, she'd only window-shopped and dreamed. Mama's words ringing in her head slowed her pace.

I'd like to buy you a dress for graduation. You certainly deserve one for all your hard work. But it seems a waste of hard-earned money. No one will see it under your gown.

Stevie shook off the memory. She was happy, and she wasn't about to let Mama's negativity get her down. Not today. She'd dreamed of buying a pretty dress for graduation and her wedding.

Stevie entered the boutique and went directly to the section where the shop displayed the most expensive dresses. Soon, she found the perfect one—light blue chiffon with a dark blue sash, accenting her small waist.

Examining herself in the dressing room mirror, she turned from back to front. The dress fit perfectly. She smiled at her reflection. This was just like a dream.

But then, she envisioned a little pink bundle. Her smile faltered as she imagined a toddling, blonde-haired girl. Oh, how she wished her little girl could be a part of her day. Her heart still ached. All she had were the pictures on the desk at the real estate office.

Shaking her melancholy, Stevie twirled around in the mirror again, admiring the way she looked. She wished things could be different, but she was happy with Gary. Maybe one day, she would see her baby again. For now, she was going to graduate high school and become Gary's wife.

On graduation day, Stevie secretly stowed her suitcase in the trunk of Gary's Mustang, as they'd planned. By eloping, she saved Mama the strain and expense of a wedding and reception, and Gary would no longer nag her about their physical relationship. Her future looked bright. She giggled to herself.

Sitting with her classmates on graduation day, Stevie sat erect, sucked in a breath, and blew it out. She'd maintained a 4.0 GPA during her senior year while working nights. Her gaze scanned the crowd of spectators. She knew Mama was there, yet she was unable to spot her.

Before Stevie had left the house, she'd written Mama a note and placed it on her pillow.

Mama,

Gary and I will be eloping right after graduation. Please be happy for me.

I love you.

Stevie

After the benediction, Stevie found Rachael and grabbed her, giving her a fierce hug. "We did it."

Everyone was hugging and congratulating each other when Gary slipped up next to Stevie and grabbed her hand. "Come on. Ted and Darla are waiting at the apartment for us." They raced to the parking lot, climbed in his car, and headed to his apartment.

Pulling up to the curb in front of the apartment, Gary honked. His cousin Ted and Ted's girlfriend, Darla, were going to Las Vegas with them to witness Gary and Stevie's marriage. Ted and Darla came out the door with their suitcases. After cramming their bags in the trunk, they squeezed into the tiny backseat.

"Stevie, this is Ted and Darla," Gary introduced them.

Stevie turned around and faced the backseat. "It's nice to meet you finally. Gary has told me how close you were growing up."

Ted lit a cigarette. "We're like brothers."

"It's nice to meet you, too, Darla," Stevie said.

"I've never been to Vegas before." Darla looked like she was half-asleep.

Soon, the pungent odor of stale cigarette smoke filled the car. Stevie waved her hand in front of her face and coughed, then cracked the passenger window. When Ted and Darla weren't filling the car with cigarette smoke, they were noisily kissing.

Stevie sat on the edge of the seat as they drove along the Las Vegas Strip at three o'clock in the morning with the colorful lights on both sides of the street.

"I'll get two rooms—one for us and another one for Ted and Darla," Gary said as he pulled into a cheap motel.

Inside the room, Stevie looked down at the worn carpet and said, "Gary?"

"Yeah?" He plopped the suitcases on the bed.

"I appreciate you respecting me wanting to wait until after we're married to make love."

"Whatever." He took off his boots and dropped them on the floor with a thud. "I don't get it. It's not like you're a virgin."

Gary didn't look up to see the reaction his words had on Stevie. Tears filling her eyes, Stevie stumbled to the bathroom, undressed, and got into the shower to cover her sobs.

He was right. She wasn't a virgin. But didn't he realize it wasn't her fault? Mama used to say, "Sticks and stones may break my bones, but words will never hurt me." Well, that wasn't true. Words hurt her deeply—more deeply than any physical pain she had ever experienced. On the eve of her wedding, she ached for her baby. Would anything ever fill the hole it left in her heart? After she and Gary were married, she'd find happiness. She just needed to get through tonight.

After some time, she turned off the shower, toweled off, and finished getting ready for bed. Exiting the bathroom, she saw that Gary had already fallen asleep.

Stevie pulled back the covers and slid into the bed next to him. Listening to Gary's soft snoring, Stevie lay awake with the red neon sign blinking on and off outside their window, her mind unable to shut off the words her soon-to-be husband had said.

The next day, after an early morning breakfast, they applied for their marriage license and quickly picked one of the many white chapels on the strip for their wedding.

Gary stood on one foot and then the other as Stevie attempted to repeat the minister's words. She wore her graduation dress and fumbled with the bouquet provided by the wedding chapel. Gary wiped his hands on his blue suit pants and couldn't seem to make eye contact with Stevie as he stammered, "I . . . do."

Later, being too young to gamble, Stevie and Darla lounged by the pool while Gary and Ted gambled at the casinos. When the guys returned, the couples separated. Gary took Stevie out to a restaurant for a lovely dinner. Not used to eating steak, she would remember it forever as the best dinner she'd ever had.

Later, in the privacy of their room, Stevie began to feel butterflies as her wedding night was about to begin. Gary didn't take his eyes off her as he said, "There's nothing to be afraid of, Mrs. Gilbert."

Mrs. Gilbert. She was Mrs. Gilbert.

He undressed quickly. When he laid her on the bed, a rap at the door stopped him. Then another rap, and another. He swore and pulled on his pants.

Stevie gasped when she spied Gary's scarred back in the dim light.

He opened the door. "What is it?"

"Darla's bored. She wants to go home," Ted said.

"You have got to be kidding me!" Gary punched the wall beside the door. "Come on, Ted. Can't you do something?" His voice cracked with desperation.

"I tried, man." Ted's voice was apologetic.

"Hold her off, or . . . "

"Okay, okay. I'll try."

Gary slammed the door, locked it, and returned to Stevie, who was waiting with the covers tucked under her chin. "What happened?"

"Darla's bored," he snapped.

"Not that. I mean, what happened to your back?"

"I don't want to talk about it. It's our wedding night, after all."

With his weight on top of her, she could hardly breathe.

She gasped for air when he plopped on his back. No sweet kisses. No cuddling. So, this was love-making. She turned her face toward him to kiss him when he said gruffly, "Get dressed. We're leaving. Darla is bored."

Soon, they were dressed, packed, and on the highway, headed back to Santa Ana with Ted and Darla asleep in the backseat of the car.

Stevie leaned her head against the passenger window and closed her eyes. She'd daydreamed about her wedding night—Gary holding her in his arms, telling her she was beautiful, kissing her tenderly, and whispering how happy she made him. Then the dream had burst like a balloon. She sighed. Instead, their love-making was quick and without tenderness.

Once we're home, everything will be better, maybe even romantic like I'd daydreamed.

CHAPTER 23

Two months later, Stevie stumbled to the bathroom and puked. Was it morning sickness? Could she be pregnant?

Sharing the one-bedroom, one-bath apartment with Gary and his cousin Ted, Stevie was thankful that the bathroom was available. Yet Ted appeared oblivious of her condition. He probably thought she had a hangover every morning. After rinsing out her mouth, she called Dr. Anderson's office and made an appointment.

On the day of her doctor's appointment, Gary said, "Ted needs the car today, too, so you'd better schedule it with him."

"I told you I need it today." She folded her arms across her middle.

Gary scowled. "So, I forgot. What's the big deal? Just work it out with him. Okay? I've got to get to work. Are you going to drive me or not?"

On the ride to the gas station, Gary asked, "So, why do you need the car?"

"Errands."

"What kind of errands?"

"Just things." She didn't want to tell him of her possible pregnancy in case it was something else.

"Why are you being so evasive?"

"Maybe it's a surprise for you."

Please. Stop with the interrogation.

He raised his voice. "How long will you need the car?"

She averted his glare. "I'd hoped to have it all day, but since Ted needs it, I guess only a couple of hours."

"I get off at five. You'd better be through with your *errands* by then." He pinched her arm, got out of the car, and slammed the door.

Holding her arm where he'd pinched her, she steadied herself before getting out of the car and going around to the driver's side.

When Stevie returned to the apartment, Ted was sitting on the couch, stuffing his face with snack cakes.

Stevie rubbed her arm where Gary had pinched her. A bruise was already forming. "Ted, I have an appointment, and I need the car at noon. So, please don't be late. It's important." She wasn't sure if he understood the concept of importance or not, so she gave him an extra thirty-minute leeway.

"I'll be back by then. I promise." He raised his hand as if he was taking an oath.

She had zero confidence in him, but today, she hoped he'd prove her wrong.

Stevie was showered, dressed, and waiting for Ted to bring the car back. With her hands in her lap, she twirled her thumbs as she watched the clock tick first to noon, then five after, and ten after. She wiped her sweaty hands on her skirt—a quarter after, twenty after, twenty-five after. Stevie jumped up and called Rachael. She paced, waiting for Rachael to answer, feeling ashamed that she'd ignored her best friend while working, cleaning house, and learning how to be a wife.

"Hello?"

"Rach, I need a huge favor. Can you pick me up and drive me to Dr. Anderson's office? I have a one o'clock appointment, and if I don't leave now, I'll be late." Stevie gulped in air. "Can you do it?"

"Yeah. I'll be right there."

Stevie hung up the phone and sat ramrod straight on the couch as she waited for Rachael to arrive.

I've had it with Ted.

Rachael pulled up, her backseat loaded to the roof of her VW bug.

Stevie climbed in. "What's all this?" She motioned to the backseat.

"Don't you remember? I leave for Humboldt tomorrow."

"Sorry. I've been forgetful lately. And—"

"What?" Rachael looked over at her and raised her perfectly shaped eyebrows.

"Nothing."

Rachael pulled away from the apartment. "Do you want to tell me why you have an appointment with Dr. Anderson?"

"I think I may be pregnant."

Rachael glanced over at her. "You don't seem happy about it."

"I'm so angry with Ted right now that I can't think of anything else."

"Gary's cousin?"

"Yeah, his loser cousin."

"Wow. You *are* upset. Normally, you think only the best of everyone."

"Not Ted. He promised he'd have the car back so I could get to my appointment on time." Stevie sat on the edge of the seat, worrying the red light to change to green. "I specifically told him I needed the car at noon today. He promised." Stevie began to cry.

"Hey. It's okay. I'll get you there on time." Rachael reached over and patted Stevie's hand.

"It must be my hormones. On top of being forgetful, I cry over the silliest things."

"Maybe they aren't *so* silly. A newly married couple needs time to adjust to each other, and it has to be difficult with . . . "

"Ted," Stevie reminded Rachael.

"Right. Ted living with you." Rachael pulled up to the entrance of Dr. Anderson's office. "You go ahead. I'll find a parking space and wait in the car."

"Thanks, Rach." Stevie hurried into the office.

Mrs. Graham was standing behind the reception window when Stevie entered. When she saw Stevie, a smile spread across her face. Mrs. Graham quickly came around the partition and entered the waiting room. She hugged Stevie. "It's so good to see you. I miss you now that you're married." Mrs. Graham pulled back and examined her. "How are you?"

"Hi, Mrs. Graham. I'm fine." Stevie looked down at the floor.

A nurse came to the doorway of the waiting room and called, "Stevie Gilbert."

"I'll see you after my appointment," Stevie said to Mrs. Graham. Then she followed the nurse to the exam room.

When Stevie left the exam room, she was relieved to see that Mrs. Graham was busy with a patient on the phone. Waving goodbye, Stevie hurried out to find Rachael.

In a daze, Stevie staggered from the doctor's office and through the parking lot. She opened the passenger side door, plopped on the seat, crumpled over, hands on her face, and cried.

Rachael turned the key in the ignition and backed out of the parking space, looking over at Stevie. "Want to talk about it?"

"I'm pregnant."

"So, those are happy tears. That's good news, isn't it?"

Stevie kept silent.

"There is something you're not telling me. Isn't there?"

"I need my marriage to improve before bringing a baby into it."

Rachael didn't interrupt.

"It isn't how I thought married life would be. Ted makes me feel uncomfortable. And Gary is different than when we dated. He's controlling. He insists on knowing my every move. And he wants me to quit my job."

"Maybe that's not such a bad idea."

"Yes, it is." Stevie turned and stared at Rachael. "My job is like a haven."

Rachael nodded, then changed the subject. "I have an idea. Since I leave for college tomorrow, why don't we buy ice cream cones and walk along the beach? Like old times. Maybe it'll take your mind off of everything."

"I don't know. I probably should get home. I need to pick up Gary at work at five o'clock."

"How often does your best friend leave for college? And, don't forget, I don't plan to come home until Thanksgiving." Rachael pushed out her bottom lip. "Call Ted and ask him to pick up Gary." Rachael grinned.

Reluctantly, Stevie agreed. They stopped at a payphone near the ice cream parlor, so Stevie could call home. While the phone rang, she tried to gather some self-confidence.

Finally Ted mumbled, "Hello?"

"You promised me you'd be back by noon, Ted. Don't ever do that to me again," she said with more confidence in her voice than she felt. "My friend Rachael took me to my appointment, and I'm spending the rest of the day with her. So, you're responsible for picking Gary up from work. Got it?"

"Yeah. I got it." He sounded like a child who was caught with his hand in the cookie jar.

Stevie hung up the phone, feeling better than she had in a while. She returned to the ice cream parlor and sat at the small, round table with the red, vinyl chairs on the black-and-white-checked floor. Stevie licked her strawberry cone while Rachael enjoyed her chocolate swirl.

After finishing their cones, they headed toward the water through the sand. Taking off their shoes and carrying them, they strolled along the edge of the surf. Stevie poured out her frustration. "It isn't only Ted. It's his girlfriend, too. Darla is as much of a loser as he is. I try to keep a nice home for Gary, but it's hard with them lounging around all the time, dropping crumbs on the floor and never cleaning up after themselves."

"Do you want some advice from a college freshman who has never been married or pregnant?"

"It couldn't hurt. Besides, what do I have to lose?"

"Have Gary ask Ted to leave—tell Ted that married couples need to be together without a third party. And you're not going to like this part, but I suggest you quit your night job so you and Gary can have your evenings together. Concentrate on your marriage and school." Rachael picked up a shell. "That's my two cents' worth. You can take it or leave it."

"Thanks, Rach. I'll think about it."

Rachael put the pretty pink shell in her pocket. "Mom and Dad will follow me tomorrow in the station wagon with all of my stuff that doesn't fit in my car. Mom's having a hard time with me leaving. Even though I'll still be in the same state, she thinks I'm moving to the other side of the world." Rachael stopped and looked at Stevie. "Will you go by and see them once in a while? It would mean a lot to them and me."

"I'll try."

"Thanks."

Stevie's stomach constricted when she saw the Mustang parked in front of the apartment. Had Ted remembered to pick up Gary from work? Was Gary still in a foul mood from this morning?

Rachael let the VW idle as she turned to Stevie. "My parents love you like a daughter. Remember that, okay?"

"I will."

Rachael leaned over and hugged Stevie. "I'm going to miss you."

"And me you." Stevie clung to her best friend, unwilling to be the first one to release their hug. Although tears filled her eyes, she tried to be brave when they finally broke apart. She filled her lungs with air. "Have fun at school." Stevie opened the door and got out of the Beetle.

"I plan to." Rachael smiled before pulling away, leaving Stevie standing on the curb.

Stevie stood outside the apartment door, hearing an argument happening on the other side.

Gary bellowed, "Just forget it. She's emotional."

"She was pretty mad," Ted stated.

"She'll get over it. Besides, I'm the man of the house. What I say goes."

He was the man of the house, and she was his wife. As Mama would say, "You made your bed. Now lie in it." He was in a bad mood, and she'd need to bide her time. She needed to wait until he was in a better mood to tell him about the baby.

She opened the door. "I'm sorry I'm late. I'll get dinner started. How do pork chops sound?"

Days later, Stevie built up enough courage to confront Gary with her concern and tell him about the baby. It was her night off from cleaning office buildings, and Ted was out with Darla. Gary sat watching TV with one leg hanging over the arm of the overstuffed chair. She inched toward him, trembling as she stood in his line of vision. "Gary, can we talk?"

"Sure, babe. What's on your little mind?"

"It's Ted."

Gary leaned around her to watch the TV screen. "What about him?"

"He doesn't work, and he sits around the house all day." She inhaled deeply. "He makes me uncomfortable."

"He tried to find a job, but no one would hire him. It's not his fault. I'm his only family." Gary pulled his eyes away from the TV, his face red with anger. "What are you asking? You want me to kick him to the curb?"

"N-n-no. I just think with the apartment being so small and—"

He grabbed his can of beer from the TV tray and took a sip. Then he crushed the empty can, making a fist. "Go get me another one."

Stevie turned and, with tentative steps, went to the kitchen, grabbed a can from the fridge, and returned. Should she tell him about the baby?

Gary snatched the can out of her hand and snapped the tab. He jumped out of the chair and yelled at the TV set, "You idiot. He was safe."

I can't tell him while he's agitated. Maybe later when he's not so angry.

Stevie tip-toed to the bedroom, went to the dresser, and dug deep to the bottom of the drawer. She pulled out her spiral notebook and held it to her chest. She settled into the soft mattress. Easing her tense muscles, she leaned against the pillow and daydreamed about her precious daughter before she began to write.

September 1, 1969

My darling daughter,

A lot has happened since my last letter. I did graduate from high school, and Gary and I did get married. We eloped. My biggest news is that you will be a big sister next spring.

I haven't told Gary yet. I'm waiting until he's in a better mood. So, you should feel special hearing the news. I told Rachael. If you remember, Rachael is my best friend, and she has moved away to go to college. I miss her.

My classes start Monday at Fullerton. Unfortunately, I don't feel so good with morning sickness, so I tried to schedule late morning or afternoon classes. I can't wait much longer to tell Gary he's going to be a daddy. I hope he'll be happy about it.

I'd like to tell you more about your birth father. But I don't know much more than I've already written about him. No one seems to know where he is. If you want to find him once you're grown, I'll do whatever I can to help you. I hope you'll want to meet me someday. It is my dream to have a relationship with you. It'll be a celebration with you, your brother or sister, and me.

Placing you for adoption caused an excruciating pain that left a hole in my heart, and I'm not sure it will ever heal, even with the birth of your brother or sister. I have to mourn the loss of you alone because nobody understands. When I needed understanding and support, I got neither. I was weak and let Mama win. I regret that I let her talk me out of keeping you, and I always will. Everyone said you'd have a better life with two parents—a mother and a father.

Well, my darling daughter, I'm tired. I've been sleeping a lot recently, just like when I carried you next to my heart.

Love,

Your First Mother

CHAPTER 24

Annie

Annie opened the door and ushered Jenn into the kitchen. "Thanks for coming. You're the only one I trust to take care of Zoey."

Jenn examined Annie from top to bottom. "You look nice."

"Thanks. Zoey is taking her nap and probably won't wake up until after I get back from meeting with Joe." Annie handed Jenn a long list of contact and emergency numbers, including where she'd be.

"I'm not taking sides." Jenn searched Annie's eyes.

Annie didn't respond, her thoughts elsewhere. *How will Joe take what I have to say? What will he say?*

"I see Joe every day, and he's a broken man. Won't you consider giving him a second chance?" Jenn held up her hands as if in surrender. "There, I said what I needed to say."

"I wish you were on my side. But if I think about it realistically, I'm glad you're still friends with both of us." Annie glanced at her watch, grabbed her purse, and slung it over her shoulder. "Sorry. I've got to run. We'll talk when I get back."

The bell above the door jingled as Annie entered the small deli tucked away on the edge of town. She saw Joe sitting in the corner, his back to the wall. When he saw her, he stood and pulled out a chair for her. The knot in her stomach tightened.

"Jenn told me she'd be watching Zoey today while we have lunch."

"No lunch for me. Just Earl Grey tea." Annie placed her handbag on the chair beside her.

Joe raised his eyebrows. "Okay." He went to the counter and returned with her tea and a soft drink.

Taking a seat across from her, he unwrapped a straw and poked it in his soda but didn't take a sip. Instead, he rubbed the back of his neck. "When can I come home?"

Never.

"I love you, Annie. I've always loved you." He leaned toward her.

She folded her arms in front of her. "And Mallory? Do you love her?"

"I never loved her." He slumped in his chair. "You were right. There's no reason for what I did. As you said, I was selfish." He reached for her hand, but she quickly pulled it away. "I'll do anything to make you happy."

"I don't trust you."

"I'm broken-hearted about what I did to you. But I'm not your father. You can trust me. I promise it will never happen again."

"You bet it won't. Because we're through."

"No. Please. You have to forgive me."

"I can't. I've filed for divorce."

"I don't want a divorce." He covered his face with his hands.

"Too bad. You were the one who broke up our marriage, Joe. Unfortunately, there are always consequences for our actions, and divorce is the consequence of your infidelity." She sat taller. "You should be receiving the divorce papers to sign any day now."

"Please, Annie, reconsider. I can change. I know I can."

"It's too late."

"What about Zoey?"

"What about her?"

"I'm her father. You can't take her away from me."

"I may be angry with you, but I would never take your daughter away from you. You, of all people, should know me better than that. Besides, she adores you. She's too young to understand what you've done. But someday, she'll probably learn the reason why we divorced." She stood, grabbed her purse, and placed it over her shoulder.

He grabbed her wrist. "I can't lose you."

She twisted out of his grip. "You already have."

Annie pulled over to the side of the road on the drive home, turned off the ignition, and bawled. After a long cry, she pulled down the visor and checked her red eyes in the mirror.

I'm a mess. I want to put on a confident face for Jenn. But she'll notice I've been crying.

Annie entered the house and found Jenn sitting at the kitchen table, papers scattered in front of her.

Jenn scrutinized Annie. "You're a wreck."

"Pretty much. Is it that obvious?"

"On the outside, you look like you have it all together, but you've always held everything inside."

"Yeah, you're right. I'm a wreck. Like a ten-car pile-up on the freeway." Annie went to the sink, poured herself a glass of water, and then turned around to face Jenn. "I can't forgive him."

"Why not?"

"Because he'll do it to me again. As the saying goes, 'Once a cheater, always a cheater.'" Annie repeated the phrase that echoed in her head. "That's what cheaters do."

"Not necessarily." Jenn came around the table and scooted a chair closer to Annie. Taking her hands in her own, she looked deeply into Annie's eyes. "Joe isn't your father. He's a great guy who made a mistake."

Annie slumped into a chair. "You dated him before I did. If he's such a great guy, why didn't you marry him?"

"Because he didn't love me. He loves you." Jenn's brown eyes pierced Annie's heart.

"That's what he said."

"He's devastated about how he's hurt you. He made a mistake. Please forgive him."

"It's too late." Tears filled her eyes. How could she have more tears? "I filed for divorce."

Jenn pulled her hands away from Annie and clasped them to her chest. "Oh, Annie."

Annie dabbed her eyes with a tissue and released a heavy sigh. "Can we change the subject? I can't talk about this anymore. It's too hard."

Jenn was silent.

"What's going on with you besides work? Are you dating any great guys?"

"No. I'm beginning to think all the good ones have already been taken," Jenn said with a half-hearted shrug. Then her voice turned bubbly. "I've started going to church. It's called The Rock, and the pastor is so relatable."

"I never knew you to be religious."

"It's more like . . . a relationship."

"You mean between you and the pastor?"

"No. With God." Jenn almost bounced out of her chair with enthusiasm. "It's wonderful. And the people are so welcoming. I want you to come with me sometime. I think it'd be good for you."

"You haven't become one of those Jesus freaks, have you?"

They were interrupted by baby babbles from down the hall in the nursery.

Annie stood.

"Can I have some Angel Baby time before I leave?" Jenn gathered her papers into a pile and plunged them into her briefcase.

"Of course." Annie went to get Zoey.

When Annie returned carrying her daughter, Zoey reached out her arms to Jenn.

"Come to Aunt Jenn, my Angel Baby." Zoey wound her fingers in Jenn's long, red curls, then held her face between her tiny hands and kissed her cheek open-mouthed, leaving slobber on Jenn's face. The three of them giggled. The more they laughed, the more Zoey slobbered all over Jenn.

After their giggle-fest, Jenn put Zoey down on the floor to play with her toys.

"I think dogs and children sense when someone is miserable," Annie said. "It's good for Zoey to see you because I've been so sad these past few months, and I think she senses it. I need to climb out of my bad mood and be more upbeat around her. She deserves a happy mommy. I have to change for her sake." Annie hesitated before adding, "I make no promises, but maybe someday, I'll visit your new church. Unfortunately, there are no guarantees that I'll become a Jesus freak; and I don't think the people at your church would like me because I'm jealous, unforgiving, and prideful—to list a few of my faults."

Jenn clapped. "You'll fit right in. You're a sinner just like us."

Sitting at their feet, Zoey clapped her chubby hands together.

Chapter 25
Stevie

The vacuum hummed in the distance as Stevie pushed the large trash bin into Mr. Costa's office. Entering, she stopped upon seeing him sitting at his desk, his head bent. Stevie moved toward him, picked up the wastebasket beside his desk, and dumped it into the larger trash container. She replaced the wastebasket on the floor, and her gaze went to the pictures on his desk. She bit her lower lip. *Should she say something?*

"You have a beautiful wife and . . . little girl," Stevie murmured, seeing her baby's adoptive father, wishing she was the one raising her baby, not him.

He looked up. "What?"

"I said you have a beautiful family."

He turned his attention to Annie's picture. Her hair parted in the middle and pulled away from her face was not the popular bouffant style of the day, but it was chic. She wore a black dress with a single strand of pearls, the epitome of sophistication. He looked at Stevie with tears glistening in his eyes. "My wife is divorcing me."

Stevie gasped. After gathering her thoughts, she nodded at the other picture on his desk. Then, uncertain what else to say, she blurted out, "At least, you have your daughter."

Scooting forward in his chair, Joe reached into his back pocket. Pulling out his wallet, he flipped it open and showed Stevie a more recent photo. "Zoey's eighteen months now." He ran his hand over the plastic that covered the picture. "It was difficult right after she was born. She had colic, but now she's perfect. Zoey is my life."

He closed his wallet and stuffed it back into his pocket. "I haven't seen a lot of her in the last several months because my wife kicked me out of the house. But that's about to change." He looked down at the legal document on his desk. "I plan to get shared custody of Zoey, or Annie will have a fight on her hands."

He stopped talking, then looked up. "I'm sorry. I wasn't thinking; I should never have told you that." He stood and reached out his hand. "I'm Joe Costa."

She wiped her sweaty hand on her jeans, then accepted his handshake. "Stevie Gilbert. It's nice to meet you, Mr. Costa."

"Call me Joe. Everyone does." Although weariness showed on his face, his demeanor changed. He sat on the edge of his desk. "Stevie. I like it. Are you named after someone?"

"My dad."

"Your dad. How nice. And for how long have you been cleaning my office?"

"About two years. I'm a student at Fullerton during the day, so this job is perfect for me."

"What's your major?"

"I haven't decided. I'm taking general courses right now." She grabbed a dust rag from off the cart and twisted it in her hands.

"Have you ever thought about working during the day instead of at night?"

"That would make my husband happy. He doesn't like me working nights."

He looked at her for only a second before asking, "What if I offered you a job? You have a pleasant voice, and I need a receptionist. While working here, I'll provide you the opportunity to learn the real estate business. I pay well, including medical and other benefits. And as you say, it would make your husband happy to have you home at night."

She felt as though she were on a roller coaster, climbing and dipping and then jerking back and forth. Quit school? Not work nights? Maybe she and Gary could get a bigger place to live. And it was such a nice place to work.

Joe moved a chair next to his desk for her. Then he sat down again in his swivel chair and faced her. "I love what I do. I find my clients their dream homes, and I provide opportunities for my employees. We're like a family here—a big family. I have offices throughout Southern California, and real estate is booming. It brings me a great deal of pleasure to help people grow and succeed."

Mama appeared in the doorway. "So, this is where you are."

Stevie jumped up. "Mama, I'd like you to meet Mr. Costa."

Joe stood and walked toward Mama. "Please call me Joe. And you are?"

"Margaret Shaw," Mama said, stone-faced.

"Well, Mrs. Shaw, I'm pleased to meet you." He reached out his hand to Mama. She cautiously accepted his handshake.

"You have a lovely daughter." He glanced over at Stevie. Mama remained leery. He turned his attention back to Mama. "I've just offered her a job as a receptionist and the opportunity to learn the real estate business."

"Stevie has school." Mama planted her feet in a wide stance.

"Your daughter could always take some night classes if she wanted to continue her education. But I assure you what she'll learn while working here will provide her a chance that the classroom doesn't offer." He added, "Many college graduates don't find their dream jobs after graduation. So, I'm offering her the possibility of a bright future."

Mama pursed her lips.

He turned to face Stevie. "You don't need to decide tonight. Think it over, and then talk to your husband. I don't need an answer right away. My receptionist is a temp, so I will eventually need someone full-time."

Stevie tingled all over with excitement.

Mr. Costa handed a business card to her and one to Mama. "I'll leave you both to your work." He grabbed the official-looking document from his desk. "Good night."

After he left, Mama turned to Stevie. "I don't get it. Why would he offer you a job?"

"Because he likes to help people."

"Humph. He must have an ulterior motive. Now, get back to work so we can go home." Mama started the vacuum and pushed it with more vigor than Stevie thought possible.

Stevie held her hands in prayer and looked heavenward. She could barely wait to get home and tell Gary about the job offer. And about the baby.

Later, before turning off the lights at Joe Costa Real Estate, Stevie stood beside the receptionist's desk and ran her hand over the shiny mahogany surface.

After Mama dropped her off, Stevie rushed inside the apartment where Gary and Ted were watching TV, beer cans scattered on the coffee table.

"Hey, babe." Gary raised his beer can in greeting.

Stevie cringed. The way he said *babe* sounded degrading to her. She must be wrong. After all, he'd married her, loved her, and worked hard at the gas station every day. She wouldn't bring up how she felt about it because nothing was going to spoil her excitement. "Can we talk privately?" She nodded toward the bedroom.

"Anything you have to say to me, you can say in front of Ted. I don't have any secrets from him."

She waited, hoping he'd change his mind.

Gary didn't budge out of the chair. Neither did Ted.

"I was offered a job tonight."

"Oh, yeah? You already have one." He cocked his head to the side.

"This one is better with a chance for advancement and benefits. And we need some help now."

"What sort of benefits?" He sat up straighter.

"Medical, for one."

"I guess that's good, since I sure don't get no benefits at the gas station." His face changed before her eyes as if a dark shadow had fallen over it. He stood. "Do you think you're better than me?"

"No. Never."

"Because I'm the man of the house. You got that?" He grabbed her arm and squeezed it hard.

"Of course, you are."

He released her.

Stevie had reached the point where she couldn't put it off any longer. He was in a bad mood most of the time. She had to tell Gary about the baby because soon she'd start to show. She approached tentatively. "Gary," she whispered, "I'm pregnant."

Gary's eyes widened. "When?"

"March," she uttered timidly.

Gary strutted back and forth in front of the TV, his chest puffed out. "Ted, did you hear that? I'm going to be a daddy."

"Yeah, man. Cool."

Stevie relaxed her tense muscles and walked to the bedroom. Once inside the tiny room, she cradled her tummy where her unborn baby grew. *This time, no one will take my baby away from me.*

She needed to tell Mr. Costa she was pregnant. It was the right thing to do. But would he still hire her?

CHAPTER 26

After class the next day, Stevie entered the bank and withdrew enough from her savings account to treat Ted and Darla to dinner and a movie so she could talk to Gary alone. Her bank account was no longer growing, since Gary had insisted she give him all her paychecks. The savings account was her secret from him, just like the bottle of vodka stashed in the back of the closet. She hadn't needed the alcohol in a long time, but the money was her insurance against any possible unknown. And she wasn't ready to get rid of her painkiller. It was another source of insurance against the unknown.

Stevie entered the apartment later that afternoon, carrying a bag of groceries. *I hope Gary appreciates the special dinner I've planned.*

Ted was in his usual spot on the frayed couch. After putting the groceries away, she returned to the living room, turned off the TV, and stood in front of Ted with her fists on her waist. "Ted, remember last August when you promised me you'd have the car back in time for me to go to my appointment?"

"Yeah. So?"

"Well, you owe me. Right?" Stevie sat on the couch next to him.

"I guess." He curled into himself like a beaten puppy.

"I've decided to treat you better than you did me."

"Huh?"

She pulled the money out of her pocket and offered it to him. "I want you to take Darla on a date tonight. There's enough here for dinner and a movie. *Butch Cassidy and the Sundance Kid* is playing at the theater."

"But Gary and me—we want to see it together." He waffled.

"So, be a gentleman and take Darla to see *Paint Your Wagon*. It's a musical."

"I don't . . . " Ted scratched his head.

Stevie pushed the money closer to him.

"Why are you doing this?'

"I need to talk to Gary alone, and it's difficult with you here all the time. It's important. And there's a condition to my offer. I want this to be our secret between you and me and no one else. Can you do that for me?"

He took the money from her. "I guess."

"You need to get ready and get out of here before Gary gets home."

Ted looked down at his wrinkled, stained shirt and dirty jeans. "What's wrong with what I'm wearing?"

Stevie shook her head. "Just be out of here before Gary gets home." She left the room and went to the kitchen to peel potatoes. Gary was a meat-and-potatoes man, and she wanted to broil him a steak.

Later, when Gary came through the door, he eyed the raw T-bone on the broiler pan. "What's this? Are we celebrating something? And where's Ted?"

"Ted and Darla have a date tonight." She leaned in and kissed him on the lips. "I'll broil the steak while you wash up."

She grabbed the broiler pan with the steak and a hamburger patty on it. She couldn't afford to buy two steaks on the food allowance Gary had given her. While she opened the oven door, he took off his greasy coveralls, plopped them on the floor next to the washing machine, and headed toward the sink to wash his hands. He went to the fridge, grabbed a beer, and pulled the tab. Soon, with the meal on the table, they sat across from each other.

"I got a steal today," Gary said. "This guy comes to the station needing money, so I bought his car. It needs some work, but I can handle it. It's a Karmann Ghia. It has no guts on hills, but it'll be fine for you to get back and forth to school." He gnawed on his T-bone. "So, you don't need to take the bus anymore."

She jumped up and came around the table, squeezing him in a hug and kissing his cheek. "Thank you. You're so good to me." After returning to her chair, she put her elbows on the table and folded her hands. "Gary, I've made a decision. It's something I've thought a lot about, and I want to do it. I hope you'll agree."

"So, what is it?" He dropped the bone on his plate and wiped his hands on a paper napkin.

"I want to quit school and go to work at Joe Costa Real Estate. I know I'll like working there, and I'll be contributing more money to our finances." She rushed on. "And we'll be able to spend our evenings together."

"Your mother will have a cow." He pushed his chair back and stared at her.

"I know she will. And I need to tell Mr. Costa I'm pregnant. I'm not sure if he'll still offer me the job after I tell him. But I think it's the right thing to do. To tell him, I mean."

"Yeah. And the more money we save, the sooner I can buy my own business. So, I guess it's a good idea." He stood, went to the fridge, and grabbed another beer. "Thanks for dinner."

"You're welcome."

He went to the living room and turned on the TV.

She cleared the table. *And maybe we can move to a larger place someday.*

Stevie made an appointment the following day to meet with Mr. Costa. She waited in the reception area, wiping her sweaty palms on her skirt.

When he came through the door, the receptionist said, "Joe, Ms. Gilbert, your three o'clock appointment is waiting." She nodded toward Stevie.

He looked over at her and smiled. "Stevie, how nice to see you. Let's go to my office." She followed him down the hallway.

Mr. Costa motioned to the seat next to his desk. After she sat, he lowered himself into his chair. "Have you decided to work for me?"

"I appreciate the opportunity you've offered me, but . . . " He listened. "I'm four-and-a-half months pregnant." There. She'd said it. Was she ruining her chance to work for Joe Costa Real Estate and possible future advancement?

"Congratulations." He leaned forward. "It isn't a problem. My employees have babies all the time. Some return, and others opt to be stay-at-home mothers." He added, "Do you have any idea if you'd plan to return to work after your baby is born?"

"Yes. My husband and I are newly married, and we need my income."

"Well, my offer is still open. During your maternity leave, I'll hire a temp to do your job. There's a probationary period of three months for all my employees. It gives us both the opportunity for me to see how you perform and for you to see if we are a good fit for you. If you decide to accept the job, I'll introduce you to Jenn, and she'll go over your salary and benefits package with you. How does that sound?"

"There is one more thing. I need to give my mother a two-week notice, so she can find a replacement for me."

"No problem. I wouldn't expect anything else." He stood. "Your starting date will be in two weeks. That'll give Pam, our receptionist, time to train you before she leaves."

She stood and offered him her hand. "Thank you."

After shaking her hand, he said, "Let me take you down to Jenn's office and introduce you."

She followed him with more confidence than she had felt earlier.

Stevie interrupted the usual silence while riding to work with Mama. "Gary bought me a car, and he's fixing it up for me. It's a Karmann Ghia, a German make."

"I know what a Karmann Ghia is."

They rode the rest of the way in silence. Stevie wasn't about to give her two-week notice now. Instead, she'd wait until they were on their way home.

After their work shift ended, they drove most of the way to Stevie's apartment in silence. Finally, she said, "Mama, I'm going to quit school and take the job Mr. Costa offered me. It's more money than I'm making now, and Gary and I need the benefits—especially medical because I'm pregnant. I wanted to give you a two-week notice."

There. I said it.

"Humph. Yes, I recognize firsthand how important medical insurance is."

Stevie waited. Was that all Mama was going to say?

"I'm disappointed, and I disagree with your decision. But since you're married, you need to do what's best for you and Gary. You're smart. You'll probably do fine in real estate as long as we don't have a recession." She added, "I suggest you save a nest egg for when the hard times hit. I know from experience, there'll come a day when you'll need it. Don't worry about me. I'll find a replacement for you." Mama pulled up to the curb in front of the apartment, stopped, turned, and faced Stevie. "I'm disappointed that you're quitting school. But you're a married woman now, and you must do what's best for your family. If you're happy, then I'm happy for you." *Was this what Mama meant when she had said, "Get on with your life?"*

Stevie threw her arms around Mama's stiff frame before she exited the car. The old Chevy pulled away as Stevie entered the quiet apartment. She crept past Ted on the sofa and entered the bedroom where Gary slept. After Stevie had prepared for bed, she grabbed her notebook from her dresser. Stepping into the closet, Stevie closed the door and pulled on the string hanging from the ceiling, lighting the tiny space. She nestled on the floor and began to write.

November 24, 1969

My darling daughter,

It's late, but I just couldn't go to sleep without telling you my exciting news. In two weeks, I'll be working for your adoptive father. He seems to be kind and generous, and I'm looking forward to the opportunity he's giving me to be his receptionist at one of his offices.

I understand your mommy and daddy are getting a divorce, and it makes me sad. But, while working for your daddy, I'll be able to keep an even closer watch over you.

You are always in my prayers.

Love,

Your First Mother

That night, Stevie awoke when Gary started thrashing in his sleep next to her in bed. She wrapped her arms around him and cooed, "You're okay. It was only a bad dream." She gently traced one of the scars on his back as he trembled and cried. Stevie snuggled closer to him. "Do you want to talk about it?"

"She beat me with a hot fireplace poker."

"Who beat you?"

"My mother."

She gasped. Comforting words eluded her. *How could anyone be so cruel as to beat a child? Her flesh and blood?* She held him close as warm tears escaped.

CHAPTER 27

Annie

Informed earlier about what to expect during the mediation meeting, Annie sat next to Deborah Dunbar, her attorney, in the conference room of the attorney's office. They waited for Joe and his lawyer to arrive. The knot in Annie's stomach tightened when Joe and his attorney entered the room, taking their seats across from Annie and her attorney. With Deborah representing her, all Annie had to do was sit and listen to the exchange between lawyers.

After introductions and civilities, Deborah began the mediation, including the house. "The home is free and clear. Mrs. Costa would like the deed put in her name. As you can see, child support and alimony are listed in discovery. Mr. Costa's net worth is quite substantial. Mrs. Costa's partnership in the business will remain as is. The marriage, not the business, is ending."

Bernard Schwartz, Joe's attorney, countered concerning the fairness of the negotiations.

Joe turned to his lawyer and held up his hand. "Stop, Bernie. Give her whatever she wants. All I want is shared custody of my daughter." He avoided Annie's eyes.

"But . . . " his attorney stammered.

With his shoulders slumped, Joe walked to the door and exited the room.

Annie's bottom lip trembled as she watched Joe leave. *I hate him for what he did to me, yet I still love him. What have I done?*

Over the next few months, Joe tried everything to get Annie to take him back. He sent flowers, chocolates, and even jewelry. He called her daily, trying to reason with her. But the phone calls just left her emotionally exhausted. Even Jenn tried to convince Annie that she was making a mistake. But all Annie could think of was what had happened to her mother when her father had left. The hurt was too much for her to bear.

One Sunday evening when Joe was dropping off Zoey from his weekend with her, he made a final attempt to plead for forgiveness.

After putting Zoey to bed, he came back out to the living room to see Annie curled up on the couch, pretending to read a book.

"Annie, I've told you that there's no one else for me but you," pleaded Joe. "I want my family back. I want *you* back!" He slammed his fist into his other palm, tears filling his eyes.

Annie looked at her husband, who had aged considerably over the last few months. "I can't, Joe. You lied. You cheated. I can't . . . I can't trust you anymore!" With that, she ran to the bedroom sobbing.

On Monday morning, Annie and Joe sat on opposite sides of the aisle in a courtroom. Judge Samuel Buckingham presided; his bushy salt-and-pepper eyebrows hovered above his Ben Franklin glasses. He listened intently as each attorney presented their opening statements.

When they finished, Judge Buckingham removed his glasses and spoke to Joe. "Mr. Costa, I congratulate you on your financial generosity to your wife. Your decision to provide for her with substantial child support and alimony, as well as the home, is admirable. You have been more than fair. And keeping her as a partner in your profitable business rather than dividing all assets at this time is also considerate."

He put his glasses on and referred to the document in front of him. "What breaks my heart is the dissolution of your marriage. I do not see any record of either of you trying to save it. There is no mention of a trial separation nor marriage counseling. Neither of you fought to save your marriage. You gave up."

He looked over the top of his glasses. "You, sir, were unfaithful to your wife." Then he looked over at Annie. "And you, Mrs. Costa, did not forgive your husband for his adultery. What breaks my heart most is your child, who you adopted legally only a little over a year ago." He glared at Annie and then at Joe. "You both should be ashamed of yourselves."

Joe hung his head, while Annie slumped down further into the hard, wooden chair.

Judge Buckingham continued. "I grant your divorce and shared custody of"—he referred to the document—"Zoey. On one condition. Zoey will not be shuffled back and forth from house to house. She will remain in her home, and the two of you will shuffle back and forth every other week and holidays."

Annie felt like she was being led to the guillotine, and the blade had dropped.

With the proceedings over, Joe left the courtroom first, followed by Annie as their attorneys stayed behind.

In the hallway, Jenn sat on a bench with Zoey on her lap. Zoey reached for Joe to hold her. Taking her into his arms, he buried his face in her neck. When he pulled back, Zoey touched the tear on his cheek. "Don't cry, Da-ddy."

CHAPTER 28

Joe

Joe was pretty distracted on his way into work. The past few months with Annie had been hard, and he hadn't been sleeping well. Work was suffering, too, but he was the boss and had people who depended on him.

Walking into the office, he mumbled "Good morning" to Stevie and started looking through his memos when Stevie suddenly bent over in pain.

"Whoa. You sick?" he asked.

"I think I'm in labor." Stevie held her belly. "I called Gary, but they said he'd gone to lunch."

"Well, I'm going to get you to the hospital." He stopped. "Which hospital?"

"Saint Joseph."

He yelled down the hall, "Jenn, Stevie's in labor. I'm taking her to Saint Joseph. Find her employment file and call her mother. And try to find her husband."

Jenn ducked her head out of her office door. "What about your afternoon appointments?"

"Take care of them." With his hand on the middle of her lower back, he guided Stevie to the parking lot and into his new Lincoln.

Stevie hesitated. "What if my water breaks?"

"Then it breaks." He hurried to the driver's side and sped away.

At the hospital, Joe stood beside Stevie, supporting her as she relayed her information to the admitting clerk. Soon, they brought a wheelchair for her as she moaned in pain.

Not wanting to leave her alone, Joe paced. Then he saw Stevie's mother come through the doors. He rushed to her. "Mrs.—"

"Shaw."

"Yes. Mrs. Shaw. I'm sorry. I'm usually good at remembering names."

"Well, it seems like this is an unusual situation." She looked around the room. "Where's Gary?" She arched her brows.

"We haven't been able to locate him."

"I see. Well, I'm here now. I'll see if they'll let me be with Stevie."

"Sure. I'll wait here in case you need me for anything. And, Mrs. Shaw, my office is trying to locate Gary."

"Thank you."

Joe stood when Mrs. Shaw eventually returned to the waiting room. "How is she?"

"Her contractions are getting stronger. It won't be long now." Mrs. Shaw furrowed her brow. "I hate to ask—"

"What? Anything?"

"Stevie would like her overnight bag . . . and I don't want to leave her."

"I can get her bag for her."

"You're very kind, Mr. Costa." Mrs. Shaw dug Stevie's keys out of her purse and gave him the address and directions to the apartment. "Where is Gary, anyway? He should be here," she mumbled.

Joe found the apartment easily. He knocked loudly; but when nobody answered, he used the key Mrs. Shaw had given him and entered. Looking around the apartment, he was disgusted by the trash that littered the room, the broken window that needed fixing, and the furniture that desperately needed to be replaced. How could Stevie live in such a place?

He pushed open the bedroom door and gasped when he discovered Gary in bed with a woman. He wasn't shocked, though. He'd never liked Gary coming around the office pestering Stevie—keeping her under his thumb, controlling her. It seemed to him that Gary was stalking Stevie—typical signs of an abusive husband.

"What the—" Gary sprang to a sitting position while the woman pulled the sheet to cover herself.

"Stevie is in labor at Saint Joseph. Joe stated coldly. "Mrs. Shaw asked me to bring her overnight bag. Do you know where it is?" he added before leaving the room.

Joe sat on the sofa in the living room, waiting for Gary. When Gary stumbled into the room carrying an overnight bag, Joe noticed his bloodshot eyes. "Man, you're in no condition to drive. I'll take you."

They rode silently to the hospital. When they arrived, Gary said, "My wife's nine months pregnant. I just—"

"Stevie needs you right now." Joe handed him Stevie's keys and overnight bag and watched Gary go through the doors to find his wife.

CHAPTER 29
Margaret

Margaret Shaw sat beside her daughter, holding her hand during Stevie's labor. "My brave, brave girl. I'm so proud of you."

The nurse returned and said, "Mrs. Shaw, please step out in the hall while I examine Stevie."

"Sure." Margaret squeezed Stevie's hand. "I'll be right out in the hallway."

Stevie grimaced from another contraction.

In the hall, Margaret watched Gary stagger toward her, carrying Stevie's familiar overnight case. She stopped him and glared into his bloodshot eyes. "You're not going in there like this. Come with me."

She grabbed his arm and forcefully dragged him to the cafeteria, his feet stumbling, trying to keep up with her. She pushed him into a plastic chair, bought a black coffee, and plunked it in front of him, some splashing on the table.

"I like cream and sugar."

"I don't care. Drink it." She sat across from him, glaring.

When he finished it, she got another. "Drink it."

"But—"

"You heard me."

He sipped the second cup of coffee.

"Gary, I liked you when you came to my home. You appeared to be a nice person. You were ambitious, and you professed your love for my daughter. But I don't like you anymore, and Stevie deserves better. You'd better shape up, be a man, and change your ways because you're about to become a father. So get yourself into that men's room and wash yourself up. And tuck in your shirt. You look like a bum."

While Gary was in the restroom, she bought a small bottle of breath freshener. When he emerged, she handed it to him. "Here, use this." She gave him the bottle. "You smell like a bar."

They returned to the maternity ward. She stood at the door. "Go ahead. Stevie needs you. I'll be out here." She nodded toward the waiting room.

Margaret sat down and put her head in her hands. Where had she gone wrong? Oh, how she missed her husband! He would have seen right through Gary from the start and would have put a stop to the relationship before it had gotten this far.

Things hadn't been easy for Margaret since her husband had died. When Stevie had been raped, she didn't know what she should do. Stevie didn't want to pursue going to the police and filing a report, so she was left trying to pick up the pieces of her daughter's broken heart. And then having to force Stevie to sign the adoption papers . . . She wished with all her heart that she could have taken that baby into their home and raised her grandchild.

She wondered what her grandchild was doing at that moment. And now, she was waiting to meet her second grandchild. The moment was bittersweet, but she had to remain strong for Stevie. She couldn't let her guard down, or Stevie would suffer.

"Mrs. Shaw?" A nurse interrupted her thoughts.

"Yes?"

"You can come in now. Your daughter's asking for you."

CHAPTER 30
Stevie

Things seemed to improve for a while after Stevie came home with her new son, Gil. Gary was more affectionate for a while. He even helped pick up around the apartment every now and then, and he tried to keep Ted from annoying her too much.

But soon, Gary went back to his old ways and spent more and more time with Ted and less time with Stevie and Gil. He hated when Gil cried, and he refused to change any diapers. The initial thrill of becoming a dad had worn off, and Gary expected Stevie to put his needs above the baby's.

It was a lonely life for Stevie, and she often felt depressed at the way her life was going. And the ache in her heart for her firstborn only hurt more whenever she heard Gil's cries.

One hot August evening, Stevie answered the phone while holding five-month-old roly-poly Gil.

Her heart immediately felt lighter when she heard Rachael's voice on the line. "Hey, I'm about to head back to school, and Mom reminded me that she still hasn't seen Gil yet. Plus, she misses you."

"I miss her, too. It seems like all I do is work and clean the house."

"Mom would like to invite you to lunch on Saturday. Can you come and bring Gil with you?"

"Sounds wonderful. What time?"

"How does 12:30 work for you?"

"Perfect. I'll be able to feed Gil before I come."

After hanging up the phone, Stevie whirled around the small living room with Gil while he gave her a toothless smile. "You're going to meet some wonderful people, little man. And they're going to love you."

On Saturday, Mr. Graham opened the door wide for Stevie and Gil to enter. "They're here," he yelled, then opened his arms and gave Stevie a bear hug. "We've missed you." He pulled back, his eyes moist. "And who do we have here?"

"This is Gil," Stevie said as Rachael and her mother peeked around Mr. Graham, who was blocking the doorway.

"Will he come to me?" Mr. Graham asked, holding his hands out to Gil. Although Gil's eyebrows squished together, he went to him. "We men have to stick together with these females hovering around us." He carried Gil to the living room.

Mrs. Graham hugged Stevie and led her into the living room, where Gil was the center of attention. Mrs. Graham sat next to her husband and made cooing noises while Rachael sat on the floor at her father's feet and played with Gil's foot.

"Stevie, he's adorable," Mrs. Graham gushed. "I love chubby babies. They look so healthy."

Gifts wrapped in baby paper with blue bows sat on the end table next to the burgundy wingback chair where Stevie sat. She watched while the Graham family doted on her son. They seemed unable to take their eyes off Gil. Stevie's heart swelled with pride.

After a while, Mrs. Graham motioned toward the gifts. "Please open those. I'm sorry it took me this long to get them to you."

Stevie unwrapped a huge white bunny with a baby blue ribbon tied around the neck. The stuffed animal was bigger than Gil. *Where on earth am I going to put this in our tiny apartment?* "Thank you." Then she opened *Pat the Bunny.* "I love this book." Stevie stood and handed the book to Mr. Graham, who proceeded to show it to Gil, who drooled while patting the soft fabric in the book.

When Gil yawned and rubbed his fist in his eye, Stevie said, "He's getting tired. It's his nap time."

"Here, let me hold him." Mrs. Graham looked toward Stevie for approval.

After Stevie nodded, Mrs. Graham took Gil from her husband and cradled him in her arms. "It's been so long since we've had a baby in our house." She gazed at him as his eyes fluttered, then closed. Mrs. Graham shooed them away. "You go ahead and have lunch while I have some baby time. Rachael . . . "

"I know. You want me to be the hostess. We'll be fine while you have your baby fix." Rachael jumped up from the floor and pulled Stevie out of the chair, slipping her arm in the crook of Stevie's. "Come on."

Rachael pulled the luncheon plates from the refrigerator and undid the plastic wrap that covered tuna salad-stuffed tomatoes on beds of lettuce.

"Where's Buddy?" Stevie asked as they began to eat.

"He's at a friend's house," Mr. Graham said while he poured the iced tea.

"Tell him I missed seeing him." Stevie wiped the edges of her mouth with her napkin. "He's such a cute, little boy."

Both Rachael and her dad laughed. "We won't tell him you said that," Mr. Graham said. "He thinks he's a teenager."

"My mistake." Stevie joined their laughter.

Stevie listened as Rachael and her dad discussed college life. While college had once been Stevie's dream, she only felt a twinge of regret. After all, she had Gil, and he was the best baby she could have ever imagined.

Mr. Graham turned to Stevie. "Rachael told me you're working as a receptionist for Joe Costa. How do you like it?"

"I hate leaving Gil with a babysitter all day; but I do like my job, and Mr. Costa is a great boss. So, I can't complain."

Later, after Mr. Graham excused himself from the table to go to his home office, Stevie helped Rachael clean up the kitchen. Stevie and Rachael walked into the living room where Mrs. Graham rested her head on the back of the brocade sofa, her eyes closed, with Gil asleep in her arms.

"I should go," Stevie whispered. "Gary will be getting home from work soon and want dinner."

Rachael gently touched her mother's arm. "Mom, Stevie's leaving."

Mrs. Graham opened her eyes. "Oh, okay." She stood and gently placed Gil into Stevie's arms.

Rachael grabbed the gigantic stuffed animal and the book and carried them to Stevie's car. She squeezed them behind the front seats of the Karmann Ghia. Then Stevie strapped sleeping Gil into the infant seat, which he was quickly out-growing. She closed the car door and turned to Mrs. Graham, who clasped her arms around Stevie in a hug.

"Please, come again soon. We miss you so much." She stepped back, her gaze transfixed on the thumb-size bruises on Stevie's arms.

"Stevie . . . " Mrs. Graham stepped forward as though she wanted to say something.

"I've really gotta go," Stevie said hurriedly, slipping into the driver's seat. "Bye!"

Driving off down the street, Stevie thought, *I'd better start wearing long sleeves even during the summer.*

CHAPTER 31

Annie

Annie crept on her weak legs to Jenn's front porch and tapped on the door. When Jenn opened it, Annie collapsed into her best friend's arms. "What have I done?"

Jenn pushed the door closed with her foot and guided Annie to the sofa. Together, they sank into the floral-quilted couch.

"It's Joe's week to have Zoey, and I have nowhere to go." Annie sobbed. "I guess I thought it wasn't going to happen, so I didn't make any arrangements for a place to live."

"You'll stay with me for as long as you need or want. Just like when we were roommates in college." Jenn hugged Annie as she cried.

When Annie pulled away from Jenn's hold, she reached into her pocket, pulled out a tissue, and wiped her tears. "I guess I thought Joe would let me take care of Zoey during his custody week while he was at work." She looked at Jenn through tear-filled eyes. "Stupid of me, wasn't it?"

"Not stupid. Hopeful, maybe." Jenn stood. "Did you bring luggage?"

Annie began to stand on her wobbly legs.

"You stay here. I'll get it." Jenn headed toward the door. "When I get back, I'll make us some tea."

Annie sank back down into the sofa.

Jenn returned with Annie's baggage and took it to the guest room. "Have you had anything to eat?"

"I'm not hungry."

"Well, you have to eat. Keep up your strength because next week, it's your turn to take care of Angel Baby. If not for yourself, do it for her."

Annie dragged herself to the kitchen and sat at the table and watched Jenn open a can of chicken noodle soup. After pouring it into a saucepan to heat, Jenn grabbed the whistling tea kettle, poured the boiling water into a teapot, added teabags, and brought it to the kitchen table.

Jenn sat across from Annie. "I'll be gone all day tomorrow. I have appointments with clients, and I'll be seeing Joe's clients, too." After the tea brewed, Jenn poured the amber liquid into cups. "He took the week off to take care of Zoey."

Unable to concentrate, Annie sipped her tea while Jenn's voice droned in the background.

The following day, Annie awoke when she heard Jenn's voice.

"Annie, I'm home." The front door closed, followed by hurried footsteps down the hallway.

Jenn entered the darkened room where Annie lay in bed. Her mouth fell open. Although it was apparent, Jenn asked, "Have you been in bed all day?"

Annie didn't answer.

Jenn sat on the bed next to her. "Joe's been trying to get a hold of you. He's been calling you all day."

Annie sprang to a sitting position. "Is Zoey okay?"

"She's fine. Didn't you hear the phone ringing?"

"It's your phone. I didn't think it was my place to answer it." Annie lay back against the pillow.

"Well, you'd better call him. He said it's important." Jenn kicked off her shoes and rubbed her feet.

Annie went to the bathroom and splashed cold water on her face. While Jenn went to the kitchen to set the table, Annie called Joe.

He answered on the third ring.

Hearing his voice, Annie felt a pang in her heart. "Jenn said you needed to talk to me."

"I do. Tomorrow, I have an appointment with a nanny, and I'd like you to be here. The interview is scheduled for one o'clock while Zoey is taking a nap."

"So, you're hiring a nanny?"

"I am. I can't take every other week off from work."

"No, of course not."

"I think it's important for both of us to agree on whom I hire to take care of Zoey. So can you make it?"

"I'll be there."

"Why don't you come at 12:30 so I can tell you about the nanny we'll be interviewing?"

After agreeing, Annie said goodbye and hung up the phone. She went to the kitchen, where Jenn had little, white Chinese take-out boxes on the table.

Jenn looked up. "Everything okay?"

Annie nodded. "I guess. Shared custody is new to me." She looked at the floor, thankful that Jenn didn't say, "I told you so."

The following day, Annie arrived at her house at 12:30. Standing on the front porch, she sighed. *Do I enter? Knock?* She tried the handle and discovered the door was locked. She began to rummage in her purse for her house key when the door opened.

"I just got Zoey down for her nap." He held the door open. "Come in."

She walked to the sofa and sat down.

Joe sat on the matching couch across from Annie. He studied her. "You look tired."

"Do I?" She put on a fake smile. "That isn't something a lady likes to hear. Where's that charm of yours?"

"Sorry."

"So, where did you find the nanny we're interviewing?" Annie leaned back into the couch. *Just relax. Take control of yourself.*

"She's been an infant nurse for twenty years. She takes care of newborns for a week or two when mothers first come home from the hospital. The Murphys have used her for all three of their daughters. And I've talked with others who've given her glowing references. They say she's wonderful."

Annie arched an eyebrow. "But Zoey isn't an infant."

"No. But I understand Mary Jefferson—that's her name—wants to make a change to a more permanent position."

"So, what happens when it's my custody week?" Annie questioned.

"Well, she can either stay in the maid's quarters that we've never used or go home every other week. She lives in L.A."

Annie mulled the information over, picturing a stranger living in her house.

"My mother would take care of Zoey in a heartbeat. She already takes care of my brother's and sister's kids." He looked down at his clasped hands. "But I'm aware you wouldn't be happy about it."

"If you're honest, you wouldn't be either. Your nieces and nephews are brats. Your mother would spoil Zoey, too."

The doorbell chimed, and Joe went to answer it. After he greeted the potential nanny, he ushered her into the living room and offered her the place where he'd been seated. He scooted close to Annie, across from the well-groomed nanny with kind, brown eyes, who wore a white uniform, white nylons, and white shoes—a distinct contrast to her black skin.

"Mrs. Jefferson, I'd like you to meet my wife—I mean, my *ex*-wife, Annie Costa."

Annie cringed. *I hate that word,* ex. *Why couldn't he have said his former wife?*

"It's nice to meet you, Mrs. Jefferson," Annie said.

"Please call me Mary."

Joe went on to explain to Mary about their joint custody arrangement. After Mary answered all their questions, Joe asked, "Would you like to see your room?"

"Yes." Mary stood.

"Follow me." Joe led Mary to the room beside the kitchen and opened the door. "As you can see, it has a sitting area, a bedroom, bath, and a small kitchen. You could stay here even when it's Annie's week to have Zoey. Or you could go home."

Annie tensed as she followed behind. She didn't want to share her home with a stranger.

"It's very nice," Mary said as they returned to the living room.

Zoey's babbling came from the nursery.

Annie turned to Joe. "Can I get her?"

"Of course."

Annie returned, carrying her precious daughter, dressed in a denim romper trimmed with lace. When Zoey saw Joe, she smiled.

Annie said, "Mary, this is our daughter, Zoey."

Mary stood and reached out her hand. "Hello, Zoey."

Zoey looked like she was about to cry and buried her face in Annie's neck.

Mary pulled her hand back.

"We'll contact you with our decision," Joe said as he escorted Mary to the door.

Zoey trembled in Annie's arms and began to cry.

"It's okay." Annie rocked Zoey. At the same time, Zoey wrapped her arms around Annie's neck and held tight.

Joe sat silently, watching them.

"We're all learning how to cope with the changes in our lives, including our daughter." Annie rested her chin on the top of Zoey's blonde curls. "She isn't used to my absence."

"I realize that." He ran his hand through his hair. "Did you think I'd walk away and never see my daughter again?"

"She's *our* daughter. And I'm not sure what I thought. Except . . . "

He stared at Annie. "Except what?"

"Except . . . I don't think we should talk about this in Zoey's presence." Annie returned his gaze with imploring eyes.

He held out his hand to her. "Truce?"

She accepted his gesture. She'd always loved his hands. Warm. Familiar. "Truce."

Joe did not let go of her until she inched her hand away.

They spent the rest of the afternoon playing with Zoey. Joe looked up at Annie over the block tower he'd made with his daughter. "I don't think she's going to let you out of her sight. Will you stay for dinner and wait until after she's in bed before you leave?"

"I'll need to call Jenn. She's probably expecting me."

"Go ahead." He nodded toward the phone hanging on the wall in the kitchen. "And, Annie?"

She turned to face him.

"Thanks."

Annie went to the kitchen to phone Jenn. Zoey followed close behind her, not letting Annie out of her sight.

CHAPTER 32

Jenn

The knot in Jenn's gut tightened. For weeks, Jenn had watched her best friend sink deeper and deeper into a pit of depression, and she knew Annie needed help. Leaving her desk, Jenn walked down the hall and poked her head into Joe's office.

"Hey, boss, can I take a long lunch today?" Jenn focused on keeping her tone upbeat.

He looked up from his paperwork. "Of course. You don't need to ask. Tell Stevie how long you plan to be away."

"Thanks." She didn't move.

He cocked a brow, studying her. "Anything I can do?"

Jenn waited. Should she tell him? She reconsidered. "Nah. It's personal."

"Okay, then. See you when you get back." Joe bowed his head and returned his attention to the papers on his desk.

Ten minutes later, Jenn opened the door to her house and heard horrible howling, like a wounded animal. She hurried through the house to the bathroom. She gasped. Annie was slumped on the shower floor in her nightie, the water pouring down on her. Jenn rushed in and turned off the faucets. Then Jenn sat next to her best friend on the wet shower floor and held her trembling body as Annie sobbed.

Later, after her sobbing had subsided, Jenn stood, grabbed a dry, fluffy towel from the rack, and wrapped it around Annie's shoulders. She went to the guest room and found Annie's red robe at the foot of the bed. She returned to the bathroom. "I'm laying your robe here on the vanity chair."

Annie shivered. "Thanks."

Jenn went to her bedroom and changed into dry clothes. She dialed the office. "Stevie, I won't be coming back to the office today. Please call the Osborns and tell them I can't meet with them this afternoon because of a personal emergency. Offer them the opportunity to reschedule with me, or they can see another realtor if they prefer." Before hanging up the phone, she said, "And, Stevie, this is not for office gossip."

"Of course." Her voice halted.

"I realize you would never say anything on purpose. Thanks, Stevie."

Jenn hung up the phone. Remembering how thirsty she felt after a good cry, she went to the kitchen and poured two glasses of water and walked into the living room. Annie sat on the couch, her hair in a towel twisted into a turban. She stared straight ahead into the distance, lost in thought.

Jenn handed one of the glasses to Annie, then sat on the other end of the sofa and turned toward her friend, tucking her legs under her. "You need to see someone who can help you."

Annie glared at her. "Like a shrink?"

"Maybe not a psychiatrist, but you need help. At least, see someone with professional counseling experience."

Annie's brown eyes widened. "I'm fine when I'm with Zoey."

Jenn reached across the chasm between them and placed her hand over Annie's. "You can't go on living your life feeling fine every other week."

Annie sipped her water.

After a long pause, Jenn said, "At first, I understood your depression. But, Annie, it's gone on too long. You've been like this for months. Maybe you need medication to get back on track."

Annie picked at the fuzz on her robe. "I don't want to take anything that will cause me to not feel in control."

"Do you feel in control now?" Jenn glanced toward the bathroom.

Annie was silent. A lone tear escaped and trickled down her cheek unchecked. "I don't want to talk to anyone about my life. Maybe you could be my shrink. You know everything about me."

"You mean, like you're not all put together like everyone else thinks you are? That you grew up in a dysfunctional home? That you're broken on the inside?"

"So, how do you plan to put Humpty Dumpty back together again?"

"I can't. But I can tell you about Someone Who can."

"Yeah. Who?" Annie's eyes held Jenn's.

Jenn said a silent prayer. *Please, Lord, I'm so new at this. Give me the right words.* "Jesus can heal all your broken pieces if you'll only let Him."

Annie wiped the condensation off her glass and set it on the coffee table.

"We're all broken because of sin." Jenn picked up her Bible from the coffee table and flipped to the New Testament. She wasn't familiar with finding the appropriate verses as a new Christian, so she'd purchased Bible book index tabs. Some called them cheaters. She opened the pages to Romans 3:23 and read, "'All have sinned and fall short of the glory of God.'"

Annie kept her eyes down. "I've made some mistakes, but you?"

"That's just it. We're all lost and in need of a Savior. God loves us so much that He allowed His only Son, Jesus, to die for our sins. But Jesus didn't stay dead. He rose from the grave and is preparing an eternal home for us. All we have to do is accept His gift of salvation."

"And what is it you think I need saving from?" Annie asked, her eyes boring a hole into Jenn.

"You haven't forgiven your father or Joe for their unfaithfulness. And you haven't forgiven yourself for the divorce." Jenn said another silent prayer that she hadn't gone too far and scared Annie away.

Annie unwound the towel from around her head. Placing it in her lap, she ran her hands through her damp hair. "I believe in God. I went to Sunday school. I sang all the songs—'Jesus Loves Me,' 'Jesus Loves the Little Children,' and 'I Will Make You Fishers of Men.'"

Jenn listened.

"I don't blame God for what's happened. I blame Joe for being unfaithful. And I blame myself for the divorce. I know God forgives him, but I can't forgive myself. I'm not God." Annie moved closer to her. "You're passionate about your new faith—and I love that about you." Annie looked down and traced the quilted fabric of the couch. "I only wish I felt the way you do."

"I knew something was missing in my life. At the time, I didn't realize it was Jesus. When I did, I ran into His open arms." Jenn flipped her long, red curls over her shoulder. "Come to church with me. Maybe you'll find what I found."

"I'll think about it." She spied the clock on the wall. "Don't you have to get back to work?"

"I told Stevie I wouldn't be coming back today."

"You like her, don't you?"

"I do. Stevie's a sweet kid, but—"

"But what?"

"Her husband is a jerk. He tries to control her, and he's made a scene at the office a couple of times. Joe has about had it with him." Jenn took a sip of water.

"It sounds like he's not only a jerk but a fool, too. Doesn't he realize Joe's connection to the mob? He could find himself at the bottom of the ocean."

Jenn's mouth fell open.

"I'm kidding." Annie propped her feet on top of the coffee table.

They giggled.

"It feels good to laugh," Annie said.

"It sure does. Like medicine." Jenn placed her feet next to Annie's on the table. "So, about church?"

"I'll think about it."

Jenn lifted an eyebrow.

"I promise."

CHAPTER 33

Annie

The following week, Annie took a seat in the Christian counseling office at The Rock, Jenn's church. She adjusted her black pencil skirt. The counselor, John Burrows, sat across from her in a matching barrel chair. He wore a blue Hawaiian shirt with life-size white hibiscuses on it. She shifted in her chair, feeling overdressed in her cropped, black-and-white plaid jacket and black pumps.

"What, no couch for the patients to lie on while they spill their guts?" *It's not like me to sound so sarcastic.*

John grinned. "No. No couch. Would you prefer I call you Annie or Ms. Costa?" His sandy hair was cut in a flat-top, a throwback from the fifties.

"Annie." She glanced around the room at the framed documents on the wall. "Do I call you Doctor?"

"John is fine," he said. Behind him, there was a massive floor-to-ceiling window, and Annie could see water spurting into the air from a reflective pool as he looked down at the tablet in his lap. "I see you list Jenn Moore as a reference."

"Jenn recommended you."

"I'll have to thank her. She's a great gal." He eyed Annie. "We're in the same singles group here at church." He glanced at the pale circle on her finger where her wedding ring used to be.

She placed her right hand over her left. "I'm recently divorced. My husband and I share custody of our two-and-a-half-year-old daughter."

He made notes on his tablet. "Who initiated the divorce?"

"I did." She choked back a threatening sob. "He was unfaithful. And I'm unable to forgive him."

"I see."

"I'm fine during the weeks I have custody of Zoey. That's my daughter. But when Joe has her, I can't get out of bed." She took a tissue from the box on the table next to her. "That's why Jenn said I needed professional help."

John waited for her to continue. When she didn't, he looked up from his tablet. "I believe you're grieving the death of your marriage. However, depression is only one of the stages of grief. There is a slew of emotions you may or may not experience. And I'll try to help you work through your grief journey."

Annie exhaled a breath she'd been holding.

"For now, I'd like you to think about keeping a journal of your emotions. Do you like to write?"

"I used to keep a diary in high school." She relaxed in the chair. "Silly stuff. Things like, 'I washed my hair tonight.' And what Jenn and I did. Jenn's been my best friend since seventh grade. We live together on the weeks I don't have custody of Zoey." She stopped. "I'm babbling."

"That's okay. You can talk about anything." He steepled his fingertips. "Journaling is a lot like writing in a diary. Go out and buy yourself a pretty notebook. Then write about your feelings. Consider finding a pleasant place to write. The beach. A garden. On a hilltop."

"During the weeks I have custody of Zoey, I live on top of a hill. It's my house as part of the divorce, but the judge's decision was for Zoey not to be moved from place to place; so she stays at the house, and Joe and I move each week." Her chin trembled.

"It sounds like the judge deemed Zoey's comfort as a priority."

She placed her hand on her heart. "He did. And although it's uncomfortable for me, I'll always be grateful for his unique decision."

He shifted in his chair. "For now, I'd like to see you twice a week."

"Not on the weeks I have Zoey. I don't let anything come between us when it's my custody week." *Zoey's comfort is not only the judge's priority. She's my priority, too.*

"You want to spend all your waking hours with her?"

"I do."

"I understand." He looked at his appointment book. "How does twice a week every other week work for you?"

After she agreed, he stood and reached out his hand. "Annie, you're going to get through this." His reassuring smile filled her with hope.

On her next visit, Annie sat across from John in his office. Her journal was tucked inside her purse. For the past two weeks, she'd given a lot of thought to what to write in her journal. She sat for hours thinking, soul-searching, and digging deep inside her heart to pull out what was bothering her.

"How have you been since our last visit?" he asked.

Annie sighed. "Better than the last time I saw you. I'm not staying in bed all day anymore." Annie gave him a weak smile and sat taller in the chair.

"That's good to hear." He looked at his notes. "And journaling? How is that working for you?"

"Well. I think . . ." She leaned toward her purse. "Do you want to see what I wrote?"

"Only if you want me to. It's more for you than me."

Annie looked down. "It's probably best you don't read it. I was furious some days, and it came out in nasty words. Words I don't usually use."

He smiled. "Like a sailor?"

She laughed.

"Annie, your emotions are valid." He paused. "Was there anything else you discovered through writing in your journal?"

She thought, feeling more comfortable with John than she ever imagined she possibly could with a stranger, especially someone of the opposite sex—and a shrink, to boot. She gulped a breath. "Joe's unfaithfulness was the worst thing he could have done to me."

John listened.

"Because my father cheated on my mother all their married life. My mother looked the other way, and she died of a broken heart." A sob threatened to escape. "I disowned my father and vowed I'd never be a victim like my mother was. That's why I divorced Joe."

Compassion filled his blue eyes. "I'm sorry." After a time of silence, he asked, "Did Joe cheat on you repeatedly with other women?"

Annie grabbed a tissue from the box on the table and blew her nose. "Only the one woman that I'm aware of."

"Did he want the divorce?"

"No. He said that he loved me and that it would never happen again."

"It sounds to me like he is repentant. Do you believe him?"

"I'm not sure if I do or not. But I don't trust him." The knot in her stomach constricted.

"It's possible to trust again. It'll take time. But you will be able to trust once more."

"I resent Joe for what he did, how he hurt me. And I feel guilty about the divorce. I didn't even try to save my marriage. I didn't give him a chance to prove to me he could change—that he could be faithful. Do you think I was too quick to get a divorce?"

John leaned back in his chair. "Did he share with you why he strayed from the marriage?"

Her tears began to flow. "He said I was obsessed with having a baby, and after we adopted Zoey, I neglected him." She sobbed. "Zoey was colicky, and she took all of my attention. I don't know what I could have done differently."

"Is Joe aware that your father cheated on your mother and that you severed contact with him?"

"No. I was too ashamed to tell him." She rubbed her finger where her wedding ring used to be. "I didn't even try to forgive him. Am I a horrible person?"

"I don't think you're horrible. I believe you came into your marriage with baggage from your past. And you still have difficulty with forgiveness. When we forgive, we are the ones who benefit from our decision. It's up to the other person if they want to accept our forgiveness." He took a breath. "Marriage and parenting are hard work. Moving on after a divorce is hard, too. You've not only experienced the hurt and rejection of your husband's adultery, but you also feel the pain of divorce. You're here to work on yourself so that you can move forward after your divorce."

"Will it ever stop hurting?"

"You'll always remember this pain and rejection, but you can learn to live again, even be happy." He looked up from his notes. "Keep writing in your journal. But don't just write about your emotions. Write about good times during your marriage. Part of grieving is not only remembering the hurt but also the good memories, too. And think about goals. Maybe a job—"

Her hand flew to her chest. "I don't think I can even concentrate on learning a new job. Besides, I'm not interested."

"What about a hobby, or something you've always dreamed of doing? What did you do before you adopted Zoey?"

"I did charity work. I organized events." She was thoughtful. "I'm not interested in doing it, anymore."

"What else did you do?"

"I played tennis." She moved to the edge of her chair. "Jenn's been begging me to play with her again."

"Great. That's a start." He set his notepad on the table next to him. "I'd like you to think about meeting new people, too. We have a singles Sunday school class here at the church. Many of them are divorced with children. They have picnics and other activities. You can bring Zoey with you on your custody weekends."

Annie stiffened. She wasn't ready to let anyone new into her life. And she vowed that no one would pierce the wall she'd built around her heart. She had Zoey. That was enough.

CHAPTER 34

Stevie

After settling Gil down for the night, Stevie washed the dinner dishes in the kitchen sink. She cleaned as quietly as possible, hoping to not disturb Gary in the other room and risk another one of his outbursts. They had become more frequent lately, and she didn't know what would set him off next.

Gary yelled from the living room, "Come here and change the channel."

Stevie dried her hands and hurried into the living room. She clicked the dial on the TV set.

"Don't stand in front of the TV, stupid. I can't see it."

She mustered up the courage to turn and face him. "Please, Gary, don't call me stupid. Mr. Costa says I'm the best receptionist he's ever had."

"Did he now?" He crushed the empty beer can in his hand. "Well, I'm sick of hearing about 'Mr. Costa this' and 'Mr. Costa that.' You think he's better than me, don't you?"

"I never said that." She subconsciously pulled her sleeves down to cover the bruises that were still healing on her arms from the night before when she was late with his supper.

"But you think it. And you think you're better than me, too—working in that fancy office. Well, no more. I want you to quit."

"What?" Terror gripped her heart at the thought of quitting her job. What would she do instead? It was her only connection to her baby girl.

"You heard me. I'm the man of the house, and you'll do what I say or—or I'll take Gil, and you'll never see him again. And you know I mean what I say."

"But we need the money," Stevie begged.

"So, find another job if you think you're so smart."

Gil began to cry, so Stevie rushed to the bedroom. She sat on the bed as she held Gil close and rocked him back and forth, trying to soothe him. "Shh."

"Stevie! Shut that kid up," Gary hollered from the living room. "I can't hear the TV."

"Shh," she crooned as she smoothed Gil's soft hair over his head. Gil whimpered for a moment, sucked on his fist, inhaled deeply, and burst into another scream.

"What did I say? Shut that kid up, you good-for-nothing excuse for a mother!" Gary burst into the bedroom. "Can't you keep that kid quiet?" He raised his open hand to her.

She recoiled. "Please, Gary! He's teething."

He turned and punched the bedroom door, leaving a hole in the thin wood where his fist went through. He slammed the front door as he left. Soon, she heard his car rev before he sped away.

She rolled her shoulders to ease her tense muscles, went to the fridge, and grabbed a teething ring from the freezer. "Here you go," Stevie sang softly as she rocked him. "Go to sleep, my baby." Tears began to roll down her cheeks, and she sobbed quietly. How long would she be able to protect him? Would Gary ever hit him as he had her?

After a while, Gil fell asleep in her arms. She placed him in the crib next to the bed. *I'll never let him hurt you.*

Stevie awoke when the front door slammed. She glanced at the clock. It was five o'clock in the morning. *Should I pretend to be asleep? But what if Gary wakes Gil?*

Stevie jumped out of bed, grabbed her robe, and went into the living room, where Gary stumbled over a chair and fell flat on the floor. "What the—"

"Let me help you." She put her hand under his arm.

Gary jerked his arm away from her, pulled back his balled fist, and then slammed it into her face. Her head felt like wires were snapping, and she was seeing stars. Gary fell onto the couch face-first.

Holding her hand under her bloody nose, Stevie staggered to the bathroom. In shock, she turned on the light and examined her battered face as she held a washcloth under the cold water. *How could he do this to me? He said he loved me. You don't do this to the person you love.*

She sat on the edge of the tub, trembling. Her head throbbed while she pressed the washcloth to her face to stop the bleeding. When she thought it had stopped, she opened the medicine cabinet and took two aspirin, hoping and praying it would ease the pounding in her head.

Skirting around Gary passed out on the threadbare sofa, Stevie went to the bedroom. She closed the door and lay on the bed, curled into the fetal position. *God, please help me.*

Two hours later, Stevie dragged herself back to the bathroom, dabbing makeup on her almost-closed, swollen eye. She dressed and made her lunch, stuffing a cheese sandwich, an apple, and two oatmeal cookies into a brown paper bag.

Softly humming, she woke and dressed Gil. She didn't want him to feel her stress. After feeding him, Stevie escaped the apartment with Gil, her lunch, purse, and a diaper bag. Gary lay snoring on the sofa.

After parking in front of Mrs. Godsey's house, Stevie knocked on the door.

Mrs. Godsey opened the door and gasped at the sight of her. "What happened?"

"I walked into a door." Stevie handed Gil to her.

"Again?" Mrs. Godsey lifted an eyebrow.

"Gil may be fussy today. He's teething." Stevie caressed his cheek.

"Don't you worry none. We'll be fine. I'm familiar with teething babies." She stepped closer to Stevie. "It's you I'm worried about."

"I'll be fine." Before turning to leave, Stevie reminded Mrs. Godsey, "I won't be picking up Gil at the regular time today because I have a doctor's appointment."

"We'll be glad to see you whenever you get here." She shut the door as Stevie raced to her car.

Stevie tried to avoid the shocked looks of those who entered the building by looking down. At noon, a delivery man brought in a dozen red roses. He read the writing on the gift envelope. "These are for Stevie."

She took the bouquet from him. "Thank you."

Stevie read the attached card, familiar with Gary's usual apology to her.

> *Sorry for hitting you. But I meant what I said. Quit your job, or you'll never see Gil again. Gary.*

She ripped the card into tiny pieces before she dropped them in the waste paper basket.

At three o'clock, Mr. Costa came through the double doors. Upon seeing her, his jaw tightened, and his shoulders slumped. He picked up his messages on the edge of her desk without a word, so unlike his usual friendly demeanor.

"Mr. Costa, may I talk to you?"

"Of course, Stevie. I'll buzz you when I'm finished returning these calls." He held up the message slips.

A half an hour later, Jenn stood beside Stevie's desk, lightly touching her shoulder. "Joe wants to see you in his office. I'll cover your desk."

Stevie strolled to his office and tapped on the door before entering.

"Have a seat." He gestured to the chair across from his desk.

She swallowed the lump in her throat and folded and unfolded her sweaty hands in her lap. "Mr. Costa, you've been very good to me, but I have to quit."

"I'll be sorry to lose you." He leaned back in his chair, steepled his fingers, and studied her. "Have you had a better offer?"

"No."

"Is there anything I can say to make you change your mind?"

"No. Nothing. It's personal."

He sat up and leaned across his desk toward her. "Tell me something. Is Gary making you do this?"

Her chin trembled as she twisted her wedding band on her finger. It was as if he read her mind.

"I can't stay silent any longer. Gary is dangerous, and I'm worried about you. He's a time bomb that could explode any minute. I want to protect you." His eyes pleaded. "Please let me help you."

"There's nothing you can do." Looking down, she wiped her hands on her skirt. "There's nothing anyone can do. Gary is in control. He's . . ." She stopped herself before she told Mr. Costa that Gary had threatened to take Gil away from her, and she'd never see him again.

Stevie tried to hold back her tears, but it didn't work. "Mr. Costa, I'm sorry for the scenes Gary has made when he's come into the office."

"Stevie, you can't apologize for him. That's his responsibility. I'm sorry it came to this." He placed his checkbook on the desk and grabbed a pen. "I'd like to give you something for the excellent job you've done here." He signed the check and handed it to her.

She gasped at the large amount.

Before she could respond, he stood. "Will you promise me something?"

"If I can."

"Don't be his punching bag. You're worth so much more."

"You remind me of my dad. I think he would have told me the same thing."

Like Daddy, Joe is a good man and father. I can leave assured that my baby girl is loved. She looked one last time at the back of the frame that held Zoey's picture, remembering how Mr. Costa always became animated when he talked about her. She would miss his stories and sharing photos of his precious Zoey with her.

Stevie walked back to her desk. Upon approaching Jenn, she said, "Today's my last day."

Jenn gasped. "What? What happened?"

"Gary doesn't want me working here anymore."

"Is there anything I can do?" Jenn asked with a shaky voice.

Stevie looked around, and then she took the vase of roses out of the wastebasket and offered them to Jenn. "Would you like these?"

"Thank you." Jenn admired the bouquet. After a moment, she said, "I have a box in my office for your things. I'll go get it."

When Jenn returned, she said, "When God shuts one door, He opens another one. Sometimes, God has something better for us. I pray that's true for you."

"Thanks, Jenn. It's been really nice working with you."

Their embrace lasted longer than usual. Neither one seemed to want to let go of the other.

Later, Stevie walked into Dr. Anderson's office.

Kathy Graham gasped when she saw her. Putting an arm around Stevie's shoulder, she quickly ushered her into an empty exam room. "What has he done to you?"

There was no fooling her. There was no fooling anyone.

"I guess you won't believe I ran into a door?" Stevie looked at the floor.

"No." They sat across from each other, their knees touching. "How long has this been going on?"

"From the beginning." Stevie couldn't make eye contact. "But it's getting worse."

"Has he hit Gil?"

"No. I'd never let him hurt Gil." Stevie squeezed Mrs. Graham's hands, staring at her.

"Stevie, I don't think you realize how badly beaten you are." She scrutinized Stevie's swollen eye. "You can't stay in this situation any longer." Mrs. Graham leaned closer. "What about your mother? Can you move in with her?"

"I don't want Mama to know I've been walking on eggshells trying to keep my marriage intact, not making any waves. Gary's moody. I never know what to expect. I think Mama stays away because she wants us to work it out. I know if she knew what my marriage was like, she'd help me." Stevie let go of Mrs. Graham's hand and pulled back. "But Mama wouldn't help me with one baby. Two babies could be too much for her."

"You're pregnant?"

"I think so. That's why I'm here—to find out for sure."

"How far along do you think you are?"

Stevie counted on her fingers. "Five or six months."

"Why didn't you come in sooner?" Mrs. Graham stood.

Stevie shrugged her shoulders. Her tears flowed unchecked. "I quit my job today. What am I going to do?"

After a tap on the door, the nurse entered, looking at the chart. "How are you, Stevie?" Then she saw Stevie's face and gasped.

"We'll talk after you see Dr. Anderson." Mrs. Graham squeezed Stevie's hand. "Everything is going to be okay."

Mrs. Graham's reassuring words floated in the antiseptic air, but they did not land on Stevie's heart.

During Stevie's exam, Dr. Anderson tilted his head to the side when she explained her black eye was from walking into a door.

She exhaled when he left her in the sterile room to get dressed. She was pregnant! What was she going to do with two babies, no job, and an abusive husband?

As Stevie plodded toward the door, her head and heart downcast, Mrs. Graham met her in the reception area. "Let's go over to Nell's for a cup of hot chocolate." She donned her coat and slung her purse over her shoulder.

"I can't. I need to pick up Gil."

Mrs. Graham's body went rigid. "Is he with Gary?"

"No. He's with Mrs. Godsey. She takes care of him while I'm at work." Stevie gulped. "I mean, when I used to work."

"I'm sure she's a nice person and won't mind taking care of him for another half hour." Mrs. Graham looped her arm through the crook in Stevie's. They entered the warm coffee shop across the street from Dr. Anderson's office. Soon after they ordered, two mugs of cocoa with whipped cream topping arrived.

"You're like a daughter to us. And we want to help you. I called Phil, and he agreed with me. You can't stay in your abusive situation. We have the empty cottage behind our house. It's for our aging parents someday, but they aren't ready for it yet. They're too busy enjoying life. It has everything you need."

Stevie held the warm cup between her hands.

"You can't go back to your apartment." Mrs. Graham's forehead wrinkled. "The next time, he may kill you."

Stevie's chin trembled. "He's sorry. He loves me, and he even sent flowers."

"Stevie, you're a smart girl. You must realize that's what abusers do until the next time." She reached across the table. Prying Stevie's fingers away from the mug, she held them in her hand. "Please, let us help you."

That evening, Mrs. Graham shoved a frozen pizza in the oven. After dinner, Mr. Graham accompanied Stevie to the apartment while Mrs. Graham kept Gil with her. Mr. Graham stood guard as Stevie packed what she needed for the next couple of days. They planned for Mr. Graham to return with her on Saturday to move the rest of her things— mostly Gil's crib, highchair, and stroller. She exhaled. Gary was not there, yet he could come through the door at any time. *Please, God.*

That night, both Stevie and Gil slept fitfully in their new surroundings.

While the Grahams were at work the following morning, Stevie realized she'd forgotten Gil's favorite toy. She decided to drive to the apartment. Stevie felt safe because Gary would be at work. She'd be gone only a minute, just enough time to grab the teddy bear and return to the car where Gil slept in the backseat.

When she arrived, she looked around for Gary's car. No surprise that it wasn't there. *Then why am I so frightened?*

She let herself in and went to the bedroom. Not finding the toy in Gil's crib, she looked under it. Not there either. She lifted the dust ruffle of her bed. "Where are you, Teddy?"

She searched the living room, turned, and came face to face with Gary. He held up the teddy bear. "Is this what you're looking for?" His breath covered her face like a fog.

She froze.

"Where were you last night?" He grabbed her upper arms and squeezed hard.

"Please, Gary, let me go."

"No way. You're my wife. I'll never let you go." He threw the teddy bear on the floor. When Stevie bent to retrieve it, he pushed her down flat on the floor with his work boot. He began kicking her. She turned on her side and drew up her legs, hugging her unborn baby. With her other arm, she covered her head, trying to protect herself. He kicked her over and over again until she blacked out.

When Stevie came to, she was lying on an ambulance stretcher. She screamed, "My baby! He's in my car."

An officer went over and looked inside the Karmann Ghia, turned back around to face her, and shook his head.

CHAPTER 35

After Stevie was sedated and examined in the emergency room, the hospital admitted her.

Later, a detective entered her room and stood beside her bed. He held a small notebook and pen in his hands. "Mrs. Gilbert, I'm Detective Curry."

"Please, please find my baby." Stevie tried to sit up, only to fall back on the pillow.

"Do you know who might have taken your baby?"

"I think it was my husband, Gary."

"Is he the one who did this to you?" He pointed his pen at her.

"Yes." She spat out the word, angrier than she'd ever been in her life. "I was in the process of leaving him. That's when—"

"He beat you?"

"Yes."

"Do you plan to press charges against him?"

"I do." Then she thought about the possible consequences. "But before I do that, you have to find my baby. His name is Gil, and he's eleven months old."

"Do you have any idea where your husband could be?"

"No." *Think, Stevie, think.* She recited both the address of the apartment and Gary's job.

"Does he have family?" His bald head shone under the overhead light.

"A cousin, but he lives with us in our apartment." Her head was pounding, but she knew she needed to push through the fog to help find her baby. "Gary drives a red '64 Mustang. Does that help?"

"You're doing fine." He peered at her closely. "Do you know the license plate number?"

"No. I'm sorry." Tears gathered in her eyes.

A handsome doctor with wavy, blond hair entered. "Detective, I need to ask you to leave now. Mrs. Gilbert needs to rest."

"Sure, Doc. I've got what I need." He looked at Stevie with compassion. "Mrs. Gilbert, I'm personally taking on your case." He took a business card from his wallet and wrote something on the back of it. "This is my home phone number. Call me anytime, day or night, if you think of something else that could help me locate your husband." He placed the card on the bedside table. "I'll do my best to find your boy."

"Thank you." Stevie gulped a threatening sob.

After the detective left the room, the doctor asked, "Is your son lost?"

"No." She sobbed. "My husband kidnapped him."

He patted her hand, and his voice softened. "I'm sure the detective will do everything he possibly can. In the meantime, we need to help you heal."

Stevie placed her hands on either side of her stomach. "My baby?"

"Your baby was not injured during your attack. It's a miracle, really, from the looks of the beating you received. You have no broken bones, but you do have internal contusions; and I want to keep you overnight for observation. You need rest for your body to heal." He patted her hand. "I'll be back to check on you before I leave tonight. Do you have a family member you'd like us to contact?"

"I'll call my mother."

He placed the phone near her.

"Has anyone ever told you that you look like Dr. Kildare on TV?"

He smiled. "That must be the drugs talking. You rest." Before he left, he placed the call button closer to her. "Ring for the nurse if you need anything."

Pain coursed through her as she dialed the number of her mother's office. "Mama, I'm sorry to bother you at work." Her voice faltered.

"Are you okay?"

"No. I'm in the hospital." Stevie began to cry.

"Which one?"

"Orange."

"I'm on my way."

I should let Mrs. Graham know I'm in the hospital, but I don't want to disturb her at work. I'll call her later. She closed her eyes and rested her head against the soft pillows.

Within minutes, Mama rushed into the room and came to a stop at Stevie's side. "What happened?"

"Gary beat me and kidnapped Gil."

Mama grabbed the bed railing to steady herself.

"I was in the process of moving into the Grahams' cottage."

Mama raised her un-plucked eyebrows. "Why them instead of me?"

Mama's disappointed expression filled Stevie with regret. "I thought since you didn't want to help me with my first baby—"

"That was different. You were a teenager. At the time, I believed adoption was best for everyone." Mama hesitated, regret filling her face.

"I was wrong. I understand that now. It hurt you more than I could have ever imagined." Mama looked down. "Can you ever forgive me?"

"Of course. You did what you thought was right." Stevie's chest tightened. "Gary said he'd never let me leave. Then he did this and took Gil. I'm so afraid of what he might do to him."

Mama leaned closer and gently hugged Stevie. "He has no idea who he's dealing with. Shaw women are strong when we're pushed against a wall." She patted Stevie. "I'm proud of you for standing up to him."

"You are?"

"Of course, I am."

"That's all I ever wanted—for you and Daddy to be proud of me."

"My darling girl, we were always proud of you, and I still am." Mama dragged a chair closer to the bed.

Stevie sighed. "A detective is looking for Gary and Gil." Stevie felt her warm tears gathering. "Oh, Mama, I've made such a mess of everything. Gary made me quit my job. And I'm going to have a baby. What am I going to do?"

Mama paused for only a second, taking it all in. She looked so tired. "We're family. And family helps each other."

"I have some money saved from before Gary and I were married. He doesn't know about it. And Mr. Costa gave me a letter of recommendation and a sizeable check." Stevie winced from the pain. "With the extra money he gave me, I have time to sort things out and look for another job."

"After all you've said in the past about how great he is, I'm sure he'd rehire you." Mama's eyebrows arched.

"I'm too ashamed to consider asking for my job back."

"What have you got to be ashamed about?" Mama asked.

"For letting Gary control me. Abuse me. They all saw it at work. I can't go back there. I just can't. Please, drop it."

Mama stood silent, her mouth agape. Then she said, "I can understand you wanting a fresh start someplace else. We'll be fine— you, me, Gil, and the baby. I've stored up lots of sick leave at work. I'll take good care of you and your babies, just like you took care of your daddy when he was sick. It's my turn to be the caregiver. Gil deserves a healthy brother or sister." Mama smiled, but Stevie saw her mother's concerned expression, reflecting her own worry.

A nurse entered the room. "Ma'am, you need to leave. Doctor's orders."

"I'm her mother. I'll sleep in that chair tonight." She motioned to the maroon recliner in the corner of the room.

"I'm sorry. It's hospital policy that I have to abide by the doctor's orders. I don't make the rules. I only enforce them." The nurse stood with her feet apart and arms crossed, as if ready for battle.

"Okay. I'm leaving." Mama bent down and kissed Stevie on the top of her head. "I'm going to check in with the officer and see if there's any update on finding Gil. I'll let you know if I hear anything. And I'll be back in the morning. Rest and get better. You are strong, and you will survive."

Before Mama shuffled out of the doorway, Stevie called to her, "Mama, I think I'll take a nap. The Grahams should be home from work about six o'clock. Will you call and tell them what happened? I don't want them to worry."

"Of course."

What am I thinking? We'll all worry until Gil is found and Gary is arrested.

That night in the dimly lit hospital room, Stevie felt someone standing beside her bed. When she opened her eyes, her body tensed when she viewed Gary wearing a white lab coat.

"Where's Gil?" she demanded.

"He's okay." He reached for her hand, but she jerked it away. "Please, babe. I'm sorry. But you said you were going to leave me." He ran his hand through his hair. "You can't leave me."

"Yes, I can. The cops are looking for you, Gary. I've pressed assault charges against you." Her voice sounded stronger than she felt, and she hoped he didn't notice.

"Dismiss the charges, or you'll never see Gil again." He sneered.

Think fast, Stevie.

She pressed the call button hidden in her hand under the sheet. "You're not in charge. I am. Take Gil to my mother's house. When I know he's with her, then—and only then—will I drop the charges against you. Do you hear me, Gary?"

She relaxed her tense, sore muscles when a nurse entered the room, and Gary quickly exited.

Stevie turned on the light above her bed and reached for the card on the table. "That was my husband. He's the one who beat me. Please, guard my room while I call the detective."

On the third ring, he answered in a sleepy voice, "Hello?"

"Detective Curry, this is Stevie Gilbert. My husband just left my hospital room. He may be on his way to my mother's house with my baby. She lives at 1103 Fifteenth Street in Santa Ana. Please hurry."

After a quick goodbye, the phone clicked off.

Next, she called her mother. "Mama, Gary may bring Gil to you. Don't worry. The police are on their way to your house to arrest Gary."

"Why is he coming here?"

"He thinks if he brings Gil to you, I'll dismiss the assault charges against him. But he's wrong."

The nurse stood in the doorway of Stevie's room. Her eyes darted toward the nurses' station, then up and down the hallway.

Stevie closed her eyes and prayed, *God, please keep my baby safe.*

An hour later, aware of the circumstances, the nurses put the call from Detective Curry through to Stevie's room.

"We got him. He's being booked now, and your baby is safe with your mother," Detective Curry said. "Now, get some sleep. We'll talk tomorrow."

After hearing the news, the nurse brought Stevie a sleeping medication in a tiny paper container and held the straw for Stevie to sip some water. Stevie hurt everywhere. Hopefully, the sleeping pill would work, and she could begin to heal. She rested her head on the soft pillow and felt her baby kick. Rubbing her belly, she whispered, "You're safe, Little One. And so is Gil. That's all that matters."

The following morning, Detective Curry entered her room. "How are you feeling today?"

"My body hurts, but my heart is full. I'm very grateful to you." She tilted her head to the side. "You must have worked all night."

"Pretty much, but we got him." He stood beside her bed. "Are you aware your husband served time?"

Stevie's mouth fell open.

"He has a rap sheet, including a couple of DUIs, and one of his victims ended up paralyzed. Gary will probably be locked up for a while this time." He ran his hand over his bald head. "A restraining order isn't necessary any longer. You and your baby are safe now."

Her muscles tensed. *But for how long?*

CHAPTER 36

While Stevie healed, Mama and the Grahams moved her stuff into her childhood home.

A few days later, Stevie met Mr. Albert, the apartment owner, in front of the building. She held Gil on her hip. "Thank you for meeting me here, Mr. Albert." She gulped a breath. "Gary's in jail; I don't have a job; and I have no way to pay next month's rent." She looked down at the cracked sidewalk. "I'm so ashamed."

He checked out her yellow bruises. "You have nothing to be ashamed about." He scratched his head. "I never thought very highly of Gary—or his cousin, for that matter. Gary was like a wolf in sheep's clothing. I never believed anything he said. I hope they lock him up and throw away the key. I'm sorry to say that about your husband, but that's how I feel."

Stevie nodded. "I'll admit, I feel safer with him in jail."

"I don't understand why Ted looked up to him." Mr. Albert shook his head. "It's like Gary had some sort of spell over him." He turned his attention to Gil, smiling. He took the baby's chubby hand and held it. "Stevie, you're different. Not like them." He looked over her shoulder and nodded.

She looked back and saw Ted and his girlfriend, Darla, sitting in a hippie van, smoke billowing out the windows. Stevie waved. Ted and

Darla returned her gesture with sneers. A lump formed in her throat as she turned back to Mr. Albert.

"I'm not sure what to do with Gary's furniture. I don't need it because I've moved in with my mother." Out of the corner of her eye, she saw the VW van with the brightly colored flowers driving away.

"Don't you worry your pretty, little head. I've got a warehouse that I can store it in until Gary gets released from prison."

She cringed, knowing Gary's release would eventually arrive.

Mr. Albert continued, "I'll clean the apartment and raise the rent for a new tenant." He looked at her with eyes full of compassion. "I didn't want to increase the rent while you lived here. You're a good kid with a sweet baby. I say, good riddance to your husband. I'm sorry if I'm speaking out of turn. But no one deserves what he did to you. I'm glad he's behind bars." He placed his gnarled hand on her shoulder, his gaze piercing. "You take care of yourself and your fine boy. And watch your back. If he wants to hurt you, he can reach beyond those prison walls."

"I will." She frowned. *Was it possible? Could Gary hurt her even while in prison?*

Suddenly, a blast shattered the silence. Stevie held Gil snug to her body, protectively bending over him, covering her baby's head with her hand.

Mr. Albert reached for her and helped her stand. "You're okay. It was only a car backfiring."

Her heart raced, and her hands shook. *Will I ever feel safe?*

Mr. Albert's warning rattled around in her brain as she said goodbye and headed to her new home with Gil.

While Stevie's outer bruises faded, the ones inside remained. With Mama at work and Gil down for a nap, it was a perfect time to garden. Stevie grabbed a trowel from the shed and knelt in the front yard. She pulled weeds and dug in the dirt around the yellow daffodils and red tulips, the bulbs she'd planted with Daddy before he got cancer. He had loved working in the flowerbeds, and so did she.

"Daddy, I feel like you're here with me." She yanked a stubborn weed. "I miss you so. It hurts that Gil and the baby I'm carrying will never know you. But I'll tell them about you. I'll tell them how you loved gardening and dancing with me to Lawrence Welk. I'll teach them to ride their bikes and how to swim just like you taught me. I'll try to be patient with them like you were with me." She sat back on her haunches. "I need to find a job, Daddy. I heard Mr. Costa hired someone to replace me. And besides, I'm too embarrassed to go back there. I need a fresh start."

She rubbed her aching back, stood, and brushed the dirt off her knees. "Daddy, I'm worried about Mama. She's aged since you left us. Even though she quit her night job, she looks so tired. Do you know she quit smoking? She said it was her doctor's orders, but she didn't say anything more. You know Mama—she never says much." Stevie stored the spade in the shed, dumped the weeds into the trash can, and went into the house.

When Gil awoke from his nap, she put him in his stroller and went for a walk. Stopping at Gil's babysitter's house, she knocked on the door.

Mrs. Godsey opened the door with a smile.

"We're on our way to the park, and we wanted to stop by and say hello." Stevie handed a bouquet of daffodils to her.

"Daffodils! My favorite. They always remind me that spring is on its way. Thank you." Her bones cracked as she stooped to greet Gil. "How is my little man?"

"He's not as cranky today—probably because another tooth popped through." Stevie ruffled the fuzz on the top of his head. "Are you available tomorrow to take care of him while I look for a job?"

Mrs. Godsey struggled to stand. "Of course, I'm available." She checked her watch. "If you'll excuse me, I best put these in water before the children wake up from their naps. They'll be ready for their snack."

"Of course. Have a lovely day."

"I will, dear, and you and Gil have fun at the park."

Later, upon returning home, Stevie put Gil in his playpen to play, and then she unhooked the living room drapes from the rod. Wadding up the window coverings reeking of nicotine, she went outside and stuffed them into her car trunk to take them to the cleaners later. Brushing off her hands and wrinkling her nose, she went back inside and began to prepare dinner.

Mama arrived home right on time. You could set your clock by that woman.

"Dinner's ready when you are," Stevie greeted her. Gil smiled while doing pull-ups in the playpen.

"It smells wonderful." Mama walked over to Gil and kissed him on the top of his head. "I'll just wash my hands." Mama trudged down the hall to the bathroom, coughing.

Stevie lifted Gil out of his playpen and set him in his highchair. After tying his bib, she gave him a few pieces of bread.

Returning, Mama carefully slid into one of the Formica chairs, gazing at the spaghetti and meatballs on her plate. "This is lovely, Stevie. You're spoiling me."

"I don't consider fixing dinner spoiling you. After all, you've given Gil and me a place to live."

"And you, my dear, are making this house a home." Mama twirled the pasta on her fork before taking a bite. "The flowerbeds in the front yard look beautiful. It reminds me of how much your dad liked gardening." She sighed. "It was too hard for me to keep up with everything."

Stevie set her fork down and reached toward Mama. "You've got me now. You don't need to do it all yourself anymore."

"I noticed the living room drapes are gone."

"They're in my trunk. I plan to drop them off at the cleaners tomorrow. And then I'll go job hunting." Stevie swallowed some water before continuing. "I've decided to apply at a temp agency because I don't feel right applying for a full-time job when I'll need to take maternity leave soon." She rubbed her tummy.

Gil banged on his highchair tray with his spoon, more spaghetti sauce on him than in his bowl.

Stevie jumped up. "Okay, little man, it's bath time for you."

"I'll do the dishes."

Stevie untied his bib, unhooked the highchair tray, and held him away from her as she headed down the hall.

"Leave them. You've worked all day. I'll do them later," Stevie called over her shoulder.

Later, Gil smelled of baby shampoo as Stevie carried him to the living room. She couldn't get enough of snuggling his neck as he laughed. Stevie set him on the floor in the living room to play with his toys, then went into the kitchen to wash the dishes. After cleaning the kitchen, she leaned against the doorframe and watched Mama read *Pat the Bunny* to Gil. Curled up in Mama's lap, he grinned at Stevie around his thumb stuck in his mouth. Stevie's heart swelled.

The happy scene became a blur when Mr. Albert's warning echoed in her head. *Watch your back.* She hurried to the linen closet in the hallway and grabbed two sheets, one striped, the other white. In the kitchen, she rummaged through the junk drawer, looking for tacks. Finding them, she proceeded to cover the front windows. Stevie turned and saw Mama's furrowed brow.

"For privacy." Stevie shuddered from a sudden chill in the warm room.

CHAPTER 37

Holding her hand on her aching lower back, Stevie waddled to answer the knock at the front door. When she opened it, Rachael threw her arms in the air.

"Surprise!" She pushed into the room.

"Rachael! What are you doing here?" Stevie hadn't realized just how much she needed her best friend until that very moment.

"I'm home for spring break and asked my mother to keep it a secret from you. But I'm the one who's surprised. Wow! Look at you."

Stevie looked down at her tummy and lovingly rubbed it.

"Where's Gil?"

"Mama took him to the park so I could finish sewing new kitchen curtains. Come and see." Stevie ushered Rachael to Mama's bedroom. Yellow and white gingham fabric lay across the sewing machine table. Then they walked down the hall to the other bedrooms.

"My room hasn't changed, except I did wash all the walls in the house. Come see Gil and the baby's room." She opened the door.

Rachael peeked into the nursery. "What happened to all the stuff that used to be in here?"

"We got rid of the junk and stored what we wanted to keep in the garage." Stevie closed the door. "Do you want something to drink?"

"Sure. What you got?"

"The usual, including your favorite."

"Great. I'll have a Pepsi."

Stevie popped the ice cubes out of the plastic tray, filled the glasses halfway with ice, and then poured the soda pop. She handed Rachael one of the drinks. "Over the rocks, just the way you like it."

They went into the living room, where Rachael plunked on the sofa while Stevie eased down. Rachael studied her glass. "Mom told me what Gary did to you. I'm so sorry. I should have written or called to tell you I care. Although I was busy at school, it's just an excuse. I didn't know what to say."

Stevie had her own confession. "I should have listened to you. You never liked Gary. You saw something about him that I didn't."

Rachael reached over and placed her hand over Stevie's.

"He was different in the beginning. Then he changed." Stevie's chest tightened. "He said he loved me." She looked at Rachael, questioningly. "If he loved me, then why did he beat me until I was unconscious?"

Rachael squeezed Stevie's hand and shook her head. "I don't have an answer. Except that there are evil people in this world, and Gary is one of them."

Stevie thought before she spoke. "Rach, you could have said, 'I told you so,' but you never did. Our lives have taken different paths. But you're here now. That's what counts." She sipped her drink and changed the subject. "A nice detective is working on the case. He comes by to give me updates. Gary got seven years for what he did to me."

Rachael swished the ice around in her glass and listened.

"When he's up for parole, I could go, but I don't want to. I'm terrified to see him, so the detective told me to write a victim's impact statement, and he'd read it for me. Hopefully, Gary won't get paroled early."

"Hopefully."

"Your parents, Detective Curry, and Mama have been here for me; and I couldn't be more grateful to them."

"So, what's it like living with your mother?"

"Mama has been great. She quit her night job. With what I make as a temp and Mama's income, we manage financially. We're helping each other. It's nice."

"The house looks great. I can see how you've spruced it up, and the flowers in the front yard look beautiful." Rach eyed her. "Are you happy?"

"Of course, I'm happy. I enjoy my job and the people I work with." Stevie smiled. "Gil is a good baby. He brings both Mama and me so much joy." She sipped her drink. "What about you? How's school?"

Rachael set her empty glass on a coaster on the coffee table. "It's okay. I've dated a few times, but I haven't met anyone special. My roommate is a Humboldt Honey."

Stevie arched her eyebrows.

"She doesn't shave her legs or her armpits. And using deodorant would be nice."

"Oh."

They were laughing when the front door opened and Mama entered, carrying Gil with his thumb in his mouth.

"Hello, Mrs. Shaw," Rachael said.

"Hello, Rachael. How nice to see you."

"Here, Mama, let me take him."

"Okay." Mama handed Gil to Stevie.

"Rach, come into the kitchen while I feed him lunch. Then I'll put him down for a nap."

Stevie cringed when Mama walked down the hall, hacking. Her cough seemed to be getting worse.

Rachael's eyes grew big. "Is she all right?"

Stevie shrugged. "I don't know." But she did. A feeling of dread settled in her stomach.

CHAPTER 38

Annie

Annie unbuttoned her blouse and tossed it on the bed. *Too business-like.* Joe had invited her to lunch. But why? It certainly wasn't a date. Was it?

Being divorced was new to her. Did divorced couples meet for lunch? How do you dress and act while having lunch with your former spouse?

She returned to the closet and searched the hangers one by one. Taking another top off the hanger, she pulled it over her head, then examined her image in the full-length mirror and shook her head—too revealing. She yanked it off and added it to the pile of clothes on the bed.

She decided on beige, linen slacks and a white, silk blouse. Instead of her signature French twist, she combed her jet black hair into a ponytail. Gold hoops and a beige sweater draped across her shoulders and tied in front finished her ensemble. She grabbed her clutch bag and headed out the door.

It would be the perfect setting for a date if things were different— seated outside along the coast in Laguna Beach on a sunny spring day. But this wasn't a date.

Joe and Zoey were already seated when she arrived.

When Zoey spotted Annie, she reached toward her. "Look, Daddy, Mommy's here."

Smiling, Joe stood and pulled out a chair for Annie.

Annie stopped beside the booster seat, leaned down, hugged her daughter, and kissed Zoey's silky blonde locks before taking a seat next to her.

After Joe saw her seated, she looked up into his gorgeous blue eyes. "Thank you." Annie's heart fluttered under his gaze; his white dress shirt strained against his familiar golden arms, and she couldn't help but picture his warm chest beneath it. *How can he be both so kind and so heartbreakingly handsome?* She had to quickly shake her head to dislodge the image of lying next to him one more time.

Joe returned to his seat across from her, with Zoey between them at the round table. "I ordered shrimp Louie for us. I hope that's okay."

"It's fine," she said with a lack of emotion.

The waitress brought two iced teas, a glass of milk, and a basket of sourdough bread.

When the waitress left, Annie asked, "What's the occasion for lunch?" She tried to sound lighthearted.

"There's something I want to discuss, and I didn't want to do it over the phone."

She raised a perfectly shaped eyebrow. "Sounds serious."

"Zoey hasn't bonded with any of the nannies. She seems truly happy only when you're with her." He beamed his irresistible smile and added, "And me."

Annie couldn't contain a smirk.

"I've been thinking." He leaned back from the table when two shrimp Louies and a grilled cheese sandwich arrived. When the waitress left, he continued, "Would you consider living at the house full-time—taking care of Zoey?"

Annie's shocked look didn't deter him. "Hear me out. The master bedroom would be yours. During my custody weeks, I'll stay in the guest room at night. During your weeks, I'll go to the beach house like I do now." He searched her expression. "No more nannies. You'd like that, wouldn't you?"

Was it possible or only a dream? Was he asking her to take care of Zoey? Should she pinch herself?

"Of course. Nothing would make me happier. But . . . "

"But what?"

"What about the judge's decision?"

"As long as we agree, why would he even be involved?"

A million thoughts ran around inside Annie's head as she glanced at her precious daughter chewing on her grilled cheese sandwich.

The waitress arrived with the check and placed it on the edge of the glass table. "Your little girl is darling."

"Thank you," Annie and Joe said in unison.

Before she walked away, the waitress added, "You make a perfect family."

Joe smiled while Annie felt a stab in her heart. They *were* the perfect family. Once.

Zoey reached for the glass of milk, and Joe helped her take a drink.

Annie sipped her iced tea. "I'll agree to your offer on one condition. I'd still like to spend your custody nights at Jenn's. I don't feel comfortable spending the night with you in the house. I'm sorry. Besides, Jenn and I are taking art classes two evenings a week."

"Really? I didn't know that." He looked down. "I get it. I do. How you'd feel uncomfortable living in the same house with me after . . . " His voice cracked. "You can't get past what I did to you, can you?"

She swallowed a sob. "No, I can't."

"What about now? Do you feel uncomfortable having lunch with me?"

Annie thought about his question and surprised herself with her answer. "No, I don't."

"Well, then, I have another idea."

"Oh?"

"Zoey's birthday is during my custody week. I plan to take her to the San Diego Zoo. Why don't you join us?"

She sighed. *But I wanted to give her a party.*

Joe leaned toward her.

"I'll think about it and let you know."

That evening during their art class, Annie stood next to Jenn at their easels. Tonight, they were painting a still-life of blue hydrangeas. Annie wrestled with the plans for Zoey's birthday and going with Joe to the zoo.

She dabbed blue paint on the canvas. "I had lunch with Joe today."

"You did? How'd it go?"

"He plans to take Zoey to the San Diego Zoo for her birthday, and he invited me to go with them."

Jenn was silent, concentrating on her painting.

"I'm disappointed. I wanted to give Zoey a birthday party, but then I realized I don't have any friends with young children. I don't have any friends except you. I no longer see any of our couple friends. Who would I invite? And Zoey's birthday reminds me of her first birthday." Annie looked at Jenn. "That was the day I saw Joe and Mallory together, and I knew he'd been unfaithful to me." Annie choked out the words. "He broke my heart, and I don't think it'll ever mend."

Jenn put her paintbrush down and wrapped her arms around her. "Oh, Annie."

After a while, Annie pulled away. "I think I'll talk to John about it during my next counseling appointment." She wiped at her tears. "I've got to get over associating that painful memory with Zoey's birthday. I owe it to her not to relate her birthday with the worst day of my life." Annie picked up her paintbrush and swirled it around in the blue hue on her palette.

Celebrating Zoey's third birthday at the zoo was nicer than anything Annie might have planned. Joe pushed the stroller around the zoo as Annie walked beside him. Before leaving, they returned to the swan enclosure. When Zoey tried to climb out of the stroller, Joe helped her. It seemed to be her favorite exhibit. She was mesmerized by the graceful birds.

Standing beside Zoey, Joe read the plaque attached to the fence. "'The swan is a large waterfowl in the *Anatidae* family. They are generally large with long, curved necks. There are six different species of swans, including the mute swan, tundra swan, black swan, and trumpeter swan. They live in various environments, including lakes, ponds, slow-moving rivers and streams, wetlands, marshes, and more. There is a reason why swans have become a symbol of love. When these monogamous animals court, they curve their necks toward each other in the shape of a heart.'"

"Look, Mommy." Zoey pointed her finger through the fence toward the graceful birds. "They love each other."

"I see." With their necks together, they formed a heart. Out of the corner of her eye, Annie saw Joe gazing at her.

"Jesus loves me. He's in my heart," Zoey said.

"What?" Annie leaned closer to Zoey, uncertain of what she'd heard.

"I've been taking her to Sunday school every other Sunday at The Rock." Joe shaded his eyes from the sun. "She loves it—singing songs, playing with other children."

"Jenn's church?"

"Yeah. I've been going. I like it. It's nothing like how I grew up. You should come sometime."

"Jenn didn't tell me you were going there." Annie cocked her head to the side.

"I think Jenn tries not to discuss us with the other one. She's a friend to both of us. And she doesn't want to be in the middle."

"I guess." Annie was silent as she thought. It was true Jenn never discussed Joe with her.

Later, as they drove home with Zoey asleep in the backseat, Joe asked, "Have you decided if you want to take care of Zoey during the day full-time?"

"Yes. I'd like that. Thanks." Tears escaped her eyes before she could stop them.

He reached over to hold her hand, but she pulled it away as "Bridge Over Troubled Water" came over the radio airways.

CHAPTER 39

Since her counselor had reduced her appointments to once a week, Annie thought she no longer needed help until after she had spent the day with Joe and Zoey at the zoo. Her emotions skyrocketed one minute and crashed to the ground the next. She needed to talk to John.

When she entered the counseling office, John was sitting in his usual chair. Through the large windows, she viewed the serene scene behind him, including the reflective pool. Taking her place across from him, she set her purse on the carpet and slid back in the chair.

"So, how are you doing?" John asked. His notepad sat on the table beside him. He looked at her intently.

"Not good."

"How so?"

"A lot has happened."

It was good John didn't respond because she felt like a volcano about to erupt and couldn't stop the flow. John watched as she wrung her hands.

"The nannies haven't worked out, and Joe has offered to let me take care of Zoey full-time."

"I don't understand your apprehension. Isn't this what you wanted?"

"Yes. But there's a hitch. He wants to stay in the guest room at night on his custody weeks while I sleep in the master bedroom, and I'm not comfortable sleeping in the house with him down the hall."

"So, what you're saying is if you agree to his offer, you'll get to be with Zoey every day. But you're not comfortable around Joe? Am I correct?"

"Yes. What do I do?"

He thought for a minute before responding. "Sometimes, we need to make compromises in relationships—divorced couples even more so."

She watched as he picked up his notepad and wrote something. She realized she knew nothing about him, while for months, she'd revealed the most personal stuff of her life to him.

He brought her out of her thoughts when he asked, "How's your journaling coming along?"

She cocked her head to the side. "Very well. I had to buy another blank book because I filled up the first one."

"I'd like you to write how you're feeling in your journal. Measure the pros and cons of Joe's offer."

"I've sort of done that already. I've decided to do what Joe suggests, except on his custody nights, I'll continue to stay with Jenn. We were roommates in college, and we get along great. Plus, we take art classes a couple of nights a week, which I'm enjoying."

"Well, then, you've already created a solution for your concern." He set the pad back on the table and smiled.

"It's . . ."

"It's what?" He leaned toward her, his elbows on his knees.

"I've been with Joe and Zoey a couple of times. We had lunch once, and we celebrated Zoey's third birthday at the San Diego Zoo. It was so hard being with him." She looked down at her manicured nails in her lap. Her heartbeat accelerated.

John waited.

"My emotions are battling each other, and I don't have a clue who's going to win."

"Which emotions specifically?"

"Love and hate, I guess. I love him." She let out a deep breath. "And I hate him." She realized she'd finally admitted it to herself.

"I don't think you hate *him*. You hate what he did. There's a difference." He leaned back in his chair. "Think back to the man you fell in love with. Other than his unfaithfulness, is he that different now than when you fell in love with him?"

"Not really. He's a gentleman. And a wonderful father." Her heartbeat returned to a regular rhythm. "Other than cheating on me, he has integrity. He helps those less fortunate, and he's passionate about what he believes in. Everyone loves him." Melancholy washed over her. *What have I done?* "I still feel guilty about the divorce. It's always in the back of my mind, and I can't change what I did. Will I ever feel differently?"

"Yes. Forgive yourself and move forward. You've come so far. You're no longer depressed, and you get out of bed every morning. Try to concentrate on the positive changes. You can spend more time with Zoey, your new interest in painting, your friendship with Jenn."

Annie looked down.

"Remember when you first began to write in your journal?"

"Yes." She arched an ebony eyebrow.

"I told you to also write about happy memories. Do you remember?"

She nodded.

"Write about why you fell in love with Joe."

"I'll try." Annie paused. "There's something else that's bothering me."

John listened.

"It seems like everyone close to me is part of this new Jesus movement. And I feel out of the loop. When we were at the zoo, Zoey said Jesus was in her heart. I feel like she's being brainwashed." His gaze met hers. "I know this is your church, but the whole thing is a mystery to me. I believe in God, and I consider myself a religious person."

"What Jenn and I believe isn't about religion. It's a relationship."

Annie's attention was momentarily distracted as a swallow played in the birdbath outside. She focused. "Sometimes, I wish I had a faith like that."

"Faith is a belief in an invisible God. That's why it's called faith—because we can't see Him."

"Jenn tried to convert me, but . . ."

"When you've experienced something life-changing like Jenn and I have, you want to share it with the people you care about."

"If I become one of you, will all my problems disappear?"

"I'm afraid that's a common misunderstanding. Christians face trials, too. That's how God builds our character."

Annie thought about what John said.

"Why don't you visit some Sunday and see for yourself?"

She'd feel out of place. She'd never been part of the hippie movement, even in the '60s. And that's what the Jesus movement brought to her mind.

Although she felt better at the end of her appointment than when she'd arrived, she was still on the fence about visiting the church.

Yet several weeks later, she followed Jenn into The Rock and sat near the edge of the center aisle. She watched others take their seats in the pews and felt overdressed. Some women looked like gypsies, wearing long, flowing skirts or tie-dyed t-shirts and bell-bottoms. Their long, wavy hair with scarves wrapped around their heads seemed to be the style of many in the crowd.

A familiar voice said, "Is this seat taken?"

She looked up into Joe's dreamy blue eyes. "No." She fumbled her church bulletin and moved her purse from the pew to her lap. She scooted closer to Jenn.

When the music started, everyone stood. Joe opened the songbook and held it for her. Although both Joe and Jenn sang, the songs were unfamiliar to her, so she silently tried to follow along. Joe stood too close to her, making her want to move away, but there was nowhere to go. She felt trapped between Jenn and Joe.

Unable to focus on what the preacher was saying from the pulpit, she tensed when Joe's muscular arm brushed against her shoulder. All she could think about was Joe. The familiar scent of his aftershave washed over her.

I can't do this.

At the end of the sermon, Pastor Mark said, "Please move across the aisle and join hands as I pray." Joe slipped his warm hand into hers and led her. Standing in the middle of the aisle, Annie bowed her head but couldn't concentrate on the prayer. All she could think about was how Joe's soft, warm hand felt holding hers. She'd always loved his hands.

After the minister said amen, Joe turned to greet the person next to him. Annie dropped Joe's hand as if it were a hot ember. Clutching her chest, she turned to Jenn. "I've got to get out of here. I can't breathe."

CHAPTER 40

Stevie

Stevie had accepted a full-time position as an executive secretary from one of her temporary jobs. They had been willing to work around her maternity leave and had offered her a full-time position once she was ready to get back to work. After the required probation period with the corporation, she'd receive benefits as well as her first raise. Although it was a company with over one hundred employees, it felt like a family to her. The work was fulfilling, and her co-workers were friendly. However, she never accepted their invitation to go out for drinks after work on Friday nights. They knew she had two little ones at home, and they seemed to understand.

From the day Stevie had brought Gracie home from the hospital, Gil had become a loving big brother, gently patting Gracie's head and kissing her. By the first month, Gracie had started sleeping through the night, which Stevie had hoped would help with her own exhaustion.

She peered into the cradle next to her bed, where Gracie slept peacefully. Stevie eased back down onto her pillow, but the nightmare that had awakened her kept playing over and over in her mind. Her mind was as weak as her body seemed to be; she was always tired, always out of breath. *I guess it's part of being a mother.*

Closing her eyes, Stevie saw the scene again, as though it were happening in real life. *Gary chased her through a forest. Even though she tried to protect herself with her arms in front of her, branches scratched her face. He was getting closer, and she could no longer escape because her feet were running in place.*

She sprang up from the bed gasping, trying to catch her breath, her nightgown soaked with perspiration. She stifled a cough. She knew she wouldn't be able to go back to sleep, and Gracie would soon be waking up to eat, so Stevie crept to her dresser and took out her notebook.

She'd wanted to write to Zoey since the day Gracie was born but hadn't found a moment to do it until now. She poised the pen above the page and began to write.

May 21, 1971

My Darling Daughter,

Happy belated birthday. I wish I could have been with you to celebrate your third birthday. But I do have a surprise for you. Your sister was born on your birthday. Her name is Gracie, and I think you'd love her. She is a beautiful baby like you were. Unlike your soft, blonde ringlets, her hair is the color of sand; and it looks like she may have corkscrew curls like mine. Of course, her eyes are blue. (All newborns have blue eyes.)

I no longer work for your daddy. Even though your mommy and daddy are divorced, you are loved and well cared for by them.

Gary beat me so badly that I ended up in the hospital. He was arrested and sent to jail. I couldn't take the chance he would hurt

Gil. Mr. and Mrs. Graham, Rachael's parents, helped me get away from him. Gil, Gracie, and I live with Mama now.

Never let anyone hit or say mean things to you.

I love you, my darling daughter.

Your First Mother

Gracie stirred. Stevie tucked the notebook into her dresser and picked up her daughter. Easing into the warm spot in her bed with her back resting against the headboard, Stevie held Gracie close to her bare breast, where she latched on and contentedly sucked.

As she watched her tiny daughter eat greedily, Stevie heard her mother begin moving around. She flinched at the sound of Mama's horrible hacking cough as she went about her morning routine before heading off to work. The aroma of coffee greeted Stevie as she held her newborn daughter in her arms, patting the little bundle.

Soon, Gil was climbing out of his crib and making a beeline to her bed, his soaked diaper needing to be changed. Gracie needed to be changed now, too. She couldn't stay in bed forever. Her day had begun.

The days and nights flowed seamlessly into each other with little variation—babies, work, life. They crept forward without seeming to advance. Until one morning, the house was deathly quiet. Something was wrong. Very wrong.

Stevie didn't smell the familiar aroma of coffee brewing or hear Mama's horrible cough or the shower running. Stevie spied the clock on her bedside table. It was past time for Mama to be up. Stevie threw off the covers and padded down the hall to Mama's bedroom. She tapped on the door and slowly opened it a crack, peering into the darkened room. She tiptoed to the side of the bed where Mama lay so still. Too still. With her head on the pillow, she looked peaceful.

"Mama?" Stevie touched her hand. It was so cold. Stevie doubled over and gasped when the realization hit her—Mama was gone. When she could breathe again, she stumbled to the door, closing it behind her.

With trembling hands, she dialed 911.

The person on the other end of the phone asked, "What's your emergency?"

"My mother passed away during the night." She was calmer than she imagined possible under the circumstances. Stevie couldn't fall apart; her babies needed her. "I have two babies I want to take to the babysitter before anyone arrives. Please give me an hour before you send anyone." She recited her location and ended the call.

Then she entered the nursery and woke Gil and Gracie with hugs and kisses and dressed them.

Sitting at the kitchen table, Gil looked across the table at Mama's empty chair. "Nana?"

"Nana's in Heaven." Stevie swallowed a threatening sob.

"Hebin?"

"Yes, Gil. Now, eat your cereal." She fed Gracie another spoonful of peaches from the baby food jar.

After putting on their coats, Stevie put Gracie into the stroller while Gil toddled down the hall to Mama's bedroom. He reached for the doorknob. "Nana."

Stevie raced down the hall, scooped him into her arms, and put him behind Gracie in the stroller. "Mrs. Godsey is waiting for us."

When Mrs. Godsey opened the door and greeted them with a smile, Stevie leaned close to her ear, barely holding back tears. "Mama . . . passed away during the night."

The older woman gasped. "Oh, my dear, I'm so sorry. Is there anything I can do?"

"You already are by taking care of the kids."

Mrs. Godsey pulled her into a hug and patted her back.

Returning home, Stevie notified her boss that she wouldn't be coming into the office. Then she numbly waited beside Mama's bed for the coroner to arrive. She lovingly stroked Mama's brown and gray-streaked hair away from her face, remembering the stubborn, sometimes hard woman who had softened in her old age.

"I'm going to miss you, Mama." A tear escaped and trickled down her cheek. "Say hi to Daddy for me." Feeling all alone, she burst into tears.

The day of the funeral was a blur for Stevie. People she had never met before came to pay their respects. The house was filled with flower arrangements that the funeral home had delivered to her from well-meaning people. The doorbell even rang incessantly for a week as strangers dropped off casseroles for Stevie and the kids.

One thing became very clear to Stevie—she had never really known her mother after all. It had never occurred to her that her mother might have friends. She was surprised to hear stories about how her mother had been a blessing to so many—and about how much she had loved Stevie and her grandchildren.

At first, Stevie couldn't bring herself to even enter her mother's room. The door remained shut, and she refused to let Gil go in there either. She knew that she would eventually have to go through her mother's things, but the sadness and loneliness were too much for her to handle. She needed a little time. Plus, she needed to figure out what she was going to do next. She wasn't sure when the bill collectors would come calling, but she'd need a plan before too long. Sick with worry, she pushed her troubles aside for the time being and tried to focus on her children.

Finally, a couple of months later, Stevie decided it was time that she moved forward and determined that she was ready to go through her mother's belongings. After putting Gil and Gracie down for naps on a Saturday afternoon, Stevie crept into Mama's room and opened the dark drapes to let some sunshine in. She grabbed one of the cardboard boxes on the floor and moved to the dresser.

She sighed as she opened the top drawer. On top of Mama's bras and panties was an envelope with Stevie's name written on it. She slipped out the sheet of stationery and began reading the letter dated February 1971.

Dear Stevie,

If you are reading this, then I am gone. I was diagnosed with congenital heart failure a while back. So, I knew I didn't have much longer on this earth. Please try to be happy for me. I will now be with Daddy.

You are the best mother to Gil and Gracie, and I am so proud of you. You would have been a good mother to your first baby, too. I realize that now. When you were so young and pregnant, I thought I was doing the right thing to insist that you place your baby for adoption. I understand that there is a hole in your heart that only your first baby can fill. I am very sorry. I was in a bad place at that time, mourning your daddy and trying to pay off the medical bills. I know you've forgiven me. For that, I'll always be grateful.

I'm also sorry for what Gary did to you. I should have seen through him, but I didn't, and I didn't protect you.

The house is yours. It's paid for, and your name is on the deed. You need to contact my attorney, Laurence Nelson. He can help you with any legal advice.

Since you've been back, you've made the house a home for you and your children. It brings me so much joy to see you with them. Daddy and I will be looking down on you, Gil, and Gracie. Now, you have two guardian angels—Daddy and me.

Love,

Mama

Shocked, Stevie sat down on the bed to re-read the letter. Mama had not only provided her and her children a home while she was alive, but now, Stevie's financial worries were resolved.

Thank you, Mama. Daddy used to say you were stubborn. He also said deep down, you had a soft heart. I never saw your soft heart until you took us in and gave us a home. I will always be grateful to you.

With tears in her eyes and on her cheeks, Stevie filled the boxes with Mama's clothes. After folding the cardboard flaps, she stacked them near the door for the Rescue Mission to pick up.

That night, there was more bubble bath on her than in the tub with Gil and Gracie.

"Duck-ie, Gay-sie?" Gil pushed the yellow plastic toy on the top of the bathwater toward Gracie.

After the children were tired of splashing in the tub, Stevie dried and dressed them in their footed sleepers, nuzzling their necks and basking in the rewarding sound of their giggles.

Their nightly routine concluded with a bedtime story. Stevie sat in Gil's junior bed with her back against the headboard. Gracie had now been promoted to Gil's old toddler bed and shared the room with her brother.

Stevie held Gracie in one arm, and soon, Gil climbed up into bed and snuggled close to Stevie on her other side.

"Gay-sie fav-rut." He set down *Pat the Bunny* in his mother's lap. They each took a turn feeling the soft fabric on the book cover before Stevie read the story.

Stevie leaned down to tuck them into their beds and gave them kisses. "Night, night, my little munchkins." Then she went into the living room and turned on the TV. She mindlessly watched TV and quickly fell asleep from exhaustion.

CHAPTER 41

June 14, 1974

My Darling Daughter,

It's been so long since I've written to you, and so much has happened.

It's hard for me to believe that you are six now and a first-grader. I wonder if you have lost your front teeth. Gil is four, and Gracie is three now. They are the best of friends.

When Gracie grew out of the crib in Gil's room, I redecorated my old room for her. Everything is pink—a pink bedspread, a white dresser with pink knobs, a ballerina lamp with a pink shade. Gracie calls it her princess room, yet many mornings when I go in to wake her, she is not in her bed but snuggled up with Gil in his.

My best friend, Rachael, is getting married, and I am going to be her matron-of-honor. Gil will be the ringbearer and Gracie the flower girl. I made Gracie a white, satin dress with a bright orange sash tied in a bow at the back. She wears her white, patent leather Mary Janes around the house because she can't wait for the big day. Gil will look like a miniature groomsman wearing a white tux with a bright orange, silk cummerbund. We are all so excited about Rachael's wedding day.

My mother passed away a couple of years ago. She and I became closer after we moved in with her. Gil brought her so much joy during the last year of her life. I've since moved into her bedroom. I have a good job, and I like my co-workers.

Gil and Gracie are my life, but there is a hole in my heart where you belong. My prayer is that someday, maybe when you are older, I can meet you. I love you, my darling daughter.

Your First Mother

The day of the wedding was a whirlwind of activity. Getting both children dressed was a major accomplishment. Mrs. Graham kept an eye on Gil and Gracie at the church while Stevie did her matron-of-honor duties. The photographer wanted a reflection of Rachael and Stevie standing side by side in front of the full-length mirror. Rachael's wedding dress was a princess-style with a low back, while Stevie wore the same style in peach chiffon.

Stevie smiled, remembering when she'd tried on the dress at home to show her children. Gil had said, "Mama, you look like a princess."

"Twirl, Mama, twirl. Like this." Gracie had danced around her.

Standing at the back of the church, Stevie waited for the music; then she slowly walked down the aisle, carrying a bouquet of peach and orange roses with baby's breath. She concentrated on each step, hoping she wouldn't trip and fall. The scent almost calmed her as she watched her children walk down the aisle, side by side. Gil carried the rings on a white, satin pillow, and Gracie carried a white wicker basket, sprinkling rose petals as she walked toward their mother, who was standing at the front of the church. Smiles and sweet utterances from the guests floated in the air. Stevie thought her heart would beat out of her chest with pride.

Gil and Gracie stood in front of her when the wedding march filled the church, and everyone looked toward the back where Rachael and Mr. Graham stood in the doorway. A sob caught in Stevie's throat at the beautiful sight. She looked over at Jerry Osborn, the groom she'd known since high school. Rachael and Jerry had reconnected at the five-year high school reunion. He wiped away a tear before it trickled down his cheek as he watched his bride move down the aisle. Next to him stood his best man, Mike Mulligan, the boy who had asked Stevie to the winter formal their senior year.

The night before, at the rehearsal dinner, Mike had introduced his wife to Stevie. How different her life might have turned out if she had gone to the dance with him instead of Gary. She mentally shook the thought from her mind and returned her attention to her best friend's wedding day.

That night, Stevie put Gil and Gracie to bed and then soaked in a hot, soapy bath, physically and emotionally exhausted. When the water turned cold, she stepped out of the tub, dried off, and put on her old flannel nightie and robe with the missing button. She plodded to the kitchen, took out the vodka bottle from the cabinet above the refrigerator, and slumped down on the sofa. Her best friend was married and just starting her life, while Stevie felt like she was already old and had no future in front of her.

She took a sip from the bottle and then another. She felt her eyes growing heavy.

A knock at the front door woke her. She stumbled, knocking her shin on the coffee table. She peeked through the peephole. Seeing Detective Curry, she opened the door.

"I hope it isn't too late."

"Come in." She shut the door and motioned to the Boston rocking chair as she sat back down on the couch.

"I wanted to tell you what happened before it's on the news."

Stevie sobered slightly.

"Gary was stabbed today."

She cocked her head. "Is he all right?" She wasn't sure she wanted him to be okay or not. Maybe being rid of him for good would be the best thing to happen to her, but she didn't want to think like that.

"I'm sorry. He didn't make it."

Now, she really *was* sober. "He's . . . dead?"

"Yes. Inmates don't like child molesters or wife-beaters. Stabbings in prison happen more often than you'd think."

Stevie relaxed her tired muscles into the soft sofa, feeling the fabric embrace her. She looked down at the mustard stain on her robe. Her cheeks reddened from embarrassment.

"I'd better go." He hesitated, spying the bottle of vodka. "I don't want to pry, but I'm concerned. Stevie, it's not good to drink alone."

"Would you like to join me?" She stood. "I'll get a glass."

"No, thank you."

She slid down and burrowed into the sofa.

"I'm a recovering alcoholic. Ten years now." He looked into her eyes. "I hit rock bottom, and my wife left me before I sought help through AA."

Feeling sleepy, she said, "That's nice."

He hesitated again. "I'll let myself out, but be sure to lock the door behind me."

"Oo-kie dokie." *Don't let the door hit you on your way out.*

The door shut quietly behind him.

Who does he think he is calling me an alcoholic? She fell into a deep sleep.

She recoiled. Gary held a knife at her throat, the blade piercing her neck. "It's your fault I went to prison. You couldn't help yourself, could you, you little—"

She sprang up with a start, sweat dripping off her. She touched her neck to see if she was bleeding. Relieved, she fell back against the couch, trying to catch her breath. It had felt so real. Gary was dead, but he was still torturing her, even from the grave. She curled up in a ball on the couch, afraid to fall back asleep but too exhausted to fight. Soon, sleep claimed her once again, but it was not the rest of an innocent soul.

CHAPTER 42

Annie

Since her divorce, Annie had dated a few times, but no one had come close to getting a second date.

As the days turned into weeks, the weeks into months, and the months into years, Annie felt more and more comfortable around Joe. She even looked forward to seeing him. There was something different about him since the divorce.

One morning while Joe was at work, Annie spotted his Bible on the table. Curious, she picked it up and opened to where the bookmark was. She read the underlined verse of David's prayer for forgiveness and confession of sin in Psalm 51. "Create in me a clean heart, O God, and put a new and right spirit within me." Joe never read the Bible when they were married. Was this the change in him she'd witnessed?

While it was Jenn who had first introduced them to a relationship with Jesus, it was Joe who decided to follow Christ first. As Annie watched the changes that came over her ex-husband, she found herself jealous of the peace that now seemed to reside within him.

Through her counseling sessions at The Rock, Jenn's influence, and the change in Joe, Annie had found herself looking for that same peace that Jenn and Joe seemed to have found. It had taken Annie longer to receive God's ultimate death and resurrection of His only Son, but her heart now ached when she realized the great sacrifice God gave out of His love for her. No one had ever loved her that much—not her mother and not Joe.

Like Joe, she had changed, too. But she knew she needed a clean heart—a forgiving heart. "God, if You can forgive my sins of bitterness, self-righteousness, and stubbornness, then I need to forgive Joe for what he did to me. I know I can't do it on my own. I need Your Holy Spirit living in me to forgive him. Please help me, Lord."

She felt her prayer miraculously answered even before she said amen. *Does God work that fast?*

On a Wednesday evening, as she prepared to leave Zoey and Joe to spend the night with Jenn, Joe said, "Don't be alarmed tomorrow if you see workmen in the backyard."

Workers? She'd gotten the house in the divorce settlement, and she hadn't authorized any work. She hooked the purse strap over her shoulder. "What's going on?"

"Since you own the property, I probably should have asked your permission before I hired a contractor, but I wanted to surprise you." He walked over to the guest closet, pulled out a roll of plans, moved to the table, and spread them out. "Come see."

Standing close, she leaned down, delighting in his familiar scent. She didn't want to leave his side, breathing in his masculine aura.

Memories came flooding back of walking on the beach on their first date and another time when he had knelt in the sand and held open a tiny, black, velvet box with a diamond ring while asking, "Will you marry me?" She'd answered by leaning down and placing her hands on either side of his face. Pulling him up, she had kissed the man she loved.

Walks on the beach had been a big part of their courtship and sharing each other's dreams. One time, Joe had turned from the surf and pointed to the hills. "I'm going to buy some property up there and build you a beautiful house on that hilltop."

She'd shared her dream with him. "And we'll fill it with *lots* of children."

His voice interrupted her walk down memory lane.

"What?"

"I said, it's an art studio." He looked at her. "With Zoey in school all day, I thought you'd like to work in your own studio. You're a talented artist. You know you are, don't you?" His gaze lingered on her.

She blushed, looking down at the plans, feeling validated by the only man she'd ever loved.

"If the contractor is on schedule, the foundation will be poured tomorrow."

On her way back to Jenn's, Annie couldn't remember if she'd even said goodbye because she was too astonished. *He thinks I'm talented. And he's building me a studio.*

Every day she watched the studio being built, from pouring the foundation to framing. And not wanting to leave on the days Joe had custody of Zoey, she lingered later and later into the evening. Rather than an irritant, the pounding hammers brought her joy. She hummed as she carried a basket of clean clothes from the laundry room and glanced at the progress outside. Soon, she'd be moving her things into the studio Joe had built for her.

Annie and Joe sat on the sofa looking out the French doors at the winding stone path leading to Annie's completed art studio.

Joe moved closer to her. "Let's have an open house and invite our Bible study friends."

Although not as excited as Joe about an open house, Annie did enjoy the new friendships she'd made with the women in her Bible study group, and they were interested in her art and the studio. On the other hand, it'd been a long time since she'd hosted a gathering, and she wondered if she'd lost the social grace she'd once possessed. "I'm not sure."

"It's your studio and your call. I'd never pressure you into anything you didn't want to do." He rested his head on the back of the couch. "I thought since we've made some great new friends, it'd be fun to have a party."

It was true. They both had made some beautiful friendships through their time at The Rock. As new believers, both of them were growing spiritually and closer in their relationship as well. Even though they were divorced, they were friends again. "I'll think about it."

He reached across the short distance between them and squeezed her hand. They sat in comfortable silence for a while. Then Joe said, "Zoey loves spending time at the beach house. Why don't you join us tomorrow?" He smiled. "I'll barbecue chicken on the grill. You love my chicken." He caught her eye and grinned.

"Maybe I will."

When she arrived at the beach house, no one answered the door. Annie trekked around to the back of the house. She spotted Joe and

Zoey down near the water, building a sandcastle. They stuffed wet sand into pails and piled the mounds next to each other.

"I brought a potato salad," she shouted, hoping they could hear her over the surf.

"Great." Joe stood, brushing sand off his knees.

"Stay there. I'll put it in the fridge." She turned, walked onto the deck, and opened the sliding glass door of the beach house Joe had bought to live in during the weeks he didn't have custody. Like Jenn had described to her, the room's furniture was bamboo with comfortable cushions in white and blue tropical flowers. If Annie didn't know she was in Laguna, she'd think she was in Hawaii. She walked into the kitchen, opened the fridge, and put the salad on an empty shelf. With her tote in hand, she left the house and trotted to the beach.

"Hi, you two." Annie spread her towel next to theirs, sat, took off her cover-up, and slathered suntan lotion on her arms and legs.

Zoey ran to her mother and kissed her on the cheek. "Hi, Mommy." Then she rushed back to what she was doing.

"That's the best sandcastle I've ever seen." Annie shaded her eyes from the sun.

"That's because Daddy and I did it together. Right, Daddy?" Zoey said as she shoveled sand into her pail.

"Yep. We're a team." Joe stood and went to the edge of the surf, filled his pail with water, and brought it back to where they were working.

"See the moat Daddy dug?" Before Annie could answer, Zoey asked, "Do you know what a moat is, Mommy?"

"I do." Annie dropped the tube of lotion into her beach bag.

"It's to protect the people inside the castle." After a while, Zoey left the sandcastle to jump waves as they rolled toward her. Joe brushed the sand off his legs and plopped down beside Annie. "I'm glad you came today."

"Me, too."

"You look beautiful."

She blushed behind her sunglasses.

"Come jump with me, Mommy," Zoey called from the water's edge.

Joe turned to Annie. "Shall we?"

Annie smiled.

Joey grabbed Annie's hand, and they jogged down to where their daughter stood. Standing on either side of Zoey, they took her hands. When a wave approached, they lifted her into the air.

Later, a perfect day turned into a perfect evening. After their barbecue on the deck, Zoey fell asleep. They talked about everything from how well Zoey was doing in school to Joe's booming business and Annie's art. Mostly, they talked about their new faith and the Bible study groups they'd joined.

Sitting in lounge chairs on the deck, they watched the sun dip into the Pacific.

Joe turned to her. "Annie, you're the only woman I've ever loved." He hesitated. "Do you think you'll ever be able to forgive me for what I did to you?"

Annie drew in a deep breath. "I'll be honest with you. I don't think I'll ever be able to forget what you did, but I've already forgiven you."

He reached for her.

She held up her hand to hold him away. "Wait. I have more to say." She gathered all the courage she possibly could. "I never told you something about my past." She went on before she lost her nerve. "My father was a womanizer, and he cheated on my mother all the time. She died of a broken heart. When you and I met, I told you my father was dead, but he's not. I broke all contact with him. I vowed I'd never be a victim like my mother was." Annie choked on a sob. "That's why your unfaithfulness was the worst thing you could have done to me." She hiccuped. "Please, forgive me for not telling you."

"There is nothing to forgive. It wasn't your fault for what I did." This time when he reached for her, she did not push him away. With only the tiki torches for light, he took her in his arms and rocked her until her cries subsided.

"I only understand forgiveness now because of what God did for me. I know I'm a sinner. Since God forgave me, I need to follow His example and forgive others." She fingered the button on his shirt. "If it's okay with you, rather than going to Jenn's tonight, I'd like to spend the night in your arms on the deck."

He drew her closer.

I'm where I belong—forgiven and forgiving.

In the morning, she turned toward him, holding her hand over her sleepy breath, and said, "Instead of an open house, why don't we have a wedding?"

A grin spread across his face. "Are you proposing to me?"

"You bet I am."

CHAPTER 43

Annie entered John's counseling office and took a seat across from him. It'd been months since she'd seen him—ever since she had given her life to Christ, and God had become the center of her life.

John smiled. "So, to what do I owe this visit?"

Annie returned his smile. "Joe and I are getting remarried, and we want you to officiate."

"Annie, I'm honored—"

Before he could say more, Annie continued. "We plan to have the wedding in our backyard. And after our vows, we want you to baptize us in our pool, and . . . "

John cocked his head, waiting.

Annie bit her bottom lip. "Zoey wants to be baptized, too, but I'm concerned that she's too young to understand what's she's doing. She's only six."

John hesitated. "Over these past few years being in the same men's Bible study with Joe, I've observed Zoey and spoken with her during some of the church activities."

Annie nodded.

"Zoey has put her trust in God. Although she has a childlike faith, she's wise beyond her years, even wiser than some adults who have been in church their whole lives." His eyes pierced Annie's. "Baptism is a public acknowledgment of her trust in God."

"Because Joe's faith and mine are so new, I wanted to make sure we're doing the right thing by agreeing to our daughter's baptism." She laughed. "I know what you mean about her being wise beyond her years. Her faith is profound. I only wish I had as much instead of allowing doubt to creep in sometimes."

"As it says in Isaiah 11:6, 'A little child shall lead them.'" He cleared his throat. "You and Joe are doing a great job as parents." He reached his hand out to her. "It'll be my joy to officiate at your wedding and your baptisms."

She grasped his hand like a lifeline. "John, how can I ever thank you for what you've done for me—for us?"

He placed his other hand on top of Annie's and smiled down at her. "You already have."

Their wedding day arrived with warmth from the sun as their friends gathered in their picturesque backyard on the hilltop in Laguna Beach. Annie and Joe stood together in the gazebo with Jenn as Annie's bridesmaid.

John whispered in Joe's ear, "Where's your best man?"

"I don't have one. Instead, I have my best girl." Joe leaned down and kissed Zoey on the top of her head.

John began. "Many of you know Annie and Joe's story." He looked at the guests. "Though they suffered through trials, they discovered and accepted God's forgiveness and now stand before you as they take their marriage vows.

"Today, we not only witness the joining in marriage of these two friends of ours, but later, we'll celebrate their baptism as well." John took a moment and looked from Joe to Annie. "Joe and Annie, God was not a part of your first marriage. This time will be different because you've both asked God to be the center of your union. Three cords are not easily broken . . . "

After Joe kissed Annie, they turned to face their guests as John said, "I'd like you to meet—again—Mr. and Mrs. Joe Costa."

When the cheering ebbed, John announced, "Now, you're invited to join us at the pool, where the family will be baptized."

Holding hands, Joe, Annie, and Zoey strolled across the lush green lawn, blades of grass poking between Annie's and Zoey's pink-painted toenails. Their guests followed them to the pool, where Joe, as the head of the home, set the example by being baptized first. Annie crouched beside Zoey as they watched. When Joe came up out of the water, he pumped his arms in the air. While their guests cheered, Annie walked down the pool steps and stood next to John as he asked her the same questions he'd asked Joe. "Annie, do you believe Jesus died for your sins?"

"I do."

"Annie, I baptize you in the name of the Father, the Son, and the Holy Spirit for the forgiveness of your sins." She pinched her nose as John dipped her back into the water.

After she came up out of the water dripping wet and glowing, Annie stood next to Joe. Holding hands, they watched John baptize their daughter.

Joe, Annie, and Zoey stood together in a group hug, crying tears of joy for their commitment to God and each other.

Jenn handed them fluffy towels when they emerged from the pool before heading toward the house to change into dry clothing. It took a while to reach the house with all the hugs and congratulations from friends. A string trio played chamber music, and people clustered in groups enjoying appetizers and sparkling punch.

A year later, Annie felt nauseated. After relieving the contents in her stomach, she laid on the sofa. Zoey brought her a damp washcloth and placed it on Annie's brow.

"Thank you, sweetheart." Annie gazed into Zoey's angelic face. "You are so good to me. How did I get so lucky to have a daughter like you?"

Zoey patted her mother's hand. "Don't worry, Mommy. I prayed for you. God will make you all better."

Every morning was the same—feeling nauseated, vomiting, laying on the couch with Zoey by her side. Annie mentally counted. She'd missed her last two cycles. *Is it possible? Could I be pregnant?* As soon as she felt better, she'd make an appointment with Dr. Anderson.

After being examined, Dr. Anderson helped Annie to a sitting position. She scooted to the end of the table and sat wearing a gown with ties in the back.

"Well, Annie Costa, there is no doubt. You are pregnant. You should give birth in about six-and-a-half months." He smiled. "There was never a medical reason you couldn't get pregnant. It just never happened—until now."

"Joe and Zoey are going to be thrilled." She could hardly wait to get home to tell them the news.

"Congratulations." He handed her a bottle of prenatal vitamins. "I want to see you once a month."

Annie wrapped her hands around the vitamin bottle. Tears of joy overwhelmed her. *I'm pregnant. I'm pregnant!*

Annie drove home, eager to share the news with her husband and daughter. She had just put the roast in the oven when Joe arrived home from work, the knot of his tie askew and the top button of his white shirt undone. He kissed her on the cheek, and per their routine, she followed him into the master bedroom as he changed into comfortable clothes.

"How was your day?" she asked.

"I sold the Bailey place. You know, the one that's been on the market for only three days?"

"Uh-huh."

He cocked his head. "You look like the cat that ate the mouse. What's going on?"

"I'm pregnant."

His mouth fell open, and his eyes grew huge. "What?"

"I'm pregnant." She grinned widely, tears filling her eyes.

"I thought that's what you said." He grabbed her upper arms and held her away from him, gazing into her eyes. "How?"

"Really? You want me to explain how to make a baby?"

He grabbed her around the waist, and they fell onto the bed, giggling.

Joe sat up with a start. "Does Zoey know?"

"No. I wanted to tell you first." She sat next to him. "We can tell her together. She's in her bedroom writing her spelling words."

Together, they walked down the hall, and Joe tapped on Zoey's bedroom door.

"Can we come in?" Annie said.

"Uh-huh."

When they opened the door, Zoey sat writing at her French provincial desk.

Joe and Annie eased down onto the bed, saving a place between them for Zoey.

Annie reached toward her. "Come sit with us. We have some exciting news."

Zoey wiggled between them as Annie ran her hand over Zoey's blonde curls. "You're going to have a baby brother or sister."

Zoey looked from Annie to Joe, her eyes sparkling. She hugged Annie, then Joe, squeezing with all her might. "I'm going to be a big sister!" She jumped up. "I'm so happy." She stopped jumping. "Can I tell my friends?"

"Of course, you can. Would you like to start by telling Aunt Jenn?" Annie reached out her hand to Zoey. They walked to the phone in the kitchen, where Annie dialed the number.

"Aunt Jenn, Mommy's going to have a baby, and I'm going to be a big sister!"

After ten hours of labor with Joe at her side, holding her hand or feeding her ice chips, Annie gave birth to Andrew James, a healthy baby boy.

When they brought him home and placed him in Zoey's arms, it was love at first sight. Happy tears ran down Zoey's cheeks and off her chin as she gazed at him. She ran her finger over his soft, olive skin and stroked his dark hair. She looked up into her parents' eyes and said, "I love him."

Days later, as Zoey helped Annie give AJ his bath, Zoey questioned, "AJ has hair like you and Daddy. Why don't I have dark hair?"

Annie nervously shifted her wet baby. "Oh, I don't know. Can you hand me that towel?" Zoey turned away; her blonde curls cascading down her back like a waterfall. Annie's stomach tightened at her secret. Maybe they should have told Zoey she was adopted, but she was so young. And then there just never seemed to be a good time to bring it up. Had they made a bad choice? Worry gnawed at her, but she pushed it away to enjoy her children.

CHAPTER 44

Stevie

Stevie's morning shower didn't help her melancholy. She wiped the steam off the mirror wishing she could wipe away her sadness as well.

Gracie spoke through the closed bathroom door, "Mama, can I sleep over at Robin's house tonight? Her mother said it's okay, and she'd pick me up."

"I guess." Stevie tried to sound cheerful. "Tell her to pick you up at the Little League field. Gil has a late afternoon game today."

Gil, a natural athlete, caught a ball at second base for the third out. Stevie and Gracie stood cheering as Rachael climbed the bleachers with her four-year-old twin boys, Robby and Ricky. Rachael looked behind her at the field. "What'd I miss?"

"Gil made an out, and his team's ahead three to two," Gracie said as she sat down.

"Hi, Rach." Stevie stared straight ahead.

"I can't stay long. The rugrats didn't take their naps today, so they're cranky." Rachael shaded her eyes from the sun. "When they're cranky, I'm cranky."

The twins didn't stay in the bleachers but quickly scampered down to the ground.

"Stay out of the dirt," Rachael yelled after them.

Stevie mentally shook her head. What did she expect? It was a baseball field.

When Gil was at bat, the count was three balls and two strikes. Stevie chewed on her lower lip.

"Robby, stop throwing dirt at your brother," Rachael called.

"Strike three," the umpire called.

Gil headed toward the dugout.

"It's okay. You'll connect next time," Stevie encouraged.

Ricky began to cry.

"Robby, I told you to stop throwing dirt at your brother." Rachael stomped down to the ground and grabbed her son's arm.

"Mama, is it okay if I take them over to the playground?" Gracie asked.

"It's fine with me if it's okay with Rachael."

Gracie held the twins' hands as she walked with them to the swings.

Rachael plunked herself next to Stevie and sighed. "It's true what they say about twins—double trouble. I can testify to it." Rachael adjusted the sunglasses on her nose. "How come your kids were always so obedient at that age?"

"Lucky, I guess."

Rachael cocked her head. "What's the matter?"

"What do you mean?"

"You seem out of sorts. Is it work?"

"Work's fine." Stevie looked down. "I'm tired; that's all."

"Well, you'd better go to the doctor." Rachael's gaze penetrated Stevie. "Remember how your mother was tired all the time. It could be serious."

The next time at bat, Gil got to first base and stole second as the crowd cheered.

Rachael persisted in her questions. "Is there something else?"

"Zoey will be thirteen on Monday."

Rachael met Stevie's statement with silence. Then she shaded her eyes from the sun. "You know where she lives. Have you ever considered meeting her?"

"Not really. I don't think it would be appropriate. I know she's loved and well cared for." Stevie watched the activity on the field. "Plus, you remember what it was like being a teenager. It could be a shock to find out she's adopted.

"What? You don't think they've told her?"

"I don't know if they have or not. I haven't seen Mr. Costa since Gary forced me to quit my job. And Zoey was just a baby then." Stevie rolled her tired muscles, trying unsuccessfully to comfort herself.

"Every year at this time, I get depressed. I can't help it. There's a hole in my heart that no one and nothing can fill." Stevie swallowed. "I don't expect you or anyone to understand. I should be happy. I have two wonderful kids and a great job."

Gracie brought the twins back to the stands. "Mama, I'm leaving now. Robin's mother is here to pick me up."

"Have a good time and thank Robin's mother for me."

Gracie kissed Stevie on the cheek and grabbed her things. She waved to Rachael and the twins. "Bye."

Ricky began to cry and wouldn't stop, no matter what Rachael threatened. Finally, after a couple of parents in the crowd turned and stared at them, Rachael stood with the twins in tow. "I've got to go. I'll call you later."

"Thanks for coming," Stevie said.

Rachael tromped down the bleacher steps.

Stevie turned her attention back to home plate, where Gil stood in his familiar stance—his feet apart and his bat poised. The umpire hunched behind the catcher.

She tried to shake off her bad mood and reasoned that Gil deserved a mother who had the energy to bake homemade cookies, go on hikes, and play catch with him in the yard. Gil and Gracie had never given her a moment of trouble. *Maybe writing to Zoey tonight will help.*

The final score was seven to six, with Gil's team in the lead. After the game, Bobby Barrett's parents approached Stevie. "We're going to take Bobby out for pizza to celebrate, and we'd like to invite Gil to go with us. Is that okay with you?" Liz Barrett asked.

"That would be nice." Stevie forced a smile.

"We'll bring him home before dark."

After the coach dismissed the team, Gil and Bobby ran toward their parents.

"Great game, boys," Stevie said as she hugged Gil. "Mr. and Mrs. Barrett have invited you to go with them to the pizza parlor to celebrate. Would you like to go?"

Gil's eyes widened. "Sure."

"Have fun." Again, Stevie plastered on a forced smile.

"Thanks, Mama." Gil and Bobby raced toward the Barretts' car.

Later, Stevie returned home to an empty house. It was quiet. Too quiet. If she hadn't agreed to her children going with friends, she wouldn't be alone. They deserved to have fun instead of being with their depressed mother. But sadness washed over her. She went to her bedroom and took her notebook from her dresser drawer.

May 9, 1981

My Darling Daughter,

In two days, you will turn thirteen. I can hardly believe it was thirteen years ago that I gave birth to you. I remember the day you were born so vividly. All I wanted was to keep you. I did everything possible. I went to school during the day and worked nights cleaning office buildings. I saved my money to prove I could take care of you, but no one would help me.

The nurse was mean to me. She wouldn't let me hold you, even when I begged her. That's when I crept down to the nursery to see you. You were the most beautiful baby. Later, when I discovered your baby picture on your father's desk, I was elated that I could watch you grow up through pictures. But that didn't work out.

No one understands the hole in my heart or why I'm so sad every year at this time.

Stevie set the pen down, walked to the kitchen, and opened the cupboard above the refrigerator. Spying the bottle of vodka, she reached for it and held it to her chest. Moments later, she shook her head. "Not tonight. I can't take a chance of Gil or the Barretts finding me passed out."

She stowed the bottle in the cupboard and went into the living room. She rested her head on the back of the chair and closed her eyes, dreaming of a sweet baby girl with blonde curls.

CHAPTER 45

Zoey

Home alone, thirteen-year-old Zoey searched her father's desk for typing paper. First, she pulled out the drawer where it was usually stored, but it was empty. Next, she opened another drawer, and her eyes focused on a folder with her name written on the tab. Curious, she pulled it out, opened it, and began to read.

SUPERIOR COURT OF THE STATE OF CALIFORNIA FOR THE COUNTY OF ORANGE, In the Matter of the Adoption of BABY GIRL SMITH, a Minor, NO.AD 645900 DECREE OF ADOPTION.

Staring at the document and frozen in place, her mind whirled. She'd often thought about why her parents and AJ had dark hair, while hers was blonde. And their skin turned a golden brown in the summer, while hers was as red as a lobster unless Mom slathered lotion on her. Why didn't they tell her she was adopted?

With trembling fingers and unsteady legs, Zoey dialed Jenn's phone number. "Aunt Jenn, can you come over?"

"What's wrong?"

"I need you," Zoey said, with tears in her voice.

"Are your parents home?"

"No. I'm alone."

"I'll be right there." The call ended abruptly.

She paced while she waited for Aunt Jenn. *My birth mother gave me away. Why? She must not have loved me enough.* She squeezed her eyes shut, hoping it wasn't true. She was Zoey Costa, daughter of Joe and Annie Costa. If she were adopted, her parents would have told her. Wouldn't they have?

A few minutes later, pounding on the front door echoed through the house. "Zoey! It's me," Jenn yelled.

Zoey opened the door and crumbled into Jenn's arms.

"What is it, Angel Baby? Where are your parents?" Jenn closed the door behind her and ushered Zoey over to the sofa.

Zoey pushed the document she was holding into Jenn's hands. "I'm adopted." She searched Jenn's expression. "Did you know?"

Jenn scanned the sheet and swallowed. "Yes."

"My parents should have told me. Why didn't they?"

"I don't know why." Jenn set the paper on the glass coffee table and faced her. Taking Zoey's hands in hers, she said, "Your parents fell in love with you from the moment they saw you. I don't know when they planned to tell you. I only know you were theirs from the beginning."

"They have AJ now. They don't need me anymore." Zoey released Jenn's grip and felt her muscles tighten.

Stunned, Jenn said, "Zoey, how can you say that? AJ can never take your place. No one can."

"But why did they keep it a secret from me?"

"Only they can answer that." Jenn leaned against the back of the couch. "Ask them. I'm sure they'll be able to explain why."

"They must have a reason for not telling me." Zoey mulled it over in her mind. "Maybe they thought it would hurt me to know my birth mother didn't want me." She stopped to think. "I . . . I don't think I want them to know I found my adoption papers." Zoey sighed. "I'll keep their secret. I'd never do anything to hurt them. Ever."

Jenn's eyebrows lifted.

"Please don't tell them," Zoey begged. "Please, Aunt Jenn."

Jenn took a breath and drew out the word, "Okay."

Questions popped around in Zoey's mind like firecrackers. "Do you know why my birth mother gave me away?"

"No, I don't."

"I want to meet her."

Jenn sat up with a start. "I don't think that's a good idea. Plus, I'm not sure how you'd find her. Even though your adoption was private through your mother's doctor, records are confidential for everyone's privacy. Maybe she doesn't want to be found."

Zoey picked up the adoption papers from the coffee table and reread them.

"The judge's name is William Keen, and my birth mother's last name is Smith I'll never forget her name, and it gives me something to go on—so I can find her."

"Angel Baby, please wait until you're older, and then I'll do everything in my power to help you. Anyway, your birth mother's name may not be Smith. It was a closed adoption, so they probably just put a generic name on the paper. I have heard of some people petitioning the court to open their records, but you would need to tell your parents to help with that."

"Oh, Aunt Jenn, I don't know what to do! For now, let's just keep it between us. Please."

Jenn held Zoey as she cried.

After a while, Zoey wiped her tears and stood. "I'd better put this back in Dad's office." She held up her adoption papers. "I found it while I was looking for typing paper."

"So, you're sure? You're not going to tell them you know you're adopted?"

"I don't know what I'm going to do. I'm still confused, but I know Mom and Dad must have their reasons."

"Where are your parents and AJ, anyway?" Jenn tucked a lock of her red hair behind her ear.

"They took AJ to a matinee to see *The Fox and the Hound*. I stayed home because I have an essay due tomorrow."

After an uncomfortable silence, Jenn said, "Remember the story of Moses and how the Pharaoh's daughter adopted him?"

Zoey's initial shock and self-pity began to wash away. "I do. His mother loved him and wanted him to be safe." Now, feeling somewhat hopeful, Zoey said, "Maybe that's why my mother put me up for adoption—to keep me safe. And Moses had a sister, Miriam. Maybe I have a sister or another brother?" Zoey brightened. "Aunt Jenn, I want to find my birth mother and thank her for giving me a wonderful family."

"When you're older and if you still feel the same way, I'll help you find her."

"Promise?"

"Promise." Jenn stood. "I'd better go before your mom and dad get home. Plus, you have homework. Will you be able to concentrate on it?" Jenn held Zoey's upper arms and gazed into her eyes.

"I think I can." Zoey hugged Jenn around the waist. "Knowing about my adoption is between us. You will keep my secret, won't you, Aunt Jenn?"

"I don't like to keep secrets, Zoey, especially from your mom and dad. I'd rather you tell them you found your adoption papers. Pray and ask God to help you make the right decision."

"I will."

When Jenn left, Zoey locked the door behind her and went to her father's home office. She bowed her head and prayed, "Heavenly Father, help me make the right decision about telling Mom and Dad that I found my adoption papers. And please help me find my birth mother, too. Amen."

Her assignment was to write an essay of one or more pages on a topic of her choice. Zoey had initially chosen "My Hero." She'd planned to write about Dad—how he'd taught her how to swim and ride a bike, built sandcastles with her, and attended all her dance recitals. But most importantly, he'd taken her to Sunday school when he was a single dad, where she'd heard about another Hero Who had changed her life.

She decided to change the theme of her article to "Great Love Requires Great Sacrifice." And she knew the three examples she'd use—the stories of Moses, Samuel, and Jesus.

Grateful she'd taken typing the previous semester, her fingers flew across the typewriter keys as fast as ideas popped into her head. It was as if someone else was writing it. Effortlessly, she told the story of how Moses' mother had loved him and wanted to protect him from the evil pharaoh who had wanted all the Hebrew boys to be killed. Bravely, she hid her baby in a basket and floated him on the

Nile River, where the pharaoh's daughter found him and took him home to raise him as her own son.

Then she wrote of Hannah, a woman who so desperately wanted a baby that she had pleaded with God to hear her prayer. In return, she promised that she would give her child back to God and allow him to be raised in the temple. Her son, Samuel, became a great prophet for God because of his mother's sacrifice.

Then, she concluded with the greatest love of all—the sacrifice made on the cross by Jesus Christ, Who left Heaven to come to earth and become a man to die for the sins of the world. Without Christ's love, Zoey knew that she would never have been able to forgive her parents and her birth mother. But typing out the words on her essay, Zoey felt some of her sorrow lifting and a peace begin to settle over her.

Pleased with herself, she yanked her finished essay out of the typewriter. After hearing the car coming up the driveway, AJ ran into the house ahead of his parents. "Zoey, where are you?"

"Right here." She bent down and scooped him into her arms. "AJ, you are my favorite brother, and I love you."

He giggled. "You're silly. I'm your only brother."

CHAPTER 46

Annie

The following morning, after their weekly tennis match, Annie sat across from Jenn and ordered the combo plate—a taco, enchilada, rice, and beans. She spread her napkin across her lap and took a sip of her iced tea. "I need to talk to you about something important."

Jenn lifted an eyebrow.

"I read Zoey's homework this morning while she was getting ready for school.." Without taking a breath, Annie continued. "Her writing is amazing."

"We've always known she was mature beyond her years."

Annie nodded. "And she has such incredible faith, too. She titled her essay, 'Great Love Requires Great Sacrifice.' She wrote about the adoption of Moses and Samuel and how God sacrificed His only Son for His adopted children. It blew me away." Annie leaned back as the waiter set their plates in front of them.

After the waiter left, Annie leaned forward and whispered, "Although Dr. Anderson advised us to tell Zoey she was adopted, we never got around to it. Maybe it was because she was so young when Joe and I divorced." Annie looked into the distance beyond Jenn. "We never felt the need to tell her."

"Don't wait any longer. Tell her." Jenn avoided her eyes.

Annie set her knife and fork on her plate. "I'll discuss it with Joe tonight."

That evening, after AJ was in bed for the night, Zoey sat next to her mother with her dad on the sofa facing them. Her dad cleared his throat and began, "You know how much we love you."

Zoey nodded.

"We wanted a baby for many years, but your mother was unable to get pregnant." He took a breath. "We adopted you and have loved you since we first saw you in the hospital."

Zoey began to cry—softly at first and then increased to sobbing.

Joe jumped up, came around the coffee table, and sat next to Zoey. He put his arm around her and squeezed her shoulder. He blubbered through his own tears. "God wanted you to be ours. And we couldn't have asked for a more loving, sweet, caring, and compassionate daughter."

"We're sorry we didn't tell you sooner." Annie choked back her tears. "We just always considered you our own. You didn't grow under my heart, my sweet daughter, but in it."

The three huddled on the sofa in silence.

"Did Aunt Jenn tell you I found my adoption papers?"

Annie pulled back and looked into Zoey's red rimmed eyes. "No."

"I found them in Dad's desk when I was looking for typing paper to write my essay." Zoey looked at her hands in her lap. "It was when you were at the movies with AJ. After I found them, I called Aunt Jenn and she came over. I told her not to tell you because I thought you didn't want me to know. So, I didn't want you to know that I knew." She looked from her mom to her dad for what seemed like reassurance.

"I'm glad Aunt Jenn was here for you. You've always been her Angle Baby." Annie looked at Joe. "We were wrong to keep it from you. We should have told you."

"I didn't like keeping a secret from you." Zoey wiped her tears. "Can I ask you something?"

"Anything," Joe said.

"Why did she give me away?" Zoey searched their expressions.

"We don't know why. We know she was very young, and we think she just wanted to give you a home where you'd be loved and cared for." Annie was glad for what she was about to say next—never wanting Zoey to think she wasn't wanted. "Like you wrote in your essay, great love requires great sacrifice. That may be what your birth mother did for you."

Zoey wrung her hands in her lap again. "I'd like to meet her."

"She may not want to be found," Annie said.

Joe patted Zoey's hands. "When you're older, we'll do whatever we can to help you find her."

When he looked into Annie's eyes for agreement, she knew her response was a glare instead of the smile he was hoping she'd have for him.

CHAPTER 47

Stevie

Wearing the same clothes she had worn to work the day before, Stevie awoke on the sofa, a blanket over her. Realizing one of her children had found her passed out during the night and had covered her, she jarred herself completely sober.

She grimaced, tasting her foul breath. *What am I doing to my children?* Laying her head back, she put her arm across her forehead, closed her eyes, and got lost in her thoughts. *I must stop drinking for my children's sake.*

After ideas ping-ponged in her head, she stood and stumbled to the kitchen. Taking the bottle of clear liquid, she poured it down the drain and dropped the bottle into the trash. Brushing her hands back and forth, she went to the bathroom to shower.

She'd already signed the permission slips for Gil and Gracie to go on a mission trip to Mexico. Gil and Gracie had been attending Calvary Church with an active youth group for a while. Now, she'd drop them off in the church parking lot.

At the end of the week, Stevie opened the drapes, cleaned up the mess, and drove to the church. She hummed—looking forward to her children's return.

After Gil and Gracie hugged her, they stowed their duffle bags in the car's trunk. Gil plopped into the passenger seat. His long legs stretched out in front of him as Gracie chattered in the backseat.

"Mom, it changed my life. The children are so poor. They live in shacks. Some are even worse than a shack. Right, Gil?"

"Uh-huh," Gil mumbled.

"Yet they're happy. They smile all the time. I want to go back again next time. Can I, Mom? Can I?"

"I'll think about it."

Gracie giggled. "That's what you always say."

How did I get so lucky to have such great kids? Not one selfish bone in their bodies like other teenagers. Mama would be so proud of her grandchildren.

The following week, Gil and Gracie's enthusiasm was contagious. They begged her to join them at church. Their group was going to give a report on their mission trip, and the kids wanted her support. Although she would have chosen to rest on a Sunday morning instead of listening to a boring sermon, she'd do it for them.

That night, sitting around the table after eating tacos for dinner, which was Gil's favorite, especially how his mother fixed them, Stevie announced, "I've decided to go to church with you tomorrow."

"Really? That's great," Gil said.

"I think you'll like it, Mama," Gracie added. "I hope Pastor Andy will be speaking. He's my favorite."

That first Sunday, Stevie had been apprehensive about what church would be like. But she was immediately drawn in by the friendliness of the people, the powerful praise music, and the not-so-boring message given by a young pastor.

Since that day, Stevie no longer dropped her children off in the church parking lot but joined them. During one of the services, while reading the bulletin of things offered at Calvary, she read about Restoration, a twelve-step program for those who need healing from their past. And it was on the same night as the youth group that Gil and Gracie attended. *Do I need healing? From the trauma of a rape I don't even remember? Healing from giving up my baby for adoption? Healing from the hole in my heart? Healing from my abusive husband? Healing from grief?*

The following week, she entered the meeting. A few sat in the semi-circle of chairs, and others gathered around the refreshment table drinking coffee.

A woman approached and reached out her hand. "Hi, I'm Amy. And you are?"

Stevie accepted her handshake. "Stevie."

"Welcome, Stevie. It's nice to meet you," Amy said.

While some continued with their conversations, others curiously looked in her direction. Should she turn and run? No. She'd made a vow to herself that she owed her children a sober mother, and if a meeting such as this one could help her keep her vow, then she was willing to face her fear of the unknown.

"Take a seat, everyone," said an older woman with gray hair, who appeared to be in charge.

"Come sit with me." Amy led Stevie to a seat next to her.

Although her strength was zapped, she forced herself to attend church and the twelve-step group faithfully. Stevie felt connected to her new friends as she listened to the heartfelt stories week after week.

When it was her turn to share her story, she rubbed her sweaty palms on her pants. "Hi, I'm Stevie."

"Hi, Stevie," the group responded in unison.

"I had my first drink when I was a teenager." She swallowed, but it didn't help her dry mouth. "I'd just lost my dad, and someone told me the alcohol would ease my pain. He was right. It did dull the pain at the time. There have been long periods when I didn't drink, so I'm not certain that I'm an alcoholic or not."

Some in the circle nodded their heads.

Feeling encouraged, Stevie continued her story, including the hole in her heart with the loss of Zoey and living with an abusive husband. She concluded, "I always drank alone after my children were in bed asleep. I was able to hold down a job and raise my children. Then one morning, I woke up wearing the clothes I'd worn the day before with a blanket over me. One of my kids had covered me during the night while I was passed out. I knew then that my drinking was a problem. I felt so ashamed and vowed I'd never drink again. I'm grateful because this group is helping me keep my vow." She brushed one of her corkscrew curls off her forehead.

While her physical body declined, her faith grew, and she gave her heart to her Savior six months later and was baptized. When she came out of the water, Gil, Gracie, and her new friends rejoiced with her.

CHAPTER 48

Zoey

"Mom! Mom!" Zoey burst through the studio door. "I thought I'd find you here."

"What's all the excitement?" Annie looked away from her easel, paintbrush poised in her hand. "You won sophomore class president!"

Zoey took the paintbrush from her mother's hand and placed it in the container. Then she led her by the hand to the accent chairs and eased her into one of them. "Yes. But that isn't the best news." Zoey sat in the matching chair. "Our new youth pastor has asked me to be a mentor to younger girls in the church—and he's going to call you and ask if you'll be the adult leader for this new ministry." Zoey bit her lower lip. "Please, Mom. Please, say you'll do it."

"I don't know."

Zoey imagined the wheels turning behind her mother's expressive eyes. "It'll be perfect for us to volunteer together. You always say you never see me anymore. And Pastor Paul said girls this age need mentors to help them through their early teenage years. He explained we'd be like their spiritual family. I'd be like a big sister to them, and you'd be their spiritual mother." She pleaded. "John

Burrows recommended us to Pastor Paul to lead the ministry." Zoey squeezed her mother's hands.

"I've never thought about working with young people."

"You're perfect for it. And my friends agree with me." Zoey's eyes widened as she waited for her mother to respond."

Annie frowned. "It would be an opportunity for us to spend more time together. And when you go away to college, I don't know what I'm going to do. It'll be like cutting off one of my limbs."

Zoey reached over and placed her hand over her mother's.

"It may be my last opportunity to spend quality time with you." Annie's frown turned to a smile. "And it does sound like a ministry that's needed."

"So . . . you'll do it?"

"Okay."

Holding her mother's hands, she pulled her out of the chair. And unable to contain her emotions, she jumped up and down.

"We'll need guidelines. Is there a curriculum?"

"No. It's a new ministry. So, we can write the guidelines for it."

A couple of days later, after meeting with Pastor Paul and hearing about his vision for the mentoring group, Zoey and her mom returned home excited to begin planning. Pastor Paul had suggested having it in their home instead of the youth building.

With tablets and pens, Zoey and Annie sat at the kitchen table. "I think the living room is way too plush for the girls. Can we use your studio?"

"It sounds like a perfect place. I'll move my easel into a corner and add a rug to one end of the room. A few beanbag chairs and some pillows should do it."

"We need to have food. What about having pizza at the first meeting?"

Mom noted it on her tablet. "What a great idea. Teenagers love pizza." She stopped abruptly. "I think we're getting ahead of ourselves. We need to pray, seeking God's guidance and will instead of running ahead of Him. This isn't our ministry. We need to follow His example of being servants."

Zoey set her pen on the table and bowed her head. "Lord, forgive me for rushing ahead of You. I want to follow Your lead. Help Mom and me serve You in this opportunity of mentoring young teen girls. Amen."

"Lord, I, too, seek Your guidance. Heavenly Father, as we serve young ladies, I ask that we be Your hands and feet. Bring the ones that need mentoring the most. Help us listen to their concerns and their needs. Fill us with Your compassion and grace with ears to hear. Amen," Annie prayed.

AJ and Joe, with towels wrapped around them and wet hair, came into the kitchen from an early evening swim.

Curious, AJ asked, "Whatcha doing?"

"We're planning for the mentoring group," Annie said.

AJ cocked his head to the side. "What's ment—?"

"It's like someone older and wiser helping someone younger," Joe explained.

"Like Zoey is to me." AJ tied his towel around his neck, letting it flow down his back.

"Okay, superhero, it's time for your bath and PJs."

AJ dashed away.

"I'd better make sure the water stays in the tub and not on the floor." Joe followed AJ.

Returning to their planning, Annie asked, "Where were we?"

"We need to write the guidelines for the meetings."

"Right."

"I think the first one should be, 'This is a safe place.'" Zoey tapped her pen on the tablet.

"Absolutely. And another one is 'whatever is said here, stays here,' so the girls will feel comfortable sharing their concerns with us."

They continued until they had a few basic rules written.

"What about calling it something other than a mentoring group?" Zoey tucked a soft, blonde curl behind her ear.

"You're right. Mentoring doesn't sound inviting for early teens. We need something else." Annie looked off in the distance. "What do you think about The King's Daughters?"

"I like it . . . but—"

"But?" Annie searched for Zoey's response.

"Let's ask the girls to suggest what to call the group and then have them vote on it."

"That's a great idea! It'll give them a feeling of ownership." Annie smiled. "I'm so proud of you. I know your influence will bless their young lives."

"Thanks, Mom. Don't forget—your influence on them matters, too. They're going to love you just like I do."

Annie blushed.

"What about a Bible verse?" Annie picked up her Bible from the table and flipped through the gold-edged pages.

Zoey turned to the concordance at the back of her Bible and ran her finger down one of the pages. "I like 1 Peter 3:8." She read, "'Finally, all of you, have unity of spirit, sympathy, love of the brethren, a tender heart and a humble mind.'"

"I like it. It's too bad we can't change 'brethren' to 'girls.' But that would be sacrilege to rewrite the Bible." Annie grinned.

They wrote their goals for the group, and Zoey had just finished making a sign for the studio door when AJ sped back into the kitchen, smelling like soap and wearing his superhero PJs. He read the sign laying on the table. *No Boys Allowed.* Hey, why no boys? I want to come," he whined, pushing out his lower lip.

Joe came up behind AJ. "Don't worry. While the girls have their meeting, we're going to have a guys' night out." Joe ruffled AJ's wet hair.

"Just you and me?"

"That's right. Just you and me."

AJ gave his dad a high-five.

"Now, kiss Mom and your sister goodnight," Joe said.

AJ kissed his mother.

When he pecked Zoey's cheek, she cuddled him in her arms. After he was gone, she said, "He is so sweet. I hope he never changes."

Zoey caught her mother staring at her.

"What?"

"He has a heart of gold—just like you."

The first night of mentoring went better than Annie or Zoey had expected. Ten girls had arrived, all of them a little shy at first but warming up quickly under Annie and Zoey's encouragement. The girls had voted, and The King's Daughters was chosen as the group's official name.

"Now, girls, I want you to know that what happens in this group stays in this group," Annie admonished. "Don't go sharing anything you learn about each other with anyone else."

"That's right," chimed in Zoey. "We need to be able to trust each other if we're going to be able to open up to one another."

The girls had all agreed to the rules and had enjoyed the games that Annie and Zoey had planned to help break the ice.

Near the end of the evening, Zoey led the girls in a devotion from God's Word and then prayed for each one of them. "Father, as we leave here tonight, may we remember the blessings we have shared and the burdens we carry. May we be a light in the darkness to others who need Your love. Amen."

As the last girl walked out the studio door, Annie looked over at Zoey, who had started to clean up the empty pizza boxes. "I'm so proud of you," she told her daughter, tears shining in her eyes.

Zoey looked back at her mother and grinned, then walked out the door to take out the trash.

"Where did the time go?" Annie brushed a tear off her cheek. The last of the teens had left after giving Zoey a going away party. Annie busied herself, picking up paper plates and cups and dropping them into a garbage bag. "I don't know what I'll do when you're gone."

"I'm going to miss you, Mom. But I know you're going to be fine." Zoey choked back her own tears, trying to be stoic in front of her mother. "I'll come home as often as possible, and we'll talk on the phone, too."

"I need you in my life. You're my best friend."

Zoey hugged her mother fiercely, feeling their hearts beat in unison. "Mom, I'll always be in your life, even when I'm not here."

Eighteen-year-old Zoey sat at her dressing table, brushing her blonde hair. After each brushstroke, her tresses bounced back into soft curls. When she looked in the mirror, she wondered if she looked like her birth mother. Did they both have the same nose? Eyes? *Would she be proud of me?*

Her body tingled with the excitement of leaving for Pepperdine University along the California coast. Boxes were packed and stacked in the corner of her room.

During her teens, she had excelled academically and enjoyed every minute on student council and all the activities at school and in her youth group at The Rock, including going on many mission trips to Mexico and starting the mentorship program. She glanced at the picture taped to her mirror of children surrounding her. Their dark skin contrasted with her pale complexion. She'd loved telling them about her Jesus. And the girls in her mentorship program had challenged her in ways that made her continue studying her Bible more deeply. What a sweet life she had been given!

While busy being an active teenager, she'd put her thoughts and fantasies of the mother who gave birth to her on the back burner.

Maybe someday, she'd revisit the possibility of finding her, but for now, Zoey was content to head off to college and what awaited her.

She spied AJ's reflection in the mirror. Wearing tennis whites, he leaned against the doorjamb, watching her as she pulled her hair into a ponytail. "I'm waiting."

She turned to face him and smiled. "And not too patiently either." She grabbed her racket and walked toward him. She poked her arm through the crook of his. "Well, let's go." They headed for the tennis court.

"I'm going to miss you, Sis."

"And I'm going to miss you, Little Brother, more than you'll ever know." When tears threatened, she changed the subject. "Now, let's see if you can beat your big sister."

CHAPTER 49

Stevie

Stevie lay in the hospital bed with sixteen-year-old Gil and fifteen-year-old Gracie on either side of her. Dr. Ferber, Stevie's heart surgeon, entered her room with a smile and announced, "I have good news. You are at the top of the list the next time a heart that matches yours becomes available."

Stevie had inherited her mother's congestive heart failure. All the years of exhaustion had been signs of a heart problem. It wasn't until she had collapsed at work and been rushed to the hospital that she found out how sick her heart had become. For weeks, Stevie had grown weaker while waiting for a heart.

After Dr. Ferber left the room, Stevie held her children's hands. She scanned Gil's and Gracie's faces. The hardest part of being trapped inside her decaying body was to abandon her two beautiful children. Stevie tried to muster up her strength, but her voice was only a whisper. With all the strength she could gather, she slightly turned her head on the pillow toward her son. "I've been keeping a secret from both of you." She took a shallow breath. "I had a baby before your father and I got married, and I placed her for adoption." She turned toward Gracie. "You have a half-sister. Her name is Zoey."

Gil silently listened while Gracie gasped.

Stevie gazed into Gracie's eyes, so like her own. "It was the night of my dad's funeral. I was sad, and my friends wanted to cheer me up. So, I went to a beach party with them and drank way too much. I'm ashamed to admit it to you both. I got so drunk, I don't remember being raped." With her mouth dry, she let go of Gil's hand and tried to reach for the glass of water sitting on the rolling hospital table. Gil stood and added cool water to the glass from the pitcher. He held the straw to his mother's lips.

After taking a sip, Stevie said, "Thank you, darling."

He returned the glass to the table. Then he retook Stevie's hand like he'd been doing every time he visited.

"That was the night I got pregnant." The tears came like they always did, sliding from her eyes onto her temples. "I wanted to keep my baby and did everything I could think of to do that." Stevie looked in the distance, remembering. "I was a teenager, and I worked nights with my mother cleaning office buildings so I could earn money to take care of my baby. But no one would support my decision. Everyone wanted me to place my baby for adoption and get on with my life." She choked on a sob.

Gracie leaned down and hugged her mother. "Mama, I'm so sorry."

"It was the worst decision of my life." Stevie's breathing became labored.

Across the hospital bed, Gracie and Gil shared a concerned glance. "Mama, you need to rest," Gracie said.

"No." Stevie lifted her head off the pillow slightly. "This is important because I don't know if I'll get a heart in time. There is something I need you to do for me."

"Anything." Gracie patted Stevie's hand.

Stevie nestled her head back into the pillow. "Your half-sister's name is Zoey Costa. I've written letters to her all these years, especially on her birthday. I never sent the letters. They are in a notebook at the bottom of my top dresser drawer. Zoey is eighteen now. She's old enough to know about me and that I love her and never wanted to give her away." Stevie struggled for breath. "Gracie, if I die, I want you to take the letters to her."

Stevie tried to lift her head off the pillows but fell back against them, too weak to do anything but wait for a heart donor. *Is it too late?* If it was, she'd made her peace with God. "Please, Gracie, in case I don't make it, I want you to mail the notebook to Zoey. The address is 1010 Ocean Vista, Laguna Beach."

Gil cocked his head. "You know the address?"

Stevie turned her face toward her son. "I've never forgotten it." Then she pleaded, "Gracie, you will do this for me, won't you?"

"Of course, I will, Mama." Gracie dug in her purse for a pen and wrote the address on the cover of a magazine.

Chapter 50

Gracie

Arriving home, Gracie raced to her mother's bedroom, opened the top dresser drawer, dug under her mother's things, and unearthed a dog-eared notebook titled, "Letters to My Daughter."

She sat on Mama's bed and began to read.

A tear escaped Gracie's eye as she reread the words, *Maybe someday, we will be together.* Even if her half-sister was unaware she was adopted, Gracie felt she owed it to her mother to deliver the letters to Zoey. She didn't plan to wait until the unthinkable possibility of Mama's death.

Feeling time was of the essence, she grabbed the car keys and headed for 1010 Ocean Vista, the notebook beside her on the passenger seat.

Although, her hands shook, she gathered her strength, knocked on the massive door, and waited. A pretty blonde wearing tennis whites opened the door.

CHAPTER 51

Zoey

Zoey didn't know who the girl was standing at her front door. "May I help you?"

"Are you Zoey?"

"Yes."

"I'm not sure how to say this or how you'll feel when I tell you." The teenager pushed a sandy-colored corkscrew curl off her forehead. "I'm Gracie." Gracie gulped. "I'm . . . I'm your half-sister."

Zoey gasped and then opened her arms wide. "I've always wanted a sister." She squeezed Gracie in a fierce hug. "I've been waiting for this day for a long time."

Zoey pulled Gracie into the house. "My mother's in her studio out back, and my little brother is home, so let's talk in my bedroom."

After settling side by side on her bed, Zoey held her hand next to Gracie's. "We have the same hands and eyes and nose."

They giggled.

Gracie said, "You have a half-brother, too. Gil is sixteen, and I'm fifteen."

"I want to meet him and—"

"Did you know you were adopted?"

"I discovered my adoption papers when I was thirteen." Zoey's chest tightened as she remembered. "It was a shock at first until I put the puzzle pieces together."

"Did you ever want to find her?"

"I did. But I didn't follow through at the time, and life went on. It was always on my mind that someday I'd try to find her."

"She's in the hospital with congenital heart failure. If she doesn't get a heart, she'll die."

Zoey's eyes widened. "I'm leaving for college in a couple of days. I'll go see her before I leave." Zoey glanced at the notebook Gracie held in her hands. "Is she a good mother?"

"The best." Gracie handed Zoey the notebook. "She wrote letters to you. When you read them, you'll see that she loved you very much and never wanted to give you up for adoption."

Zoey gulped a sob that threatened. *She never wanted to give me away.*

Gracie tilted her head to the side. "Are the pictures in the hallway of your parents and brother?"

"Uh-huh."

"What are they like?"

"They're wonderful." Zoey smoothed her hand over the notebook's lettering. "But I always felt different, and I had questions like why I had blonde hair while both my parents and brother had dark hair. Things like that."

"I'm sorry I can't stay longer, but I need to go. Visiting hours start soon, and I don't want to miss a minute with Mama. Gil can't be with her today because he's working, and I don't want her to be alone."

Zoey handed Gracie a tablet and pencil. "Give me your address, and I'll write to you." They hugged before Zoey escorted her out to the car. When she went back inside the house, Zoey raced to her room to read the letters.

While reading about her birth mother's sad life, Zoey's heart ached for the young girl who had given her life.

After reading "Letters to My Daughter," Zoey closed the notebook, wiped her tears, and grabbed a sweater. She called to her mother in the kitchen as she headed out the door. "I'll be home in time for dinner."

"See you then," Annie answered. "I love you."

"I love you too, Mom."

While driving to the hospital, excitement and nerves caused butterflies to flit in her tummy. "Lord, I believe Your ways are higher than mine. I believe You predetermined today for me to meet the woman who gave birth to me. Your plan for me was for a teenage girl to give me life. Although she never wanted to give me up, Your will for me was for Mom and Dad to raise me. I couldn't be more grateful. And now, I'm on my way to meet her. I trust You, Lord, whatever—"

Zoey did not see the car that ran the red light and crashed into her, leaving her trapped inside her mangled vehicle. She only heard a voice in the distance.

"Stay with me."

CHAPTER 52

Annie

Joe sped to the hospital while Annie prayed, "Father, please let Zoey be okay."

He held firmly onto Annie's waist as they entered the emergency entrance of the hospital. Reaching the counter, Joe exclaimed, "I'm Joe Costa. Dr. Armstrong called. Our daughter, Zoey, was in an accident."

The nurse behind the desk said, "Please have a seat. I'll page Dr. Armstrong."

Soon, an older man with gray hair and wearing a white lab coat approached as Joe and Annie stood. "Mr. and Mrs. Costa, please, come with me. I'll take you to your daughter."

They followed the doctor to the ICU, where Zoey lay in a hospital bed.

Annie's hand covered her gasp as her legs gave way. Zoey, her face swollen, lay wired to beeping machines, almost unrecognizable while a ventilator whooshed.

Joe eased Annie into a chair.

"We'll know more after we see her test results," Dr. Armstrong said. "I'll leave you now."

With Annie unable to pray, Joe prayed for both of them. "Heavenly Father, You know our hearts. We are asking You to restore our daughter. Heal her with Your mighty touch. Lord, I'm not ashamed to ask for a miracle. Amen."

They sat in silence, holding onto Zoey's battered hand and arm, willing her to live.

Later, a nurse ushered them into a room where Dr. Armstrong said, "I'm sorry. There is no easy way to say this, but there is no brain activity."

Joe and Annie clung to each other as she collapsed to the floor. "No. No. No," Annie cried. "Not Zoey. Not my beautiful daughter."

After a while, Joe asked, "What happened?"

"I understand a drunk driver ran a red light and hit her on the driver's side." Dr. Armstrong shook his head. "She didn't have a chance." He stood. "You can go back into the room and be with her."

Time stood still in the dimly lit hospital room. The ventilator hum and heart monitor beeping faded as Joe clutched Annie's hand across their dear, sweet Zoey. They prayed in the Spirit. For the first time, Annie understood the Lord's teaching that the Spirit hears our groans when there are no words.

Later that evening, a woman they recognized from The Rock but didn't know personally entered Zoey's hospital room. "My name is Mary Dodge. I was one of the chaperones who went on a Mexico mission trip with Zoey—an amazing young woman." With tears in her eyes, she spoke softly. "I witnessed how much she loved people and how she would do anything to help them. Zoey always lit up while telling the children that Jesus loved them." After relating more stories about Zoey, Mary asked, "Will you join me for a cup of coffee in the cafeteria?"

Sitting in the cafeteria, steaming paper cups of coffee on the table, Mary said, "I'm the organ and tissue donor director at the hospital." She blew on her coffee before taking a sip. "We have a patient in the hospital waiting for a heart. If she doesn't get one soon, she'll die." Mary sipped her coffee, leaned toward them, and spoke quietly. "Will you consider donating Zoey's heart to her?"

Annie glared at her. "How dare you. You want to cut up my daughter! No. I can't do it. I will not donate my daughter's heart." She reached for the cup of coffee to throw in Mary's face when Joe stopped her.

After a long silence, Joe spoke. "It's late, and we need to get home to our son. I'm sure he's worried. He knows only that his sister was in an accident—nothing else."

Annie tried to stand, but her whole body felt weak. Her knees were shaking, and each time she thought of Zoey, her heart nearly stopped. Joe moved to her, wrapped his arm around her waist, and helped her stand. *The nerve of that woman asking us to give Zoey's heart to someone else. Who does she think she is?*

At the house, Annie saw AJ and Jenn watching but not seeing the TV. After Joe told them about Zoey's condition, AJ stood, kicked the couch, raced to his room, and slammed the door.

"He's in shock," Jenn said, clutching her chest.

"We all are." While Joe bent over, buried his face in his hands, and sobbed, Annie sat next to him on the sofa, rubbing his back.

Jenn stayed for a while, bringing them coffee and holding Annie as she cried. "I should probably go."

"Don't go. Please stay. We need all the family we can get. Will you stay here with AJ? I don't want him to remember his sister the way she looks now."

Jenn answered in a tight hug, "Of course. Whatever you need me to do, I'm here."

Eager to return to the hospital, yet feeling the need to comfort her son, Annie slipped into AJ's room and lay down next to him. She draped her arm over him as he cried himself to sleep.

Numb, she eased herself from AJ's bed and tiptoed out of his room. Hearing muffled voices, she glanced into the living room and saw Pastor John sitting on the sofa, his hand on Joe's shoulder. For some reason, she felt drawn to Zoey's room. She turned on the light switch, and while her eyes adjusted, she moved to Zoey's bed. Annie sat down and spied a notebook laying on the bed. Picking up "Letters to My Daughter," she opened it and began to read. Shocked and confused, she read the story of Zoey's birth mother and realized she was not alone in her love for Zoey.

After reading the last page, she felt a peaceful presence in the room. Was it God? Zoey? She wasn't sure. Annie pondered over what she'd read—the teenage girl who was raped and placed her baby for adoption under duress.

"Father, You know my heart is breaking not only for myself but also for the mother who gave birth to my sweet Zoey. She had a hard life, Lord, while I enjoyed my beautiful daughter for eighteen years. I ask that You bless the woman who gave birth to my Zoey. Amen." Annie laid her head on the pillow and breathed in Zoey's familiar scent.

Joe crept into the room. "Annie, we need to get back to the hospital. John's here. He'll drive us to the hospital and stay with us while—"

She handed him the notebook.

He cocked his head. "What's this?"

"Letters to Zoey from her birth mother. I found it on her bed. I don't want you to think I've gone crazy, but after reading it, I felt a peaceful presence in Zoey's bedroom. I don't know if it was God or Zoey." She gulped a sob. "Joe, I don't want to do it, but I think Zoey wants us to donate her heart so someone else can live." She swallowed hard.

He stood, and with red, puffy eyes, he wrapped Annie in his arms and rested his chin on top of her raven-colored hair. "We'll go to the hospital together and say goodbye to her."

Annie walked robotically as Joe led her gently by his supportive hand into Mary Dodge's office. Annie gripped the pen and couldn't move. She was numb. *How can I give away my baby girl's heart? How is this happening? Please, God, make it stop.* She raised her eyes to God and hesitated at the painting on the wall behind Mary. It was a Mexican cathedral, doves soaring above the wooden cross.

Zoey's plaintive voice from the past echoed in her head. *Please, Mom, please let me go on the mission trip. I'll be with Pastor Paul and the other kids. I have to go. Why else am I alive if not to give my gifts back to God? I know this is why I'm here. Please trust God and let me go.*

Annie clutched the pen as she scrawled her name. *God, she's Yours. She always was.*

Annie set the pen on the table. "Is it possible to meet the person who will receive"—she choked on her words—"our daughter's heart?"

"Let me ask the patient." Mary stood.

"We'll be in Zoey's room," Joe said.

Later, Annie and Joe stood in the doorway of the patient's room. A frail woman lay in the hospital bed with a teenage boy and girl on either side of her.

"Stevie?" Joe asked.

"Mr. Costa?" the patient whispered.

Annie glanced around the room at the surprised faces. "Joe, I'm confused. Do you know her?"

Joe led Annie into the room. "Stevie worked for me for a while as a receptionist. Stevie, I'd like you to meet my wife, Annie."

"It's nice to meet you, Annie." Stevie's breathing was labored. "These are my children, Gil and Gracie."

"Wait." Gracie gasped. "You're Zoey's parents. I recognize you from the family portraits in your home."

"You know Zoey?" Annie questioned.

"Um, we met today."

"Zoey is why we're here. She was in an accident . . . We wanted to meet the person who will receive her heart."

Annie noticed as a sadness invaded the room, like a black cloud hovering over them. Gracie threw herself across Stevie as the dying woman moaned.

"What's happening?" Annie asked.

Stevie, unable to speak, whimpered like a trapped animal. Gracie held her mother's hand and said, "Mama was Zoey's birth mother."

Annie leaned against Joe before her legs gave out on her.

After gathering some of her strength and voice, Annie said, "I found your letters to Zoey in her room and read them."

Gracie began to cry. Between sobs, she confessed, "I brought Mama's letters to Zoey yesterday. I think she was on her way to the hospital to meet Mama when the accident happened. It's my fault."

"No, it isn't." Annie walked over to Gracie and put her arm around her. "It was a drunk driver's fault. Not yours."

While Stevie recovered in the hospital, Zoey's memorial service took place. Held at The Rock, the church filled with mourners and overflowed out to the manicured grounds. The night before the service, Annie, Joe, and AJ said their goodbyes to Zoey at the funeral home. Annie placed "Letters to My Daughter" in Zoey's hands before the white casket was closed.

In the front of the church, eighteen pink rosebuds covered the casket, with Zoey's senior picture displayed on an easel beside it. The crowd came to pay their respects to the girl with a heart of gold. Annie, sandwiched between Joe and AJ, felt numb in the warmth of the cocoon they had provided for her. Gil and Gracie sat with the family as John gave the eulogy.

He told Zoey's emotional story, concluding with, "Annie and Joe have given me permission to read Zoey's last entry in her prayer journal." He opened the book and read, "'Dear Father God, You are my Rock. I worship, praise, honor, and glorify You. I love and adore You. Thank You for living in me and for Your plan for my life. I seek only Your will in Your time, and I put my complete trust in You.

"'You know, I tried to find my birth mother, but Dr. Anderson was on vacation and won't return until after I'm settled at Pepperdine. So next year, I'll start my search for her earlier in the summer.'"

John took a breath. "'I want to meet her and tell her how grateful I am Mom and Dad raised me. They've always loved me unconditionally and provided everything any girl could need or desire.'"

John turned the page. "'One more thing, Lord. Please watch over AJ while I'm away at college. He's at a crossroads with doubts of which way to go. I so want him to know You personally as I do.'"

John closed the journal. "We'll be singing Zoey's favorite hymn, 'Blessed Assurance.' Please turn to page 319 in the hymnal." As pages rustled, John said, "For those of you who may not know, Zoey's name means 'life.' I think we all know that Zoey breathed life into everyone she met, but most of all, she wanted to share the eternal life that only Jesus can give."

Blessed Assurance, Jesus is mine
Oh, what a foretaste of glory divine.

While others cried during the singing, Annie wasn't able to shed a tear. She didn't understand why. Maybe someday, she'd be able to let her tears flow.

Heir of salvation, purchase of God
Born of His Spirit, washed in His blood.

Annie and Joe were slowly surrounded by mourners sharing their grief. Loving embraces comforting them in their mutual sorrow.

Perfect submission, perfect delight
Visions of rapture now burst on my sight.

Annie turned for another embrace, and a young man she recognized from church collapsed on her shoulder. "I need you to know that Zoey changed my life. I was messin' up real bad, and she saw me. She saved my life. I wish I could've told her." He muffled a sob.

Angels descending bring from above
Echoes of mercy, whispers of love.

"She knows." Annie comforted the boy like a mother, and she knew, for the first time, that she had her own mission from God. And she'd find it in His time.

This is my story, this is my song
Praising my Savior all the day long.

Outside, after the service, Annie watched AJ standing apart from the others. She turned to Jenn. "I'm worried about AJ. He loved her so much."

Jenn choked back a sob and dabbed her tears with a tissue. "We all did."

EPILOGUE

Two years later, Annie stood back and watched Joe hang her most recent painting over the fireplace in the living room. Annie had painted it from a favorite photo she'd taken at the beach house. Zoey and Joe were covered in sand, building a castle. In the background, the sun glistened over the water, creating a halo around Zoey's blonde curls.

Jenn saw Zoey as angelic from the first time she saw her, calling her Angel Baby. Jenn was right. Zoey was an angel on earth, and now she was one in Heaven. Annie swallowed a sob as she gazed at the image of her precious daughter.

What if I hadn't forgiven Joe of his infidelity? What if God hadn't softened my hard heart toward Joe? What if we hadn't remarried? What if I hadn't taken the opportunity God gave me of a second chance—a chance to be a family again?

Joe stepped back and stood next to Annie. "That was a perfect day."

"It was, wasn't it?" Annie slipped her arm around Joe's waist and leaned her head on his chest.

AJ came into the room carrying a flashlight. "Mom, I need batteries."

"They're in the laundry room, lefthand bottom drawer next to the broom closet."

"Thanks." AJ headed in that direction.

"Do you need help packing for camp?" Annie asked.

"Nah, I got it."

Annie followed AJ into the laundry room. "I'm going to miss you while you're at camp."

He stopped and turned toward her. "Mom, I don't have to go. I can stay home if you need me."

"I want you to go. Besides, I'll be busy while you're gone. I've got a MADD speaking engagement scheduled."

Thank You, Lord, for giving me a purpose. She stared at her handsome son as he rummaged through the junk drawer, looking for the correct size batteries. *And thank You, Lord, that AJ is no longer angry and has followed Zoey's example of being active in his youth group and serving You by going on mission trips. I'm grateful, Lord.*

Finding the batteries, AJ put them in the flashlight and placed it on the counter. She noticed his furrowed brow. "What is it?"

"I . . ."

She waited.

"I'd never want to do anything to hurt you. You know that, don't you, Mom?"

She nodded. "What is it? You can tell Dad and me anything. You know that."

"I want to meet the woman who gave birth to Zoey." His eyes searched for her reaction.

"I see."

"I'm not sure you do. I don't even understand it myself. It's like something is pulling me toward her."

"If you feel the same way when you get home from camp, I'm sure we can help you find her." Annie embraced him.

Wrapping his arms around her waist, he said, "Mom, I miss her so much."

Annie held him for a long time. "I know. I do, too."

When he pulled away from her grip, he wiped his tears and rushed to his room.

Annie was grateful that finally, after two years, she was able to cry for her beloved daughter. She clutched her chest over her aching heart, knowing, like her, AJ and Joe needed to travel their own grief journeys.

She walked back into the living room, where Joe sat on the sofa reading. Annie stood behind him and looked at the painting for a long while. She knew, with God's comfort and peace, that even while grieving, there would be more happy days in their future.

Stevie came in from gardening, washed her hands, poured a frosty glass of iced tea, and sat at the table. Taking a sheet of stationery, she began to write.

May 11, 1988

My darling daughter in Heaven,

Happy Birthday. I was in the hospital waiting for a new heart when you were on your way to meet me. That's when it happened! The gift your parents gave me was your heart to replace my broken one. I probably should start from where I left off in my letters to you. Gracie told me she gave you my letters.

Since I received your heart, my life has changed. God has given me a second chance. He has forgiven all my sins, and I no longer feel the need or the desire for alcohol. I am healed, and like you did while you lived on earth, I long to tell others about Jesus and His saving grace. So, I tell my story to everyone who will listen.

Amazingly, Mike Mulligan came back into my life after all these years. I saw him at a high school reunion. He'd been a widower for ten years after his wife died from cancer. They never had children. He said he'd always thought about me and wondered what happened to me. Boy, did he get an earful when I told him my story. He's a Christian—kind, gentle—and he loves me—and Gil and Gracie, too. He's stepped into the role of the father they never had. He is a developer and invests in real estate. He has done very well financially and is helping Gil and Gracie with their future career plans.

Both Gil and Gracie want to become doctors and eventually go into the mission field. They are both intelligent and compassionate. And they love Jesus. They will not only mend bodies, but they will also share the story of Jesus and His redeeming grace. Some say they got their smarts from me, but I don't feel like I can take the credit.

A rap at the door brought Stevie out of her thoughts. She opened the door and saw a teenage boy with dark, curly hair and dreamy, blue eyes standing on her front porch. There was no doubt that she was looking at Joe Costa's son.

"I'm—"

"I know who you are." She opened her arms wide.

AJ stepped into her embrace, and Stevie held him close to her as Zoey's heart danced against his chest.

About the Author

B.J. Bassett encourages others as an author, teacher, and speaker. She teaches writing workshops at Umpqua Community College, Roseburg, Oregon, and at writer's conferences; and she is a speaker for Stonecroft Ministries. She enjoys reading, jigsaw puzzles, and munching warm scones oozing with butter and jam while sipping Earl Grey tea.

Contact Info:

bunny1940bassett@gmail.com
www.bjbassett.com
bjbassett.wordpress.com
www.facebook.com/bunny.bassett
B.J. Bassett (@bassett106) Twitter

More Books By B.J. Bassett
Fiction

Lily
Gillian's Heart
Sweet Charity

Non-fiction

The King's Daughters—A Women's Devotional

For more information about
AMBASSADOR INTERNATIONAL
please visit:

www.ambassador-international.com
@AmbassadorIntl
www.facebook.com/AmbassadorIntl

Thank you for reading this book. Please consider leaving us a review on your social media, favorite retailer's website, Goodreads or Bookbub, or our website.

More from Ambassador International

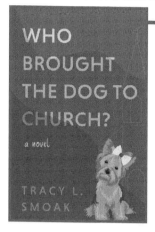

Betty is sure that Ida Lou does not belong in their church when the woman shows up to the Good Friday service with her small dog in tow. But before she knows what's happening, Betty—along with the other women of the WUFHs (Women United For Him)—is pushed into helping the woman. God works in mysterious ways—and through ordinary people. The town of Prosper is about to experience some drama—and it all starts with a dog who comes to church.

Niamh is a devout Catholic living with her parents in Ireland in 1908. She has never doubted their faith, but when she joins a suffragist movement, Niamh suddenly finds herself being introduced to women from who all believe that women deserve to be treated as well as men. As Niamh begins to imagine a world where women and men are equal, she meets Fred, the brother of one of her sister suffragists. Based on a true story, The Last Letter is a tale of overcoming prejudice and finding love against all odds.

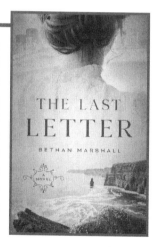

Sam Anthem has always been a team player, leading his Home Team on secret missions around the world. When he is forced on a vacation, he is introduced to a former covert ops soldier-turned pastor. But the vacation takes a turn when the Home Team comes under attack. As the team fights to stay alive against an unknown adversary, Sam begins to wonder if there is more to life than just the job. With his life on the line, Sam must decide between the job or his newfound faith and possible love.

Made in the USA
Columbia, SC
04 July 2023